The Vulture

Books by Frederick Ramsay

The Ike Schwartz Mysteries
Artscape
Secrets
Buffalo Mountain
Stranger Room
Choker
The Eye of the Virgin
Rogue
Scone Island
Drowning Barbie
The Vulture

The Jerusalem Mysteries
Judas
The Eighth Veil
Holy Smoke
The Wolf and the Lamb

The Botswana Mysteries
Predators
Reapers

Other Novels
Impulse

The Vulture

An Ike Schwartz Mystery

Frederick Ramsay

Poisoned Pen Press

Copyright © 2015 by Frederick Ramsay

First Edition 2015

10 9 8 7 6 5 4 3 2 1

Library of Congress Catalog Card Number: 2015932059

ISBN: 9781464204760   Hardcover
      9781464204784   Trade Paperback

Poisoned Pen Press
6962 E. First Ave., Ste. 103
Scottsdale, AZ 85251
www.poisonedpenpress.com
info@poisonedpenpress.com

Printed in the United States of America

Acknowledgments

This latest "Ike" book should be considered some sort of milestone. When I wrote *Artscape*, the first in the series, and the Poisoned Pen Press took it, my hope was that I would be lucky and given the chance to write a sequel. This is the tenth in the series, so it seems my luck held. It has been fun writing about Ike, Ruth, and the rest of that band of characters, cops, and criminals, who are Picketsville, Virginia.

There have been changes over the years. The Ike you find here is mellower in many ways than the sheriff introduced in *Artscape*. In life, people change. So they must do in fiction as well. All of this is by way of acknowledging my debt to my publisher and editor who liked Ike in the first place and allowed him to endure since. Thanks to Robert, Barbara, and all the folks at the Poisoned Pen Press who make the magic happen.

Foreword

Some time ago I took my car in for some routine maintenance; probably an oil change. I was called to the desk to pay my bill and pick up my keys and, although it seemed they were the keys that had been used to drive the car to the ready line, I realized that they were not mine. I said so. The clerk smiled and said, politely, yes they were, that those keys were the ones used to bring my car to the pickup point. I looked over his shoulder and saw my keys hanging on a pegboard behind him. I had put an attachment which was quite distinctive on the ring, and the keys hanging had it. We argued and, finally, with an "indulge the customer look" on his face, the supervisor, for that was the level we had reached by then, marched me out to my car. I inserted my key in the ignition and started the car. Next, and to the supervisor's chagrin, I inserted the other set and started the car again.

I have no way to calculate the odds that two nearly identical cars would be at the same location on the same day and both keyed alike. It boggles the mind, yet sometime later, when I told this story at a meeting, one of the participants reported that the same thing had happened to her. So, the odds must not be as great as one might think.

They say that "truth is stranger than fiction." Perhaps, but strange or not, truth certainly does suggest some really strange fiction. Read on.

Pursuant Executive Order No. 10834, August 21, 1959, President Eisenhower established the official flag of the United States as a banner with 50 stars. This flag was raised for the first time at 12:01 a.m. on July 4, 1960, at the Fort McHenry National Monument in Baltimore, Maryland, and is currently the official flag of the United States of America.

Chapter One

Smoldering flames and a streetlight leaning at an acute angle and flashing on and off like a badly programmed strobe, and firemen's work lights illuminating the street bright as day. Frank Sutherlin's head spun. In spite of the glare, he sensed only darkness. Nauseated and short of breath, he felt his knees start to buckle. *Darkness comes. In the middle of it, the future looks blank. The temptation to quit is huge.* Frank read that somewhere. He couldn't remember who wrote it…Piper…somebody Piper. It seemed eerily strange, remembering that line just now, but also appropriate. He was a tempted to cut and run, to get as far away from this place as possible. He took a deep breath, steadied, and forced himself to focus on the awful truth: that the otherwise unrecognizable, charred body behind the wheel in what was left of the twisted and scorched Buick must be all that remained of Ike Schwartz. The car's trunk had sprung open from the blast. He studied what was left of its familiar contents and the blistered and twisted just-readable license plate dangling from the bumper. Ike had used his own car again. He was funny that way.

Frank pivoted on his heel, his gaze took in everything—the glass shards from broken store windows, twisted bits and pieces of automobile, and still-smoking chunks of what might have been upholstery or…he didn't want to think or what…scattered over a quarter of an acre of downtown Picketsville, Virginia.

It had to have been one helluva bomb.

The Volunteer Fire Department had arrived almost as quickly as he had and made sure that fire did not spread. Some of its members, still booted and helmeted, stood by keeping watch on the smoldering wreckage while the rest were busy rolling up hoses and storing equipment. A low haze, part steam, part smoke from burning upholstery and gasoline, drifted over the area. Those who spoke did so in hushed voices. EMTs, seeing that their medical skills would not be needed and having been assured that the vehicle had cooled sufficiently, donned gloves and began the grisly task of removing the body and placing it in a body bag and thence onto a gurney to be taken to the morgue for autopsy. What they expected the medical examiner to find was anyone's guess.

Frank's head swam: Ike Schwartz dead. He had a hard time getting his mind around that. Sure, Ike had enemies. What cop doesn't? And Ike had served time in the Agency; there could be some bad stuff left over from that, but this was Picketsville, Virginia. What were the chances? He took one last look at the scene, turned and went back to his cruiser to think, to plan.

Who would tell Ruth? Frank assumed that, as second in line and now acting sheriff, it fell to him to make the call to Ike's wife. Once he'd done that, he'd call everyone in—all shifts, part-timers and retired. They would mount a taskforce the likes of which had never been seen anywhere. Vacations off, leaves canceled. He wanted everybody on this for as long as it took. He'd ask Karl Hedrick to call in some favors from the FBI, that is, if he had any left to call in. And Sam, he'd ask Sam to jump on the Internet. If there was anything lurking out there in cyberspace, she'd surer than hell would find it. Whoever had done this was about to find out they'd made the worse mistake of their life.

⟩⟩⟩

The phone's insistent ringing woke Ruth. At night, she made a point of disconnecting the answering machine on the assumption that any call made after midnight would likely be an emergency and need her attention.

"Okay, okay, in a minute." She fumbled for the phone and picked up at the same time as her mother. "Hello," they said in unison.

"Hang up, Mother, I've got it."

"How do you know it's not for me?"

"What are the chances? I'll holler if it is, now go back to bed." Ruth waited for the click that indicated the line was clear. "Hello, who's this?"

She listened. Her expression changed from sleepy annoyance to concern, to fear. "You're sure? Oh, God, you can't be… Tonight? Where? Yes, I understand. I will. What? When? Three days from now. I don't know. People will be all over the place. How will I…? Where? Will you be able to do that? He will? You're sure? How do I reach you? Okay, yes, yes. I still don't understand. Okay, I will, I promise."

She hung up.

"Who was that?" her mother shouted from her third floor studio.

"Nothing, wrong number. Okay, since you're up, you take the next one, Mother. I'm wide awake for a while and I'm headed downstairs for something to drink."

Ruth slipped on a terrycloth robe with the logo of a Las Vegas hotel on the pocket—she called it her honeymoon souvenir—and descended to the first floor. She poured herself a brandy snifter full of red wine and downed half in a single draught. She needed fortification. She also needed a few minutes to prepare before her mother rushed downstairs and broke the bad news and all hell broke loose.

The phone rang again fifteen minutes later. She hugged herself closer in her robe. God in Heaven, what was going on?

〉〉〉

Several miles away the County medical examiner received a similar call. He grumbled at first and then listened carefully. A frown squeezed his eyebrows so closely together it seemed his face was reduced one third its size. He shook his head, barked "No" several times, listened some more and reluctantly agreed to do as the caller requested. He didn't like it, but he would do it. It meant lying, a lot of lying, and he did not fancy himself a good liar. His ex-wife might have disagreed, but that was another story. More importantly, lying could lead to an accusation of perjury later and that could threaten his job and cost him his medical license. He hung up and started to dress. The next call he knew would come at any second and then he'd need to move.

The phone rang. He answered, was predictably shocked, and hung up. He had things to do. There would be DNA to process, naturally, and dental records. There could be no mistake about who had ended up on the slab. Then there would be the reporters, the State Police, the FBI probably, and God-only-knew who else would poke in their nose. Bombs tended to attract far more attention that simple shootings, or stabbings, or deaths by the old reliable, blunt force. Worse, he'd made it clear there might be a need to stall the release of the body for days, possibly longer. That would be the difficult part.

He started to slip his necktie under his shirt collar and then tossed it aside. What need had he for a tie at two in the morning? Later, maybe, when the crowds arrived to ask their questions, he'd dress up, but not now. Once in his county car, he headed straight to the highway. He ignored the speed limit all the way to the morgue. He wanted—no, he needed—to be the first one there. The problem with owing someone a favor is that they inevitably wanted to collect. People expected miracles from him. They probably watched too much television.

⟩⟩⟩

Felix Chambers had watched the car pull out of the parking lot. It had turned east, not west. The guy wasn't going home after all. He'd rigged the bomb to detonate when the odometer initiated a countdown and he'd calculated the miles with some care. This had not been a spur-of-the-moment job. Computer-monitored automobiles made his job so much easier now, no more guessing times or road conditions. Just hack into the car's "brain" and you could do damned near anything. All he had to do is measure the distance from a fixed point—for this job a convenience store a few miles away where the mark usually stopped for coffee—the point where he wanted the thing to blow. He'd intended for it to go off on the Calland University campus, with luck near the guy's house—at least blow out some windows. The man said he wanted to send a message. Some message. Well, it wasn't his fault that the cop didn't go straight home. Probably had to go somewhere else or maybe he had a little something going on the side and needed a dip first. Small-town cops were like that, right? So, okay, it didn't bust out some windows on the college. So what?

He called it in, skipped the part about where the thing went off, and waited. The man seemed pleased and said he'd move the money in the morning. No soap there. The deal was, pay on delivery. Move the money now. Then some bullshit about banks, but in the end he'd done it. He tapped off and checked his offshore account, saw the transfer completed. He lit a Cuban cigar and exhaled. Life was good. He ditched the burn phone, and headed to Dulles. He'd be on the next flight to Aruba one hundred thou richer and no one would ever put him in the frame.

Nobody shared the road when he pulled onto I-81 and headed north. He shook his head and smiled. Some guys really go to all kinds of trouble to get even. This last guy took the cake. One hundred K to snuff a small-town cop with a car bomb? Like, that was way over the top, like swatting a mosquito with a hand grenade or something. Hell, to do the job like that, he coulda got himself a hit man off the street for a short stack of Benjamins—or one, maybe even two, Clevelands, seeing as how it was a cop. Cops went down in the line of duty all the time. Nobody would have even noticed. Dead is dead, right? He flicked the ash from his cigar and smiled.

Chapter Two

Charlie Garland had a title at the CIA which did not match what he really spent his time doing. In that secretive and institutionally paranoid environment, no one dared notice or even suggest this to be unusual. Few people outside the director's office knew what his job entailed and if asked, they would mumble something that sounded official but which, on reflection, meant nothing. All anybody knew for certain was he occupied an office in the basement of the main building at Langley which contained a battered and very old Government Issue oak desk left over from another era, a wall full of mismatched filing cabinets, and an array of electronic devices including two computers. The title on his door read Public Affairs Annex, but no one had ever heard of such a division or function, nor was a there a line in the budget so named. No one thought it politic to mention that either. A newer computer sat on a makeshift credenza against one wall; the older one sat on his desk. Whereas the one on the desk had all the markings and characteristics of Government Issue, the newer one did not and it was this latter, off-budget, machine which at that moment had begun filling the room with alerts and chatter.

Charlie stood with his hand on the doorknob having every intention of going home. After all, it had already been a long day and it was late, but the incessant pinging from his computer made him hesitate. He dropped his briefcase, returned to his desk, and swiveled to stare at the computer screen.

The mandate given the CIA by Congress limits its purview to foreign affairs, covert and otherwise, international terrorism, spying, and so on. Domestic surveillance remained the clear responsibility of the FBI and Homeland Security. There would be no reason for the CIA to keep tabs on any activity within the borders of the United States or its territories. Any suggestion that it might be doing so would be vigorously denied. There were, however, certain gray areas that the Agency believed needed to be accounted for and which they were not entirely confident other law enforcement agencies would cover to their satisfaction. For instance, international borders, particularly the more porous ones in the Southwest, were a concern. Mixed in with migrant workers, children fleeing gangs in Central America, the gang members themselves, and people seeking a shot at a better life in general, terrorists and double agents found them easy entry points. So, where did the Agency's mandate really end in an era marked by shape-shifting enemies and ambivalent allegiances? A threat on one side of an arbitrary line drawn on a map would be its responsibility, but ten yards farther on, it fell to the forces monitored by Homeland Security? How efficient was that? Then there were acts of terrorism within the borders which, until their sources had been identified, might be linked to cells outside the country.

Thus, to cover its bases, the Agency had undertaken some passive domestic surveillance. Deniably, of course.

Part of Charlie's job was to be the one who "watched the watchers." Therefore, almost every program run by the Agency could be mirrored in his office. When the electronics geek had arrived to install some new programming and the alternative computer, Charlie made sure that not only would the obvious cities be covered—New York, San Francisco, Detroit, and so on, but that links to less likely places, places like Picketsville, Virginia, for example, could also be monitored if required. He did not explain why and the young woman had not asked. Obviously, the Shenandoah Valley did not rank anywhere near to the top of anyone's list of terrorist hotbeds.

Ike Schwartz was the sheriff of Picketsville and the closest thing to a best friend Charlie had—maybe even his only friend. They maintained that friendship by keeping each other at a distance, which might seem counterintuitive, but in the world of cloaks and daggers, as they used to say, it had been necessary. Charlie wanted to know what Ike was up to, whether Ike liked it or not. That was how he discovered the wedding, for example, but that was then and this was now.

Anyway, Picketsville or Podunk, any explosion bearing the signature of a professional bomb maker would trigger alerts up and down the line in all of the agencies now affiliated, however loosely, with Homeland Security. A car bomb with enough explosive power to crack and scorch asphalt and blow in windows in adjoining buildings fit the criteria and had set computer screens dancing across the country. As unlikely as it seemed, Picketsville had made the list of possible terrorist sites after all.

Alerts streamed across Charlie's alternative screen. He scanned each in turn, barely able to keep up with the volume of messages as they came pouring in. His gut told him, even before the dispatches confirmed it, that whatever had happened down there had to somehow involve Ike. Why he believed it, he could not say. There was something about Ike Schwartz, about his unyielding—some critics would say, insufferable—rectitude that seemed to attract trouble. People who always insisted on doing the right thing seemed to find themselves in the path of more than their fair share of enemies, critics, and untimely violence. When Charlie saw the burned-out shell of the Buick, he slipped off his coat, and sent the night porter for a pot of coffee. Whether Ike was alive or dead, Charlie would dig until he knew if he was, and then who, and what, and why all it had come about. He settled in to his desk chair. The coat slipped to the floor. He didn't notice. No one else would either. Charlie wore clothes that Alice, his administrative assistant, referred to as permanent un-pressed. One more wrinkle or a dozen would not be remarkable.

Once he'd determined the scope and magnitude of the bomb, Charlie put out a BOLO for any suspicious person to every airport within two hundred miles of Picketsville. He particularly wanted the explosive-sniffing dogs deployed. If he knew his bombers, and Charlie believed he did, he knew the person responsible for this last one would either be on the way out of the country or he would go to ground. The latter would take some digging, but the possibility of the former dictated tighter security at the nearer exit ports. He also knew that bomb makers, for all their cleverness at manufacture, rarely appreciated the evidence left on their clothing. If one were headed through an airport any time soon, the dogs would sniff him out. A wipe down would confirm it. The BOLO would also call for the facial recognition programs to be cranked up and not just the "usual suspects," but tourists, persons flying for business or pleasure, parents visiting their children or vice versa—everyone would be subjected to an increased TSA scrutiny for the next week. They would not be happy about that and mutter darkly about what the country had come to since 9/11, but there it was.

Charlie was still at his desk at noon the next day when the footage from the few, the precious few, surveillance cameras came online. Over the rest of that day and most of the next, and with only an occasional break to eat and nap, he scanned them repeatedly. Back and forth, again and again. A car pulls out of the lot and drives east. Why east? The University is west. Back it up to where the car pulls in. Is that Ike? There is another car. It is almost the same. When did it arrive? Who is that? Fast forward…back…forward to the second camera showing the explosion. Stay with that one a moment longer. You never know.

"Mr. Garland, you should take a break."

"Thank you, Alice. Can you get me a sandwich?"

"Sure. Would you like me to take a shower for you while I am at it?"

"It's that bad?"

"You see me standing six feet back from your door. Does that tell you anything?"

Charlie rolled back and stood. Alice was right. He needed to stop. He had been going in circles for over forty-eight hours.

"Anything else?"

"They've detained a man at Dulles. The dogs found explosive residue on his clothing. He already lawyered up. The FBI has him."

"Good. We will want to talk to him, too. Send someone over there."

He packed up and went home to sleep. He would awaken after six hours and realize what fatigue had made him miss.

Two drivers and two cars. There were two cars, two nearly identical cars and their drivers—not identical.

⟩⟩⟩

The rain began as a drizzle and then morphed into a hard downpour, the kind that soaks anything and anyone unfortunate enough to be caught in it for more than a few minutes. At least one person fit that description; caught standing in the downpour because he had been ordered to. He had crouched in the brush beside the A-frame since late the previous night. Before he took up his watching post he'd slipped into the house to make sure no one was there. Then he'd crept into the forest's edge and waited. The rain had not been expected. It began to rain and the temperature dropped ten degrees. Only a sodden Hudson's Bay wool shirt over a tee-shirt separated him from the damp. He had no rain gear and he was miserable.

"I tell you, ain't nobody here. No man and no woman," he muttered into his phone. No response. "Hey, you there or not?"

"I hear you. Give it another hour. Did you find anything before?"

"There's nothing. There's just this old broken-down Jeep and a car under a tarp. It doesn't look like it's been run in a while, either. It is covered with a year's worth of dust and has expired Virginia tags. I called them in to Manny and he says they are for this guy's old man, like he's storing it for him or something. Come on, Jack, the guy's dead. You saw the video. I'm drowning out here."

"Another hour, then come in."

"Christ, Jack, it's been like fifteen already."

"Fourteen and a half. Just do your job."

Chapter Three

The rain didn't seem so overwhelming under the canopy of hardwoods and pine. Ruth pulled deeper into the driveway. The car's headlights swept across the steps leading up to the glass sliders to the right, then into the shed-like structure that served as an areaway for the vintage Jeep that Ike rarely used but could not bring himself to part with. She braked in front of the A-frame and slid out of the front seat. Dripping branches and wet piles of leaves cluttered the way to the areaway which also held a utility closet and the electrical panel. She cinched her raincoat tighter and walked to the structure. She threw the main as Ike had taught her years ago when they'd spent their first weekend there. The water pump caught and hummed to life. The light next to the door lit. She had power and water. She'd need to adjust the thermostat inside and, if all went well, if the pilot light had not blown out, there'd be heat. It was wet and cold and the idea of building a fire with wood soaked by a driving rain did not appeal to her. She would do it if she had to, but then, telltale smoke would beg the question—a question she did not want to entertain just now.

It had been a terrible three days. Police with endless questions, well-meaning and sympathetic faculty with more, friends and people she hardly knew, all crowded into the house. Flowers, sympathy cards, and casseroles—the latter from the townsfolk who seemed to have a better grasp of what she needed than her academic colleagues. It wasn't that she didn't like flowers and sympathy, but who wants to cook at a time like…? And then more questions. Frank, now acting in Ike's stead as sheriff, solicitous but firm, and maybe feeling embarrassed at the circumstances that had put him in charge, needed to know what Ike had been up too. *You don't know? Then why should I?* Colonel Scarlet from the State Police had a few questions of his own—something about a man named…*what was his name?* The FBI also wanted to know who Ike had met and why. As if she knew. Car bombs were naturally high on their list of things they wanted to track, they said. Of course they did. Terrorism, domestic and foreign, had everyone on edge, and to them, bombs meant terrorists. Fortunately, Karl Hedrick had arrived in time to short-stop some of the more aggressive members of the late J. Edgar's boys intent on lecturing her on anti-terrorism and her responsibilities thereto. Her head swam.

She needed to get away, she'd said. They'd demurred. Why not? she'd asked. There might be an attempt on her life, they said. Why? No answer. Finally she'd persuaded them that she'd be better off in the A-frame than on campus. The Board had reluctantly granted her a leave of absence from her duties as president of the university. What else could they do? She needed space, she'd said. Reluctantly the FBI, the Sheriff's Department, and the rest of the gathered law enforcement community agreed, but only on the condition that she would call in every day at a specific time to tell them she was safe and well. She declined her mother's company. That had hurt, but there was no way around it. She had to come here alone. Finally they'd left her in peace and it began to rain. A hard, driving rain, the sort that washes away all the accumulated detritus that collects in gutters and lives.

The steps bore their share of leaves and branches knocked down by the deluge. The debris was as undisturbed as that littering the driveway, which showed no evidence that anyone had been in the cabin for weeks. Good. She kicked aside a pile in front of the door, unlocked it and let herself in. She had her hand on the light switch, but did not throw it.

"Okay, I'm here. Do I turn on the lights or not?" No answer, only the rustle of blinds in the sitting area and footsteps in the dark. "Okay, now?"

"Now."

She flicked the switch and the single lamp on the sofa's side table blazed. The room remained more in shadows than lighted.

"Where are you?" she said. Her eyes darted from corner to corner.

"In the hallway to the bedroom. Don't come here just yet. The draperies are closed."

"I know. I heard you close them."

"If no one was here, they should have been. I had them open to watch the slope down to the valley. I closed them so that your opening them wouldn't seem unusual."

"What? Jeez, does everything need to be this complicated? Is there someone in the valley?"

"As far as I can tell not anymore."

"Not anymore? Was there someone before?"

"Oh yeah. He left late yesterday afternoon. Poor jerk. He stood in the rain out in the bushes for nearly fifteen hours. Probably has a case of double pneumonia by now. Look, this is the obvious place for me to go if I wasn't killed, so I figured if they didn't get an absolute confirmation, they'd check around. They were probably at the farm, too."

"Your dad's in Richmond."

"Good thing, too."

"So, okay, why close the curtains?"

"Because I couldn't be sure someone else didn't follow you here. You open them, have a look around, and close them again. I'll meet you in the bedroom."

"If you say so. I hope you know what you are doing."

Ruth went through the motions of settling in. She swept the curtains back, peered out and let them fall. She switched on the lamp over the stove and banged her overnight bag around. She shed her raincoat, gloves, and scarf, called her mother to say she had arrived safely and no, she didn't want company...no, Eden was not to come out in the morning, or anytime. No, that was final. She shut her phone down, slipped into the bedroom, and launched herself at Ike.

"You have some explaining to do, Sheriff, but first, are you okay, are you hurt? God, I was so worried."

"I'm fine, really. Not a scratch. You?"

"Me? Hell, what's not to like? My husband is reported blown to bits. There are cops and people all over the house and I am doing my best to be a grieving widow all the while knowing you are lurking somewhere in the dark, thank God. Did I say I was worried? I was. No, not worried—sick. All I had was your call and then everybody barging in and questions, my God the questions, but from you, nothing, and…Jesus, I began to wonder, did you really call or was I in denial and just made that up? Ike, what's going on?"

"It's complicated"

"No shit. Complicated! That's your answer? I was nearly thrown into early onset menopause and all you can say is, 'It's complicated?'Well, as people who live on their iPhones would type, WTF, Ike?"

"I'm sorry to have to put you through all this—"

"Sorry? Sorry doesn't even come close. Not just me. Ike, the whole town is either in shock or mourning, or ready to lynch somebody—anybody they think might have had a hand in this. They want to go to a funeral and I can't tell them a damned thing."

"I am sorry. It's not what I want but…I wish I knew what happened. All I know is that was a bomb for the ages. Not just a 'let's kill Ike' bomb, but a 'let's kill Ike and the rest of you better take notice what happens to people like him or you could be next' kind of bomb. It had to be about something bigger than just me, Ruth. I wish I knew how much and why, but I don't. All I can say is a slightly drunk Mike Holloway jumped in my car by mistake, made it halfway to his motel, and got blown into tiny bits and I am sure it was meant to be me driving that car. I must have really pissed off somebody, big-time."

"No surprise there. But I still don't get it. How did what's-his-name manage to get in your car and drive away?"

"Holloway? Damned if I know. All I know is that I left right after he did, got into what I thought was my car and then realized it wasn't. It took me a second or two to figure that he must have taken mine by mistake and, in the condition he was in, he probably wouldn't have noticed, so I took off after him."

"Okay, and your key fit his ignition?"

"Yeah, it did. I had the car started before I realized it wasn't mine. It figures mine must have fit in his. We were parked next to each other, and since he had his usual overdraft, so to speak, he didn't notice he was in the wrong car."

"You're sure about the keys?"

"How could I possibly know? My key worked in his. It follows his worked in mine. He drove off in it, right. If the key hadn't fit, he'd be alive and I'd be dead. Of course it fit."

"No need to bite my head off."

"Sorry. I'm still a little edgy. Look, if my car had been hotwired, Forensics would have been onto that right away and all this would be moving in a different direction by now. His key and my key both had to be the same. I do not know what the odds are of two nearly identical cars being in the same place at the same time with keys that are interchangeable but…Anyway, he took my car, off he goes, and blam! He's blown to bits and I'm alive."

"There's no chance that he was the intended victim?"

"Slim to none, I should say. Remotely possible, but…he was undercover, a man who moved in and out of the drug smuggling business so there's always a slim possibility he was the target, but remember, it was my car that blew up, not his. Also, it would be an overreach hit for an informer. Holloway was one of Colonel Scarlet's people, by the way."

"Explains why the Colonel hovered. That's the name Scarlet kept asking about. So, not likely it was Holloway. It had to be you. Okay, I get it. But, won't they be looking for him, for Holloway?"

"Not right away. He has no family and is always on the move. It would not be remarkable if he disappeared for a period of time. I got the impression he hadn't told anyone that I was meeting him, though it seems now that Scarlet must have known or suspected something. I guess that leaves me as the target."

"Yes, well…Ike…" Ruth's knees buckled and she collapsed on the bed. Seventy-two hours and the enormity of what had happened…what was happening…finally caught up with her. Someone tried to kill Ike—wanted him dead. No, not just kill him—atomize him—erase all trace of him. "Jesus, I was worried before. You know, confused and worried and a little scared. You call, Frank calls." Ruth's breath had become ragged. "He tells my mother who then tells me that you were killed in an explosion only I know you're not and I can't say…can't say anything And everybody saying how bravely I was taking it, that I should go ahead and have a good cry. I did, you know. I just let go one afternoon. People thought it was grief. It was because I couldn't take any more, you see?"

"Got it."

Ruth took a breath and let it out. "Okay, that part was scary and confusing then, but just now the enormity of it all hit me and I'm past scared. I'm terrified. Who wants you dead? Why do they want you dead? What happens when they find out you aren't?"

Ike shrugged and squeezed her hand. "I wish I knew, Ruth. They'll try again, I guess." He put his hand on her knee. "That's why I'm here, not in the office. Whoever is behind this obviously has means and resources not available to your average assassin. Right now, I need time and a safe place to stay. I need to work this through."

"By yourself? You plan to do this alone? Is that what you have been doing for the last three days?"

"Trying to, you know, making lists of names, dates, places, and crossing them off, listening, and waiting."

"Waiting? Waiting for what?"

"Two things: first, to make sure the people who did this feel sure they're in the clear that I am certifiably dead, and second, for the other half to arrive."

"The other…you mean me? I'm the other half?"

"You are a major part of the other half, yes. Right now, we need to take a breath and celebrate the fact that I am not dead and I have you for a little more time."

"What about your killer?"

"He thinks I'm dead. Until he finds out otherwise, he won't be looking."

"So, then—"

"Later."

Chapter Four

The tech arrived about noon and explained to Charlie how the enhancement programs could sharpen an image on the screen but would not add details. "Pixels are pixels," he said, as if that made sense. Charlie murmured something about tautologies. Tautologies are the sort of thing liberal arts graduates like to natter on about, for IT guys, not so much. The young man nodded and muttered something about the number of pulses per second. At least that's what Charlie thought he heard. He showed Charlie how to execute the facial recognition programs and repeated the pixels mantra. Charlie smiled, thanked him, and sent him on his way.

The director called and wanted to know what Charlie was up to. Charlie smiled and waited until the door closed behind the tech and then briefed the director. He left out the part about his belief that Ike might still be alive. He knew the director was the soul of discretion, but his secretary had been known to gossip and though in the past she kept it to office scandal, Charlie dared not risk it. Not yet, not until he'd actually talked to Ike, assuming he was correct about Ike being alive and he could.

Right, talk to Ike, but would Ike talk to him? By now Ike must be wondering what part of his past had come into play to destroy him. His first guess would be the CIA—that the Agency had decided he might have to be a necessary pawn in some game involving that past. He'd be wrong, but that would not stop him from thinking it and consequently he would, by now, be someplace where he felt certain the Agency could not track him. Or would he?

Ike had survived all his years in the agency and in his latest iteration as rural cop by convincing people they were cleverer than he. "Dumb like a fox," Charlie's grandmother would say. Well, he and Ike had played this game of cat and mouse before. Charlie sat back in his ancient oak desk chair and dropped into a coma-like state that removed him from the world and allowed him to focus on the problem at hand. Alice knocked twice, recognized the thousand-mile stare, and said she'd come back when he returned to Earth.

〉〉〉

"Woof, it's been a long time since we made sheet music like that, Ike."

"Absence makes the heart grow fonder."

"It's only been four days...nights."

"Nevertheless. Glad to discover you haven't misplaced your playbook."

"My what? My playbook? You think? You have no idea. Oh, Lord. I say, you have no...no idea. Listen, Buster, with you presumably dead, I've done some research. Just in case you really are/were...dead, that is. A wake-up call, you could say."

"A what?"

"Take this as a cautionary tale, Copper. There are many fewer hot male catches out there than there are female hunters. I know that's hard to believe but there you are. Don't ever tell anyone I said that or that it's even important, by the way. So, if I have to go back into the lists to compete—you being dead and me a widow and all—I want to be a first-rounder. Keeping up with the next generation, see. Kids these days read the *Kama Sutra*, for God's sake. So, I'm always learning, staying ahead of the curve. *Fifty Shades of Gray*, the aforementioned *Kama Sutra*, CineMax, *Busty Cheerleaders Camp*...I've been busy. Hey, a woman can't just rest on her laurels, you know."

Ruth grabbed a tissue and blew her nose. "Allergies."

Ike wrapped his arms around her. "Right. I wasn't imagining your laurels or you resting on them. Hey, it's okay…shhhhh. I'm here and I don't plan on leaving."

She shook her head and a tear finally escaped and rolled down her cheek. "I was so scared, Ike. I thought, 'Okay, I know he's not really dead, but he could be. Cops die LOD all the time, don't they?' And I thought what if it was true, you know? What if it *had* been you in the car? You know it could have been, might have been. Except for a drunk who took the wrong car…I mean identical keys? Two cars and keys? That's the difference between the now and the what-might-have-been? What are the fucking odds? God! And then the worst part, I thought about what life would be without you and it…and my heart almost broke. Ike, don't do this anymore."

"I won't, I promise. But until I find the person who thinks he killed me, there can be no end to it. And you don't have to drop the F bomb. You're the president of a University, not one of your students."

"Not drop the F…what? Why? You and your high octane testosterone-fueled cops say it all the time and you know it."

"They do as do the ladies in the beauty parlor, at least half a dozen clergymen I know, editors, school children, and nearly everyone else. Eighty percent of the world's English-speaking population and probably most of the rest of the world, too, often in everyday conversation, I'm told. I know, but I don't. I did, but I don't anymore."

"You do know how sanctimonious that makes you sound."

"Yes, I do. I don't care. Sanctimonious sounds a little pejorative, though. How about prudish? I sound prudish…no, stick with sanctimonious. Prudish is for little old ladies. Sanctimonious sounds more macho, don't you think? Anyway, why not simply respect a decision made and not judge it at all?"

"Macho? Jesus! Okay, I won't judge, though you do know that others will. Why have you given up the F bomb, as you say?"

"Well, believe it or not, when every upper-middle class housewife drops it into conversation on the mistaken notion it adds to their sense of relevance, it loses its punch. I mean when it ceases to shock, it ceases to be useful. Also, it has become a word that has lost its meaning. It is now used as an adjective, verb, adverb, object, and noun and often in the same sentence. You might as well say, 'oatmeal' or its euphemism, 'fudge.' Same impact."

"Wow, so if it is no longer meaningful, why do you care if people say it?"

"Aside from I find it disconcerting, maybe I just don't want to be like everybody else."

Ruth took a deep breath and straightened up. "Surely you kid. 'Not be like everybody else?' Jesus, Ike, there is no way in hell you will ever be mistaken for anyone else in this life or the next, assuming there is one. Oh, God, that's not quite true, is it? Someone already…Okay, no more verbal fucking. Just the actual kind. Gottcha. So, what can we do?"

"First, I have to consider who I can trust and then begin to poke around. I wish I had Sam Hedrick in my back pocket."

"Well, you don't. She's been exiled to Washington, DC, the navel of the Universe. So, except for her, you don't know who to trust?"

"I am not ready to rule anybody in or out."

"Frank, Karl. None of your deputies? They're your friends."

"Yes, in time…soon. I have to figure how to limit the number of people who know."

"Because? Never mind. Then, how about Charlie Garland?"

"Nope."

"Charlie is out?"

"He's CIA, Ruth. The Agency is a screwy place. They work hard at what they believe is the best interests for everyone at any moment in time, but times change and alliances shift. Today's friend is tomorrow's enemy. Their loyalties can be powerful, but at the same time, fickle. Who knows what trade-off might have required me to be the bait in some larger dodge? I have a history, but I am ex and therefore, very expendable. The Agency has few scruples in matters like that."

"I hate your past."

"Yeah, well it sucks but it has it perks. Anyway, if Charlie is involved he will react one way. If not, another. I will wait and see which way he jumps. When that happens and I have a line on its direction, as much as you will not like it, he could become a necessary part of our lives for a while."

"If it gets you out of this, I'm okay with that, but you're right, I won't like it. What will you do while you wait for him to, as you say, jump?"

"Catch up. How's our ward, Darla, taking this?"

"Darla is a 'Wednesday's child,' Ike. Her life has been one of nearly continuous awfulness. For her, this is just one more crappy thing to absorb in a lifetime of crap. I suspect she will take it all in better than any of us. Besides she's at that GED prep program and I haven't told her yet. Maybe I won't have to."

"Your mother?"

"My mother is the ultimate Drama Queen. She's in her element. So, again, what now?"

"At this exact moment, I need to realize what I could have lost. You are not the only one who was scared. With that in mind, I think for now I'll start exploring all the new additions to your playbook you implied you'd added."

"Dare I say the word?"

"Not say, do."

Ruth frowned and looked at the man who was supposed to be dead, but wasn't and who, but for a twist of fate, should have been. Ike Schwartz, her husband. Peculiar word, husband. It means "dutiful manager" or something stupid like that. How many women really think of their husbands as their manager, dutiful or otherwise? How many women would introduce their spouse as their "dutiful manager?" How many in her world could do so and live? She shoved Ike backwards. Some managing might be in order here, but not by the manager.

Ike cocked an eyebrow. "You did say you've done some research."

"Do we have any plum sauce?"

Chapter Five

A dozen frustrated and angry deputies crowded in and around the door of what used to be Ike Schwartz's office—well, technically, still was. Frank Sutherlin held up his hand in a feeble attempt to quiet them down. Billy, his younger brother, stood in one corner, his wife, Essie, in the other. Where Billy's face was beet red, Essie's showed the ravages of three days of steady weeping.

"We have been shoved aside like they think we don't know what we're doing, or something," Billy said.

"That's because they don't think we do. They think all rural cops are some version of Buford T. Justice." This came from a recent recruit fresh from the Police Academy, shiny bright and togged in a too-new khaki uniform, and filled with the confidence that only the young and inexperienced possess. Frank was startled that he knew who Buford T. Justice was. A late night Jackie Gleason movie marathon?

"One of the guys from the State Police said we were the junior varsity and it was time for the first string to step in."

"Okay, okay," Frank said. "We all know how the suits from the big city view us. Nothing new there. So what? We still have a job to do and no matter what they may believe to the contrary, this bombing took place in our jurisdiction. The FBI, the state, and the rest of them from wherever they came from, can swagger around all they want, but in the end, it's ours. Look, instead of bitching and moaning about them, why don't you all tell me what you've got so far?"

The room fell into silence.

"Nothing?'

"The Feds took all the surveillance tape from the store across from the restaurant where Ike was eating, so we don't have any idea when Ike came or left. Same with the shots of the explosion. Nothing there. No, wait, I think I heard one of them say there were two cars at the store that left about the same time."

Frank shook his head. "That's it? No report from the ME? We're sure the body was Ike?"

"He says the dental records are a match. That's one piece. Frank, it don't look good."

"I know, I know, it was wishful thinking maybe, but the fact remained that until we had positive ID, the death was still booked as possible. I guess we have it now."

Essie grabbed her box of Kleenex and bolted from the office.

"There has got to be something we can do." Charlie Picket said.

"There is," Frank said. "Colonel Scarlet from the State Police told me that it was his understanding Ike was meeting with a guy named Holloway. Holloway works for the state undercover as a NARC and he was supposed to be bringing Ike up to speed on the traffic through the area."

"So?"

"So, Holloway is missing, too."

"If he's undercover, he would be, wouldn't he?"

"Yes, except this explosion is all over the news. So, why hasn't he called in by now?"

"Maybe he thinks the hit was drug-related and then he might be dead, too. That way, he's laying low until he can get a line on who put out the hit."

"It's possible. Since the FBI and their buddies have shut us out of the investigation, I think we need to go looking for Mr. Holloway. He had to have seen something, noticed someone."

"Great. How, Frank? He's undercover, remember. He won't be easy to find. Hell, he won't want to be found."

"I don't give a shit what he wants, Billy. I want him. He has a car. The car has a tag. We put out a BOLO and look for it. Wait. Just to make sure the Feds don't scotch our attempt to get involved here as well, make the BOLO for…a Deadbeat Dad. They won't even notice. Damn, I wish we had Sam back. She could scour the Internet or whatever for us…at least keep tabs on what everybody else is doing."

Billy looked at Frank as if seeing him for the first time. "Damn, you're right. Frank. You know that the Bureau figured that since Karl was so familiar with the town and all, they made him Agent in Place for this investigation. How about, because Sam is his wife and all, maybe we ask if she could drop in like for a visit or something and we could put her on all that computer stuff she assembled and then left behind when she got herself sent to Washington back then?"

"Karl Hedrick is a friend, but he is still FBI. We can't expect him to compromise his position that way."

"Well, why the hell not? We got us a frickin' tragedy here and they are…sorry, they were…both really close to Ike. Why wouldn't he jump in? It's not like he would be working for us, just Sam. Come on, Frank. We've been dropped into the equivalent of a ten-foot pothole here. We need to climb out. Screw the Feds."

Frank cocked one eyebrow and smiled. "Right. Why the hell not? I'll make the call."

⟩⟩⟩

Samantha Hedrick heard the news late in the morning. Now, dressed in yoga pants and a bright red hoodie with USMC emblazoned on it, she was on the road headed southwest. She'd driven not quite an hour when Frank's call came through. She took it on her cell phone just as she reached junction of I-66 and I-81.

"I'm way ahead of you, Frank. I already called your mother and she is expecting me. Karl has to be officially out of the loop on this one and the party line is that I am taking some personal leave time. There may be some flack headed your way and you can bet some close scrutiny of any Internet activity emanating from your office, but I'm on my way."

"Will there be trouble when they find out you're attacking their databases?"

"Well, if I know one thing, I know how to keep them from noticing. Hey, I work for NSA, remember? We do this stuff all the time."

"That part I really don't want to know. Just get here ASAP. We're being stonewalled big-time."

"Give me a couple of hours and time to get the kid settled with your mom, and I'm on it."

Sam tapped off and stared through the windshield, aware of the traffic and her place in it, but otherwise a thousand miles away. Her mind raced through protocols she would need to establish, the cloaking she would need to do to keep other agencies in the dark, and the excitement of using the skills honed at NSA to go after some local bottom-feeder without needing an order from a supervisor or a warrant from a judge. Except for the horror of losing the nicest man she knew, her husband excepted, this was going to be the best vacation ever.

>>>

"She's on her way," Frank announced. "Now, the rest of you hit the road. I need the witnesses at the restaurant re-interviewed. I don't trust the reports from the FBI. I want you, Billy and Charlie, to plot the distance to the explosion and then figure where else it might have happened, like, if Ike had headed straight home. Also, get us fresh pictures of the site where the thing went off and the restaurant parking lot. Tire tracks, anything and everything."

"On it. Anything else?"

"If I were the Feds, I would have put out a BOLO and alert at exit ports within a couple of hours from here in case the bomber decided to skip the country. Check around and see if they picked anybody up in the last day or so."

Bill clapped his hat on. "Okay, it's a start. Let's see if we can out-maneuver these candy-assed big shots from DC."

Chapter Six

Martin Pangborn acquired wealth the way magnets attract iron filings. At least that is the way he liked to describe his success. His critics were less generous in their estimation, comparing his success to be more like how excrement attracts flies. He made millions from the misfortunes of corporations facing financial collapse. Once he'd spotted them, like a carrion bird, like a vulture, he would circle until his prey's struggles appeared terminal and then swoop down and devour the flesh. The bones he left to be picked over by other, lesser operatives. Small companies dealing with money problems, companies with credit lines that had become stretched to the breaking point, were his targets. Once acquired, he'd sell off the viable assets, and dump the remains onto the scrapheap of corporate failures. The people left behind faced a future without jobs and pensions. Not his problem. He moved on to the next acquisition, the next corporate dismemberment. Broken dreams and men were detritus in his wake.

He was not a popular man. Popular or not, money, he discovered did buy him a cadre of sycophants and friends eager to bask in the aura of wealth and notoriety. Among them were celebrities—movie stars primarily, and politicians, a great many politicians, all with campaigns to finance—and the shady individuals with indeterminate pasts who possessed certain skills and connections he found useful. Even the President of the United States had been persuaded to have his picture taken with Pangborn and his prospective nominee for a high government position.

Ranked against that array of beautiful and influential people were the legions of broken men and women, their families and, indirectly, their friends whose lives had been destroyed by his financial predation and who had to stand helplessly and watch as their lives imploded. If any man could be said to have more enemies than friends, he would be Pangborn. Also, it should be noted, that there were a few people who had had the audacity to stand up to him, or threatened to expose him. If anyone had been keeping track, had made the connection between them and Pangborn, they would have been struck by how many others like them had died unexpectedly. In accidents, mostly, a few from natural causes. At least that was what their death certificates would say. Pangborn was not a man to be trifled with.

His was not the usual rags to riches story—certainly not a Horatio Alger narrative. He started out poor. That part was true, but his rise to fame and fortune had a darker thread than the "hard work is its own reward" line one would like to read in *Fortune*. His mother deserted the family of six when Martin, the youngest, was three. His father celebrated her departure by getting very drunk, beating up two of his older sons and attempting to rape his only daughter. One of the brothers, the one who'd suffered the lightest beating, split the old man's head open with a Louisville Slugger. The family was remanded to Child Protective Services and sent to a series of foster homes. All but Martin ended up in jail at one time or another. The daughter, his sister, died of a drug overdose on the Southside of Chicago late one December night. The heroin had been a Christmas present from her pimp.

For the most part, Martin, because of his age, managed to avoid these and similar disasters and, indeed, was unaware of any of them until years later, after he had achieved some measure of success occasioned by the suspicious death of his foster father who had built a modest acquisition business. There was one important exception to an otherwise uneventful life as a foster child. Martin, fearful for his young life, would never reveal to anyone the things which occurred in his bedroom almost nightly, which was why the caseworker assigned to him would report that his life in foster care had been unremarkable and, given the usual foster care statistics, a positive experience. She did remark as an afterthought that he seemed reticent to communicate with her. Those terrible and painful nights defined the relationship Martin had with his male foster parent and ultimately conspired to bring that man to an early, deserved, but quite unexpected death.

Later, Martin would spend a great deal of money to discover what had happened to his siblings. He bought a modest annuity, anonymously of course, for each of those who remained alive so that they would not starve—unless they chose to—and then proceeded to erase them from his conscience.

In his search for guidance, for a lighthouse, he would say later, he came to admire one man, a conservative thinker and blogger named Drexel Franks. Franks claimed to be distantly related to Bobby Franks who, everyone knew, was the thrill-killing victim of Leopold and Loeb from the nineteen twenties. Martin had never heard of either Bobby Franks or Leopold and Loeb. He Googled their names and read the story. He'd had several clashes with Jewish business owners in the past and the story turned his nascent dislike of certain men into a simmering anti-Semitism. It was about this time he started his journey from cutthroat entrepreneur to demagogy.

Drexel Franks also had a highly filtered view of the American Constitution and its provisions. In his view, the current administration was populated with "One Worlders" (it was never clear what he meant by that, but Martin grasped the essence), bleeding heart liberals, and traitors. The Second Amendment became Franks' pivotal talking point. It was intended, he said, not just because the framers of the document wanted a well-armed militia, but equally, to enable the people to rise up against it when the government departed from the simplicity of the ideal and turned to totalitarianism. That turning point was never defined either, but seemed to have more to do with ideology than action. His mantra was to arm for the coming revolution, the one that would put the country back on the track the Founding Fathers had intended.

Franks also founded the Fifty-first Star, an organization dedicated to his idiosyncratic world view. The name referred to a concept he developed over a period of time and then promoted on his website; true representation was no longer available to real people. Not in the Congresses and not in the executive branch. (He had no use for the judicial branch one way or the other.) The present system, however well-intentioned the Founding Fathers might have been in its ideation, had since become, he opined, another example of "taxation without representation" and justified separation. Thus, he called for the establishment of a new state, one without geographical borders, but composed of people joined together in a commonality of ideology. It was needed, he said, so that representation of like-minded people could be assured, a sort of sociological gerrymandering. Thus, if he had his way, a fifty-first star was to be added to the current flag. To that end, he declared himself governor of his new (as yet unnamed) state and proceeded to enact laws that reflected his political thinking and to lobby for recognition by the government. Further, claiming state supremacy, he ruled that laws he believed to be at variance with his understanding of the Constitution were null and void and were not to be obeyed by those who shared this skewed notion of democracy.

A full recognition of his delusional state would require an amendment to the Constitution, naturally, but in the interest of democracy as he understood it, Franks saw no reason why such an amendment could not be passed and had lobbied state legislators across the country for its introduction. He had no takers, but did receive several encouraging letters, usually accompanied by a solicitation for campaign funds.

Martin Pangborn joined the Fifty-first Star shortly after he determined the reason America was losing its soul. He stood shoulder-to-shoulder with men like himself who were under attack by society for their greed and lack of ethics. People, Martin and his colleagues believed, simply did not understand capitalism. It was to be understood in Darwinian terms and these soft bleaters on the left did not get it. Survival of the fittest did not include any notion of fair distribution or wage reform. Workers worked and the few men, like himself, who knew how, raised themselves by their bootstraps and left to become managers, owners, and so on. The Founding Fathers understood that. Why not these wooly thinking do-gooders?

Martin joined this fantasy but not completely. He realized that if the movement was to have any traction it would need more than Drexel Franks' rhetoric. And that the idea of amending the Constitution was ludicrous. A sovereign state—a new one based on ideology—within the current fifty states would never fly. But it had enormous potential as a movement that could draw people to it and exert pressure in the right places at election time. Influence, he knew, could be purchased. He already had several lawmakers in his pocket. He could buy more. He had the money to do that, and if the Fifty-first Star could be effectively mobilized, he believed he would soon own the government—figuratively, of course.

That change, he believed, would be brought about by the judicious application of money to certain politicians and the concomitant assembling of a group of people, men primarily, who shared this burgeoning ideology and were willing to act on it. With the right people in office, the need for Franks' dreamy new state would not be necessary. Pangborn assumed control of The Fifty-first Star. Franks, he set up as its titular head and sent on a prolonged sabbatical to write a book. He recruited like-minded people to his vast acreage in Idaho. There he established the militia he believed the Second Amendment envisioned, set up training camps, armed his people, and—constitutionally empowered, he believed—sent them out to right the wrongs he'd identified as contrary to the commonwealth or, occasionally, to right the wrongs of those who'd caused him personal pain. The country's youth, he knew, were the future, if his plan were to be permanent. To that end he established the New Pioneers, boys between the ages of ten and sixteen, who were to be placed under his personal aegis. He would train them and provide their education. His fascination with the organization soon became evidenced in the number of times Fifty-first Star or some variant appeared in one of his myriad corporate names—Five/one S, five one Star, New Star, etc.

There were some who had concerns about his drive to power. They were dealt with variously. Money or coercion usually worked. The more difficult undertakings, he contracted out. Ike Schwartz had caused him pain the previous year. Ike Schwartz had confounded one of his moves toward the White House and Ike Schwartz was a Jew. As far as Pangborn was concerned, that was a double whammy. Ike Schwartz was eliminated. Ike, of course, had no idea that he'd ever met, abused, or caused pain for Martin Pangborn. Martin did not care. Cross the Five-One Star and you pay. People would learn soon enough what it was and what it stood for.

When he'd confirmed the hit, he paid the man for a job well done. Later he'd heard the idiot had been apprehended at Dulles Airport. Not as professional an assassin as he'd been led to believe. The word on the wire was that the bomber had lawyered up and had not, as yet, told the Feds anything. Martin did not take chances. People like this contract killer, people with no loyalty except to the highest bidder, with loyalty only for the money they were paid, could never be trusted to keep silent. He dared not take the risk that this weak link wouldn't break, so he sent two of his close associates to Washington, DC to tidy up that loose end.

>>>

The FBI had been able to detain Felix Chambers, but with no supporting evidence beyond explosive residue on his clothing, they could not hold him and his lawyer had already produced a writ of *habeas corpus* to the hearing judge. They had to let him go. They were embarrassed a day later when the only lead they had in the Picketsville bombing was killed while under their surveillance. Apparently someone had dispatched him through the motel's bathroom window while the agents sat in an unmarked car across the street.

Chapter Seven

Charlie Garland had finally mastered the art of enhancing the grainy images from the surveillance cameras and was studying the restaurant parking lot one last time when the news of Felix Chambers' shooting came across his desk. The Bureau lost its only solid lead in the bombing and thus, had egg on its face. To lose a witness or suspect, or even a "person of interest" while under close surveillance was a definite no-no. An agent or two were about to be given a winter assignment in Duluth.

Charlie scanned the new crime scene images which he'd pirated from the Bureau's secure website. The accompanying report stated that the alley behind the motel had not been subject to observation for two reasons: There seemed no reason to believe there was any risk to the suspect from the outside, and the windows were too small for him to exit should he wish to escape further scrutiny. The report speculated that only a lucky shot from a distance could have produced the result and therefore no dereliction of duty could be ascribed to the surveillance team.

Charlie snorted. "It's a good thing they weren't working for me or they'd be on their way to the farm for retraining by now."

The ever-present Alice, stepped into the office with the latest analysis. "What?"

"Lucky, my sweet patoot. Look in this picture…right here." Charlie tapped the image with a finger. "What do you see here?"

"It looks like a big box."

"A box or a crate, correct. And where is it?"

"Under a window?"

"Not just any window. Under Chambers' motel bathroom window, to be precise. So, a box on which a man can stand. Imagine then, he taps on the window. 'Felix,' he says, not too loudly, but enough so the folks in the next room can hear. 'Hey, Felix.' The guy comes to the bathroom to see what's going on. 'Over here. Come closer, I have a message from…whoever.' The dope steps closer. The report says he stood in the tub, for God's sake. As soon as his shadow fills the window, the guy with the Sig drops his laser spot on it and, pop. Lucky shot by a sniper, my foot. I bet when they do the post they'll find a nine millimeter, not a rifle slug, and evidence of a noise suppressor."

"There were men tracking Chambers?"

"I would assume so. Two, probably—someone had to watch the alley. Anyway, we need to know who hired him and why. Wait. Alice, you read that report. What did he have on him when he was arrested? A cell phone?" Alice scanned the report and nodded. "Did they dump it?"

"They did. Nada. They found calls to restaurants, the cleaners, stuff like that."

"Codes?"

"Nope."

"That means that somewhere between Picketsville and Dulles there is a dumpster, a trash barrel, a ditch, something, with a burn phone in it and we need to find it."

"Mr. Garland, do you know how impossible that would be?"

"Nonsense. First, we find out where it was sold. He would have used cash, of course, but maybe not. Look at that report again. Credit cards? Numbers?"

Alice rattled off a series of numbers associated with a half dozen credit cards found in Chambers' wallet at the time of his arrest.

"Great, we put a trace on all purchases made in the last month. Contract killers like to keep track of their expenses. Look for a phone or phones. He might have bought a series. It would be safer if he did. I would, if I were in his line of work."

Alice raised her eyebrows marginally and started to say something.

"Yeah, yeah, fine line, I get it. Okay, then trace the serial numbers, and then track GPS signals. There, we'll find it."

"Unless he trashed it."

"Possible, but why would he? A dumpster is trash enough."

"Mr. Garland, I don't think the director would authorize the resources to make that hunt, even if he believed it would work."

"You're right. He wouldn't. That's why we're not going to tell him. Hop to it, Alice, get the gang on it *tout de suite*. Oh, and you are looking very smart this morning."

"Smart?"

"You know, fetching, well turned-out…"

"Charlie, nobody talks that way anymore, but thank you. I'll get the guys on it."

〉〉〉

Frank had only a minimal knowledge of the extent of modern forensic software and its capabilities. He'd heard, but didn't really believe, that calls made one day would be retrievable days or weeks later.

"Sam, is it possible to capture any local calls made the night of the explosion?"

"Maybe. It depends if the signal triggered a watch."

"A what?"

"There are a gazillion calls made on any given day. Some are of interest to the law enforcement community, most aren't. Obviously, you can't record every call ever made, but certain phones and, ah, circumstances…will set off a keep signal."

"Certain phones and certain circumstances? That's NSA-speak and I don't think I want to hear any more. Just tell me if there are any suspicious calls made to or from the area around the time the bomb went off, and if so, can they be traced?"

"Maybe and maybe not. Let me see what's still in the air. At the very least, we might get a location for the phone if it's live. And don't worry. NSA isn't interested in your love-life, Frank. By certain phones I mean, think a minute, why does anyone need a burn phone? I know there are lots of perfectly good reasons, but at the same time, don't forget they are also the preferred means of communicating by all kinds of bad guys. They think that because they are not registered to a specific person, they can't or won't be traced. So, as a general rule, a call on a disposable phone will trigger a tap, a watch. Phones sending or receiving odd-sounding messages might be recorded. After a period of time the recordings are erased to make room for the new stuff. I can go searching the call bank for local off-registered phones if you want me to."

"Do that."

"Okay, but first, there is some stuff you should see here. The FBI is not the only group with eyes on this business."

"No? Who else?"

"Well, it appears the CIA has its nose in at least, and then I get the feeling there is someone else. I can't figure out who the last one is. It's pretty well cloaked."

"Will you be able to ever?"

"Oh, yeah. It's just a matter of time. Has anybody heard from Ike's buddy in the Agency?"

"Garland? No, not that I know of."

"Doesn't that strike you as odd? They were pretty close and all. You'd think he'd be all over this."

"You did say the CIA was nosing in?"

"Oh, right. That could be him. Should I 'ping' him just so he knows we know?"

"Do what?"

"I can drop a line of text into whatever he's looking at so he knows we know."

"Suppose it isn't him at the Agency that's doing the snooping?"

Sam grinned. "Then someone up there will have a minor heart palpitation and go running to their systems security people. It could be fun."

"Do it and let's see, but don't get caught. Remember what happened the last time."

>>>

The message startled Charlie at first and then he understood. Ike's people were on the trail as well and this would be Samantha Hedrick unless he had lost his touch. He studied the screen and then entered a reply.

It's nice to hear from you, Sam. You do know it's a Federal offense to hack the CIA. Of course you do. We've had this conversation before. Want to help me out here?

He waited.

Sure, we're looking for a phone. Any thoughts?

Same here. You have a lead?

"Maybe...you?

Let you know in a couple of hours

K.

Charlie smiled. At least there was some hope. If Samantha Hedrick was on the trail, that meant there was a trail. Now, where was Ike? When should he tell the others that Ike is alive? When should he tell Ike he knows he is alive? Where is he?

Chapter Eight

Ruth scooped fried potatoes and eggs from the pan onto Ike's plate and then hers. Breakfast any time of the day saved more marriages than sex, she thought. She hitched the flannel robe she kept at the A-frame tighter and sat. She had no idea why this breakfast epiphany occurred to her at that particular moment. It certainly did not carry much in the weighty intellectual department and she wondered if it were even true. Another thought popped up to displace it.

"What did you do with what's-his-name...Holloway's...car?"

"It's under a tarp parked in front of the Jeep. I was waiting for you to get here for a chance to get rid of it."

"You said one of the goons who wanted you dead was here. Wouldn't he have seen it?"

"Figured that was a possibility, too, and rigged it, just in case."

"Rigged it? How?"

"I shook the vacuum cleaner bag on the dash and seats and then all over the car. I switched the tags to some old ones that used to be on one of my father's old clunkers, covered it with the tarp and emptied the remainder of the dust on top. It looks like that buggy has been in storage for years."

"Jesus, Ike. Are you always this devious?"

"Only when someone with real chops tries to kill me."

"Okay, we get rid of the car. How and where? Wouldn't it attract a lot of attention, no matter where you put it?"

"Not necessarily. I thought that tonight we would drive down to Roanoke Airport and I would put Holloway's plates back on and leave the thing in Long Term Parking. It's where it would be if he was off somewhere. You would follow in your car or the Jeep. Are you up for a midnight ride?"

"I don't know, Paul Revere. Let me get this straight. You are proposing that we drive down to the Roanoke Airport in two cars, dump the dead man's Buick in a parking lot, and drive back here tonight?"

"Isn't that what I just said?"

"At midnight?"

"Or thereabouts, yes. We'd be less likely to run into state cops."

"Ike, I am beat. Three days of unending chaos and then finding you. Can we do this tomorrow night? What I really want right now is a hot bath and a cuddle until I drop into unconsciousness."

"That bad? Okay, tomorrow then. Go take your bath. I will light a fire and we can sample some vintage vintage."

"A classic redundancy. Great. I will prepare my ablutions. You are not...repeat...not invited to join me. Tub's too small and I am too tired to engage in soapy intercourse, verbal or otherwise. Do you like breakfast for supper?"

"I do. Every man does. Why do you ask?"

"It occurred to me that you might."

"I see, I guess. Okay, give me a five-minute heads-up when you're about to de-tub so I can have the wine open and breathing. White or red?"

"Your choice."

Ruth retreated into the bedroom with its adjoining bath. Ike retrieved a bottle of white he'd been assured was indeed "vintage." He heard the water running. Ruth's hot baths, the sort needed to un-kink muscles and untie mental knots, required no less than a half hour. He laid a fire and got it going and settled back to wait. He must have dozed off because the next thing he saw was a wet and naked Ruth pointing at the land line telephone which was ringing.

"I thought that thing had been disconnected," she said and wrapped a towel around her waist.

"It was, over a month ago. Crap."

"It's ringing, Ike."

"Yes."

"Do you want to explain?"

"I'd rather pull the towel off you."

"I mean it, Ike. The damned phone is ringing. It's supposed to be dead. What's going on?"

Ike sighed, resisted the urge to yank at the towel, and stood and stared at the phone. "I know of only one person that could be on the other end of that line."

"Someone is there? Oh, crap, it's Charlie Garland, isn't it? The bastard has found us—found you."

"Charlie, I don't know." He hesitated. "Either him or there is another group with the same capability of remotely reconnecting a telephone. Considering the magnitude of that bomb, I'd guess my man with a hard-on for me might be able to."

"What do we do?"

"We listen." He stood staring at the phone and seemed to count. "Okay, it's not Charlie."

"You know that, how?"

"Tell you later. So consider, it's entirely possible that you did not know the phone was disconnected. It is possible that other people did not know that either. They may have discovered or guessed that you are here. If you answer, it will not seem unusual. If you don't answer and it is an innocent mistake by someone thinking the line is live and expects you to answer, that might cause alarm. So, we don't have many choices here. You'd better answer. Be the grieving widow and get rid of whoever is on the other end. Oh, and either wrap up all the way or drop it. You are driving me crazy."

"Wow, decisions, decisions…drop or rearrange, drop or re-arrange…what to do? Okay." Ruth rearranged the towel in a marginally more modest fashion and picked up the receiver. "Hello?"

〉〉〉

The last person to see Felix Chambers alive, albeit through a shattered bathroom window, listened to the woman's hesitant voice. The wife?

"Hello?"

"Hello. Yes," he glanced at the script he'd memorized earlier. "This is Bill Montgomery calling from the *Washington Post*. Could I speak to Sheriff Ike Schwartz?"

There was a pause. Was she alone and consulting someone?

"Excuse me, Mr. …?

"Montgomery."

"Montgomery…how did you get this number?"

"It's in the book."

"Sorry, but it is not. Why are you calling?"

"I want to speak to the sheriff."

"You obviously have not heard."

"Heard?"

"My husband is dead. Killed in an explosion. This is a very bad time to call. Since this is an unlisted number, I insist you remove it from your files."

"I am sorry to hear about your husband's death. Can you tell me any…?" The line went dead.

He turned to his companion. "She hung up."

"Did she say anything?"

"She confirmed that Schwartz is dead." He snickered at his words.

"What's so funny?"

"The old joke. You know…'Schultz is dead…' only now it's, Schwartz is dead."

"I don't get it. What old joke? Never mind. Anything else? Did you get the impression someone else might have been in the room?"

"Nothing certain. There was this hesitation like she might be looking at someone or something. But then, she might have just been caught off guard, you know."

"Nothing else? Maybe a click on the line like another person picked up an extension to listen?"

"The sheet says there's no extension in the house."

"Doesn't mean shit. Any jackass who isn't color blind and owns a screwdriver can install an extension nowadays. Did you hear anything?"

"Maybe a click. I don't know. If there was someone else there, it don't mean it was Schwartz. Cops could have tapped the phone."

"The cops don't tap phones that are disconnected, Manny. There's no reason to. They would do her mobile."

"Well, at least we know where she's at now. I'll pass that on."

"Yeah. Jack said the guy in town lost her and the people at the top weren't too happy about that. So, confirmation Schwartz is dead, but still need to see a corpse."

"The boss sent Brattan to the ME's office. He should call in soon."

"Yeah, still…see, the car wasn't going in the right direction and that got the boss thinking. You know how he is with details."

"You and me both…and what's-his-name…Chambers."

❯❯❯

Ruth dropped the phone's handpiece back into the cradle and turned to Ike. "What do you think?"

Ike shook his head. "I don't like it. That wasn't Charlie. I'd bet my firstborn that it wasn't the *Washington Post* either. Someone with the same kind of resources as the CIA managed to reconnect the phone. I guess that just confirms it. I thought the guy watching the house—"

"He just watched?"

"Actually, he came in and searched the place. Before you ask, I was in the rafters. I have a way to get up there and—"

"Of course you do."

"Right. Anyway, something has got them doubting. I don't know what or why. The damned bomb was big enough to have qualified as one of Bush's 'Bunker Busters.' Surely they don't think I survived it. What's bugging them?"

"I guess they tried the phone for the same reason Charlie would, don't you think? They were hoping the fact that the phone rang would lure you into picking up. Since they had already been here, they were double-checking."

"Yeah, probably. There is another possibility, of course."

"Another…what?"

"Could it be that they, whoever *they* are, might be looking for you, not me?"

"Me? Why would he/they care about me?"

"I don't know. But if they were convinced I was dead, there is no other reason to open this line and call. If it is you they are after, now they know where to find you. Either way it is definitely not good news, but useful news nevertheless."

"Not good, but useful how?"

"Not good because if it's me they are looking for, they must still have doubts. Useful because it means we know that whoever it is that wants me dead is not your garden variety mook. That fact clears Charlie and his playmates at the Agency. This guy has resources and power. Finding him won't be easy, but at last we can eliminate all of the bottom-dwellers with a grudge. So, who the hell, with that kind of power, did I piss off enough to bring this on us?"

"Don't look at me. Piss me off and you sleep alone. I am definitely not into bombs."

"That is very reassuring."

"I don't rule out castrating shears in extreme circumstances."

Ike was about to reply when the phone rang again.

"What do I do, Ike"

He held up his hand and mouthed numbers—*one, two, three.* Silence. He kept counting. *Four, five, six,* ring, pause.

"I'll take this one." Ike reached for the phone.

Ruth passed him the receiver. "What just happened here?"

"Hello, Charlie. Before you say anything, put a trace on the last call made to this phone and call me back." He hung up. "That was Charlie."

"How did you know that before—?"

"Three rings, a three-second gap, and one more ring equals Charlie. It's something we worked out back in the day."

"And he can control the rings?"

"If you know how, anyone can."

"Really? How?"

"NTK."

"Oh, 'need to know.' What? I don't need to know? I think I do. Listen, we're in this together or not at all, Ike. Anyway, I think I need one of those secret code ring things too."

Chapter Nine

Tom Wexler tapped the papers on his desk into a neat pile, snapped off the desk lamp, and stood. It was late and he wanted to get out of the office and climb into a tall whiskey and soda. Between a bus rollover on I-81, a suspicious death in Lexington, and the Schwartz business with its incessant interruptions from cops from all jurisdictions, not to mention reporters, his patience had worn dangerously thin. As for the Schwartz thing, the DNA results had come back and there was no way he could hide the fact. Now, he faced the problem of finding another excuse to delay Ike Schwartz's interment. He wished he'd never agreed to this charade. He picked up his briefcase and turned to leave. A stranger stood in the door.

"Excuse me," the stranger said. "Are you the county medical examiner?"

"That's what the title on the door says."

"I can read. I'm asking if the title on the door is yours."

"And you are…?"

The guy reached into his coat. Tom had a permit to carry a gun. It came with the job, although why a medical examiner would need to pack was unclear, television depictions of the job notwithstanding. When he lived in Detroit he'd often carried a weapon, but not because of his job. It was Detroit, after all. Rockbridge County, Virginia, was not Detroit, so his Glock, still in the box it came in and coated with Class C Cosmoline, sat perched on the top shelf of a closet in his bedroom. Right now he wished he hadn't put it there. Tom reached for the alarm button on his desk instead. The man paused and held his hand palm out, and then produced a wallet. He flipped it open.

"Franklin, FBI," he said and snapped it shut again. Quickly— too quickly, but the shield looked legit.

"Okay, Franklin, FBI, what can I do for you? And yes, I am the ME."

"I just need to double-check. Is the stiff from the explosion… is it Schwartz?"

"Dental records say it is."

"I already heard that. I need something better. DNA?"

"Just arrived. See for yourself." Tom pulled a sheet from a manila folder and handed it to the agent.

"I can't read that. What's it say?"

"The DNA sample from the body matches a sample on file."

"It's Schwartz?"

"Like I said, the samples match. Is there anything else?"

"Nope, that's all I need."

Franklin turned and left. Tom waited until the door swung shut and picked up his phone and called the security office.

"This is the medical examiner. Do you have surveillance footage for the last hour?"

"Yes sir."

"How often do you overwrite the tape?"

"Unless we get a request not to, every three weeks or so. Depends on the tape and if the system is down or something. I don't know, so, yeah about three weeks."

"Okay, I need a secure copy of everything from an hour ago until my last visitor leaves. Got it?"

"Well, yeah, I can do that. Is there a problem? The guy just walked out the door. Do you want me to apprehend him?"

"No, not necessary. I just need a copy made and locked up in a safe place for a while."

"Sir?"

"It's okay, son. Maybe I worked the big city for too many years. I have a feeling. If I'm wrong, we'll dump the copy later."

"Yes, sir. Copy will be made."

Franklin, FBI, he says…flips open the badge wallet and closes it. Nothing else…What's wrong with this picture?

Tom was a belt and suspenders man. You can never be too sure. You make a copy of everything.

〉〉〉

Ruth and Ike stared at the phone willing it to ring and maybe hoping it wouldn't. It did. Three rings, pause, one ring…Ike picked up.

"Hello, Charlie, what have you got?"

"Nice to hear from you, too, Ike. I can assume that since it is you and not Ruth that answered the phone, that the reports of your death were grossly exaggerated?"

"You can, but you may not."

"Ah, English 101. Got it. You are officially dead. I may not deny that, yes. Good. Would you like to know what I discovered about your most recent call?"

"Of course."

"Well, unfortunately there is a difficulty. Whoever contacted you definitely did not want to be traced. We were able to connect the dots that bounced all over the grid and all the way to Idaho and there the path ended. It seems the line ended at a radio translator near the Idaho-Montana border. We couldn't get past that. The people in the trace group said they will have to do some analysis of the tower in question to see if its signal is directional and determine its strength. Also it likely scrambles the signal. Right now that isn't a problem because we aren't into tapping the line, but we might be later. So, depending on what they discover about direction and strength, we might be able to narrow down the general area and ultimately the sender."

"Idaho? What's in Idaho except for Boise State football, skiing, and movie stars on the lam?"

"Much more, *mon frère*. Rich plutocrats with their—you should pardon the expression—'hunting camps.' How two hundred acres can be considered a 'camp' boggles the imagination. Then there are the McMansions with stables of expensive ponies, some very nice scenery, and a smattering of survivalists of the ultra-conservative stripe, and oh, mustn't forget it's the Potato State."

"So, eliminating the possibility of an overcooked French fry, you're suggesting an irate movie star, a ski bum, a plutocrat with an itch to shoot elk out of season, or a survivalist is out to see me dead?"

"How many movie stars have you annoyed in your lifetime?"

"None that I know of. Many have annoyed me, but not the other way around."

"Okay, we eliminate Hollywood. See how easy this is going to be?"

"Cut the crap, Charlie. What have you got?"

"Beyond the radio tower in Idaho, nothing. Oh, wait, maybe one, no two other things. The FBI picked up a suspect at Dulles the morning after the attempt on your life. They couldn't hold him forever so they kicked him loose. They did keep him under what they called 'close surveillance' but didn't bother to watch the alley behind the motel and—"

"He slipped the noose."

"Not quite. Someone popped him through the bathroom window. It was an eight-by-ten-inch window. That's why the feds neglected the alley. He had a portly physique and they figured he couldn't squeeze through it. They only watched the front door. By the time they heard the shot or shots and hustled around the back, the shooter was long gone."

"Embarrassing for them."

"Indeed. Ike there is only so much I can do here. The Agency has its limitations when it comes to domestic stuff."

"Yeah, yeah, like you care. Charlie, even you don't believe that. If this was a known terrorist organization, your people would be all over it, jurisdictional niceties or not."

"Well…okay. Listen, you should know this. Your old buddy, Samantha, is in Picketsville and working the wire, so to speak. So, that is good news. We have communicated. Both of us are looking for a phone."

"What phone?"

"The FBI dumped the dead suspect bomber's phone. There was nothing on it, which means somewhere out in the countryside there is a burn phone with stuff on it that could lead us to his employer."

"And you know that even if you find that needle in a haystack, it will probably lead to that tower in Idaho."

"Maybe, maybe not, but it would at least be a confirmation. Leave the tower to me. The larger question is: Do I tell Sam and the rest that you are alive?"

"I will have to give that some thought. Lord knows I need a blanket, but how and who to tell?"

"While you muddle over that, what did you do with the dead guy's car?"

"It's parked out here under a tarp. Ruth and I were planning on whisking it away to Roanoke tomorrow night."

"Bad idea. Leave it to me. I will send a cleanup crew tomorrow. You wait for a wrong number on Ruth's cell phone and then take a cross-country jaunt in your little Jeep. Ride some trail where no one ever goes—at least this time of year no one does. Where was your contact headed, by the way?"

"Norfolk."

"Then that's where the car will mysteriously appear. Okay, think about the 'who and how.' I will check back later—on Ruth's phone. This one is going dead again."

Charlie hung up.

Ike replaced the receiver and looked at Ruth. "You finished your soak?"

"You got the wine?"

"I do. Ditch the towel?"

"Maybe later. Pour and tell me what the 'Evil Genius of the Potomac' had to say."

Chapter Ten

Earlier that year and because he needed some serious physical exertion to cut the cobwebs away from some of the darker corners in his mind, Ike had cleared a wide pathway down the mountainside from his A-frame to the state park that borders his property. Ike described it as "exercise to exorcize." The remark received a puzzled look and a raised eyebrow. He never repeated it. He'd had to stop at the edge of the state park. Three months later a state forestry crew asked for an easement through his land in order to access the meadow below. He'd agreed and that is how the path he'd started had been widened and wandered deep into the state forest before exiting out onto the open grassland to the east.

Charlie called with his "wrong number." Ike and Ruth, he said, needed to vacate the premises for two or three hours while the cleanup crew relocated Frank Holloway's Buick to Norfolk. Ike told him where the license plates were hidden. Then he and Ruth packed a picnic of ham sandwiches, chips and dip, a bottle of Merlot that the liquor store guaranteed was not too dry, and set out in his Jeep, now painted a dull olive drab with streaks of black and tan. Ike had made a stab at camouflage. A bad stab, as it happened, but even so, parked in the brush it nearly disappeared. The Jeep bounced down the path toward the foot of the mountain. Near the point where the path broke into the open, Ike had created a small picnic area. He'd tidied up an existing clearing by removing the scrub and brush from the center and hauling the fallen tree trunks to its edge. Then he'd applied a chainsaw to the stumps to make places to sit. Assuming you didn't mind a seat full of pine sap when you stood, they worked fairly well. He parked the Jeep and unloaded their supplies.

"This is idyllic, Ike. Just smell that air."

"Pine sap."

"Whatever. Why haven't we come here before?"

"I don't know. I guess neither time nor opportunity ever came together."

Ruth spread a blanket in a patch of sunshine and proceeded to shed her clothing. Ike watched, curious to see if, or where, she stopped. Finally, clad only in her panties she stretched out on the blanket.

"Don't get any ideas, Sheriff. This may be the last of the summer sun we will have and I am interested in having only it on my body this morning. Read your book."

"Right. In case you are interested, there are two of those round Band-Aids in the first aid kit that you might consider applying…um, strategically. I don't know, but I imagine a burn there would be pretty uncomfortable."

"Coconut butter, Bub, and mind your own business."

"I like to think they are my business, but I won't press the point—no pun intended."

"Read your book."

"Reading my book."

>>>

Charlie Garland sat at a picnic table in the park on the north side of Picketsville. He'd arranged his laptop and papers on the space in front of him. Passersby would assume he was a salesman, maybe between appointments, taking advantage of a warm fall day to work outside. The other three arrived within five minutes of each other in separate cars.

"You called and I came," Frank Sutherlin said. "I assume you called Sam and Karl as well?"

"I did and you are wondering why." The three took seats on the bench opposite Charlie and waited. "Okay. I called you because Ike said you were the three who could be trusted, at least at first."

"Ike said that? When? When did he say that to you and why? I mean, sure we want to get to the bottom of this damn thing, but why you and why bring it up now?" Karl frowned and drummed his fingers on the table's rough planking. Having the CIA poke its nose in at this point could not be good news. The Bureau, when it found out would have a fit.

"Okay. It's good you're sitting down because—"

"Why didn't he include Billy and Essie, for crying out loud? Those two are closer to him than any of us."

"Stay with me for a minute, please. There is a reason he left those two off the list and he said that you, Frank, would be the one to make the decision when and if to break the news to them."

"Break what news, Mr. Garland?"

"Ike is not dead." He waited for the words to sink in and then continued. "The car that took the bomb was his, but he wasn't in it."

"He wasn't…Wait, if he's alive, who's dead?"

"A state NARC named Holloway and before you ask, Ike stays dead until we find out who ordered the hit."

"Because?…I don't understand."

"The hit was too much, way over the top. If someone had just wanted Ike dead, a sniper could have just popped him or, I'm assuming it's a 'he,' could have arranged a drive-by shooting. There are too many easy ways to kill a cop and you three know that better than anybody. That bomb…well, you all saw what it did. That bomb shattered the car and a half block of storefronts on both sides of the road. That was not just a hit. That was a declaration of war."

"Sent by whom? Why?"

"If I knew that, we would not be having this chat, would we? That is what you all need to find out. I am CIA. As you know, Karl, having the Agency involved in a domestic murder will cause all kinds of not-nice, spiky memos to sail back and forth from the Bureau to the Agency. I can help, but only you people can be up front, you see?"

"But you can use CIA resources on this? That's against—"

"The Picketsville Police Department, cooperating with the FBI will crack this thing. If asked, you may concede that you had the help of a private consultant who, because of the delicacy of his position, may not be identified."

Karl sat back and scratched his head. "Does your director know you're doing this?"

"The director feels a certain obligation to Ike for his past services."

"Is that a yes?"

"That is an evasion. Anything else before we get down to cases?"

"I guess not. What have you got so far?"

Charlie told them about the radio repeater tower in Idaho and the death of the only suspect they had so far. Karl already knew about the shooting at the motel. He said he could probably requisition a team from Boise to check out the tower but would need a plausible reason to do it. Charlie smiled, pulled a burn phone from his pocket, and called him.

"You don't know me, but if you want to find the guy that killed the cop down there in Virginia, you should check out a radio tower in Idaho."

Charlie clicked off. "There you go. You just got an anonymous tip. It sounded real enough, don't you think? Hey, it's worth checking. Now, Sam, with that bit of information shared by the FBI with the local police, do you think you can zero in on some possible names in the general area covered by the transmission, assuming Karl's buddies in Boise can determine it? You have NSA files that you can access. Somewhere in them there has to be a list of people you are tracking for whatever reason—good, bad, or political."

Sam thought a moment. She absently picked some lint from the pocket of her leather jacket and gave Charlie a half smile. "We don't do political."

"Of course you don't. Just look anyway."

"What do we do?" Frank asked.

Charlie thought of Frank as a workhorse, strong, steady, and untiring. Also, he hoped, not like Orwell's Boxer, but smart, intelligent, and aware. "There has to be something that everybody has missed so far. I don't care how good the killer was, somebody saw something, heard something. There is evidence the FBI and the State Police have overlooked. You go find it."

"We can look, sure. Why not Billy and Essie?"

"Ike said that if I were to include Billy in this conversation, no matter how much Billy promised not to, and to stop Essie from crying herself sick, he'd tell her."

"So?"

"Essie, he said, hasn't a disingenuous bone in her body. The minute she found out, she'd be grinning all over herself. If anyone is watching, he will guess why. Is Ike right?'

"He's right. The trouble is, I need Billy on this. You think we have watchers?"

"I don't know, but when in doubt…Figure something out about Billy. Are the rest of you straight about keeping the fact that Ike is alive quiet for a while?"

"Ruth knows, right?"

"She does."

"Okay. How do we get in touch with you, Garland?"

"Sam will know how. Okay, we're done here."

Chapter Eleven

Frank had his feet up on Ike's desk and his chin on his chest. He'd been that way since he'd returned from his meeting. Billy asked him who he'd met and what had happened to Sam, but Frank had only mumbled something about new evidence and had stalked into the office. Billy followed him in and sat. Frank was his older brother and he could read his moods. Something important had happened in the last hour and Billy wanted to know what that was. He took a seat in the corner, fingered the brim of his Stetson, and waited.

"If you want to plant a bomb on a car, you have to have access to the car, right?" Frank said at last.

"Right."

"Did you calculate the distance the car traveled before it blew and where it might have been if Ike had gone home instead of the other way?"

"Yeah, we did. It would have exploded on the Calland campus, blown out windows in several buildings, possibly one of the dormitories."

"Or the president's house?"

"Oh, yeah. That too, I guess. Hey, you don't think—?"

"I don't know what to think. Look, if we assume that having it go off on the campus or, more likely at the place where Ike lived, was a secondary objective, it means the bomb had to have been put in the car in the parking lot outside the restaurant. We have no evidence of that so it had to be someplace pretty close to it. The bomber could not have known where or how long Ike might drive in a given day, but he would figure that late at night, his next stop would be home. Sam looked at that surveillance tape a dozen times and if the device was placed on the car there, she would have spotted it. Whoever rigged it, couldn't have known that Ike would make a stop on the way first, but it wouldn't matter if home was the final destination. He had to rig it somewhere else, but not too far away."

"Yeah, I never thought of that. Wait, there's another thing. If you're right, the bomb had to be linked to the odometer, not on a timer, otherwise it would have blown while he was meeting the NARC. That means it would have to be a pretty sophisticated device."

"So, it had to be installed somewhere else. I'll ask Sam to draw a circle with a twenty-mile radius with the restaurant at the center and then pull the surveillance tapes of every parking lot, gas station, and mall inside it."

"We should ask Ruth if she knew where Ike went that night," Billy said.

"Yeah, we should but I'm guessing she won't know. Ike was careful about bringing work home, he said. "Ruth! Oh my God. Look, if that thing was set to go off at the university, it follows that whoever did this, wanted more than just Ike dead. He wanted to hurt Ruth as well, maybe even catch her in the blast."

"Jesus, I hadn't thought of that. You think?"

"If we're right, they could be after her. We let her go off to the A-frame to have some time alone. If they're keeping tabs on us, they know that. There's nobody up there to protect her. Billy, grab a couple of deputies and get your butt up there. If she bitches, tell her what we figured out and bring her back here ASAP."

"What if she won't come?"

"Cuff her and drag her back."

>>>

Ike put down his book. His attention span had run its course after two hours. Now he was having an inner debate whether he should disobey Ruth's declaration to leave her body to the sun alone when he heard the blast. Ruth sat up and looked at him, then reached for her blouse.

"That came from up there, toward the A-frame."

Ike leapt to his feet. "Get dressed and follow me." He grabbed the remnants of their picnic and blankets and tossed them into the Jeep. "Hurry."

Ruth pulled on her clothes and scurried to the Jeep. Ike attempted to fluff the grass crushed by her blanket and restore the site to some semblance of naturalness. He released the Jeep's brake and pushed it toward a slope away from the area. He let it drift ten yards and into a thicket. Ruth had to duck to avoid being plucked out of her seat by a tree branch. Ike quickly arranged some scattered limbs around the rear of the Jeep. He put his finger to his lips and motioned to her to follow him. He led her deeper into the thicket and motioned her to squat down.

"Ike, what just happened?" She whispered.

"Shhh…someone is coming."

Two men wearing pricey Pierre Cardin shirts and slacks worked their way down the path toward them. One had a rifle in the crook of his arm, the second a large nickel-plated automatic in his hand.

"Hunters?" Ruth whispered.

"In those clothes and wearing three hundred-dollar loafers? I don't think so. Scrunch down, wait, and see."

"Who then?"

"Shhhh…"

The man in front, tallish, pale blond hair and carrying the rifle, paused, bent over and studied the ground at his feet.

"These tracks look fresh."

"According to the map, the state has an easement down through here. Besides, her car was still in the driveway."

"Where is she then?"

The second man was short and heavy, the near opposite of his companion. Mutt and Jeff. "Probably out shopping with a friend or taking a walk. We can wait for her at the front of the driveway."

"Why not at what's left of the house?"

"Don't be stupid, Hugo. She takes one look at that mess and she's off to the cops in a New York minute. We'll catch her on the way out or the way in. We got her either way."

The men glared at the bushes and, satisfied no one was nearby, started back up the path. When they were well out of earshot, Ike sat back and turned to Ruth.

"You get that?"

"They were looking for me, and you don't think they were here to help me because of something that happened at the A-frame?"

"Hang on." Ike grabbed the burn phone from the Jeep and dialed 9-1-1. "There's been an explosion, maybe a gas leak." He gave the address of the A-frame and hung up. "That ought to get some people here and make those guys think twice about hanging around."

"You're saying they were not Good Samaritans?"

"The guns and the reference to the cops pretty much blew that theory, don't you think?"

"Okay, I'll buy that. Who wants me dead?"

"No idea. Maybe not dead, maybe just bad hurt. So, it's not just me they are after, whoever they are. It's us. Who hates us that much? Me, I understand. As a cop and former field agent for Spook Central, I made a lot of people unhappy. But you…? You didn't kick out a student with 'connections,' did you?"

"You're joking, right?"

"I am. Now it appears we both need to disappear. Any suggestions where we might go?"

"What happened to the house?"

"Judging by the sound, I think the A-frame will be mostly pick-up sticks and twisted plumbing. In a minute I will skulk back and see."

"If you think I'm staying back here in the woods alone, you are nuts. You go, I go."

"They said they would wait by the road for you. I better go alone. Two people are far easier to spot than one."

"Nevertheless, I go. Hey, remember me? I'm your intrepid shooting partner from our fun-filled summer vacation on the island."

"We are unarmed and your buttons are in the wrong holes."

"It's the latest from *Elle*—slovenly is the new *chic*. You have a revolver in the Jeep. I saw it."

"Not much against a rifle with a scope."

"You're a crack shot. I saw you hit a tin can at twenty yards."

"That was with me standing and using a finely calibrated pistol. The piece in the Jeep is a snub-nosed Police Special .38. You need to be within ten feet to do any damage with that."

"Still, you'd be armed."

"Ruth, right at the moment, the last thing I want to do is get in a fire fight with a pair of heavily armed goons. Even in the unlikely event I win it, we lose. If they don't go back to their boss, he or she will get suspicious that old Ike ain't dead after all.

"That's bad."

"Very. I need to talk to Charlie. This puts a new wrinkle on an already very creased plot, I think." Ike stood and retrieved the pistol from the Jeep and handed her the phone. "You call."

"What do I say?"

"You'll think of something, you're a university president."

"Very funny."

Ruth tapped in the number Charlie had given them earlier and waited. Charlie answered with a simple "Hello?" Ruth cleared her throat and asked if she was speaking to Mr. Garland.

Pause.

"Tell Ike I just heard about your house. My crew cleared the area and the car is on its way to Norfolk. Ruth, we need to get you into protective custody. Billy and two other deputies should be there in a half hour. Wait for them."

"There are two men at the end of the driveway looking for me."

"Roger that. Wait for a call."

Ruth sat back and opened the hamper with their picnic. She handed Ike a sandwich and poured each of them a cup of wine.

"He said wait for the call. Eat up. Your deputies will deal with the bad guys at the end of the lane."

"I'm going to check anyway."

"What's the matter with you, Ike? You missed one date with death this week already. Why do you want you to risk another? Okay, if I take my clothes off again, will you stay?"

"You're bad."

Chapter Twelve

Billy Sutherlin grabbed Charlie Picket and the new kid and hopped into the Department's only available cruiser, the Ford Vic with two hundred thousand miles on the odometer and slated for trade-in as soon as there was some wiggle room in the budget. They headed east toward the Blue Ridge Parkway. Ike's A-frame was situated on a six-acre plot down the mountainside and off a road that briefly paralleled the parkway. The radio crackled. Sam forwarded a 9-1-1 call that reported an explosion, possibly at the A-frame. Billy lit up the cruiser and stomped on the accelerator. The old-school siren howled as they climbed up into the mountains. A second message from Sam told them to be on the lookout for two perps possibly hanging out near the house driveway and also that Ruth was okay and staying out of sight. She would come out when they signaled an all clear.

Charlie Picket said, "Did that voice on the 9-1-1 call sound familiar to you?"

Billy's answer was lost when a sedan with rental tags roared past them headed the other way. Billy reckoned that the bad guys must have heard the siren and decided to take off. He suppressed an urge to put the car into a drift-spin and chase after them. Instead, he had the kid call in as much information about the sedan that the three of them could recall and request anyone in the area to intercept.

The A-frame appeared past rescuing by the time they arrived. The front wall had been blown out and the floor buckled upward at a sixty-degree angle. Fire licked at what was left of the interior. Broken glass, shards of plasterboard, and timber littered the driveway and adjoining wooded area. The stone fireplace still stood, but leaned to one side at a dangerous angle. Billy thought it lucky Ike wasn't there to see it. It would have broken his heart. The three men spread out and scoured the surrounding area for any sign of the bombers/arsonists, even though Billy felt sure they were the pair he saw blow by them in the car earlier. The fire trucks arrived a few minutes later.

First Ike, now his retreat. What was going on? Were they after Ruth like Frank thought? It sure seemed like it. Why? Billy understood that Ike might have made a shitload of enemies in his time and would be a candidate for killing, but Ruth? Who wants to kill a college president? The fire captain strolled over.

"You're local?"

"No, Picketsville. Our boss…that is our former boss, owned this place. We came up to pick up his wife is all. What happened?"

"I'm no expert, but it looks to me like the propane tank blew. Funny thing is, I can't for the life of me see how. Them things' usually pretty inert unless you work at it and then they mostly sit off to one side of a house, you know? Just being careful means putting them against a non-life-threatening wall, and isolated from any kind of a spark. This one looks like it might have been located right under the damn floor and that doesn't make sense. And the other thing—"

"Could it have been knocked there by the explosion?"

"It'd be a stretch but maybe. I don't know. We'll have to wait for the arson investigator to say. It don't seem likely to me. Lucky nobody was here when she went up, though."

"Yeah, lucky. You started to say something else, 'another thing' you said."

"I did? Oh yeah. That's way too much damage for a blown propane tank."

"Something else exploded?"

"Can't say, but I'd bet the rent on it."

"How long you reckon you'll stick around here?"

"Another hour or so. Long enough to douse the hot spots and be sure she's plumb out."

Billy checked in. Sam said to hold, then told him to work his way down a path behind the house. Ruth would be waiting for him. He did as he was instructed and met Ruth on her way up the mountain in Ike's old Jeep. She didn't look too good. Her clothes were all crooked like and buttoned wrong. Probably pretty shook up.

"You okay, Miz….Doctor…?"

"I'm okay, Billy. What happened to the house?"

"It's pretty busted up. Propane tank blew. Maybe an accident, maybe not. The fire guy thought the tank might have had some help. Do you know if it was situated up under the house?"

"The propane tank? No, it was out in the areaway on the side of the main building. Why?"

"No reason, only it seems like it got relocated under the floor and the fire marshal reckoned that was a peculiar place to put one."

"I guess it would be. How would you fill it? You think somebody moved it? Could they? It must weigh a couple hundred pounds."

"I don't rightly know. Anyway, it's okay to come out. We been thinking, Miz. President—"

"Could you call me Ruth? Maybe not on campus and so on, but…you know…"

"Right. Okay. So, me and Frank reckon that whoever killed Ike…sorry, umm…Whoever done that is out to get you too."

"It's a thought."

A thought? "Well, more than just that, see—" Billy scratched his head. Ike's wife didn't seem even a little surprised about what him and Frank had figured out. What the heck was going on here? His radio crackled again. Sam.

"Billy, here's the thing. The FBI plans to put Ruth into protective custody. Wait for a black SUV and a guy named Hitchens to arrive. He'll take Ruth. You three stand down, Okay?"

"Hitchens? FBI? You sure? Sam, we can protect Ike's wife just fine. We don't need no Feebies doing our job. No offense to Karl, and all."

"Sorry Billy, that's the drill. Hand her over to Hitchens."

Billy did not like this at all. Nobody ever believed he was stupid. Not and live. He studied Ruth carefully. She seemed too calm to be still grieving, to hear she might be a target, and what was up with the FBI suddenly putting themselves in the play? He frowned and tried to think of any circumstances that would reconcile all three. The SUV arrived. It did not look like an FBI vehicle. Billy did not know why he thought so, but his gut told him that something was about to go down.

Hitchens introduced himself and took Ruth aside. They had a few words then Hitchens said, "Okay, Deputies, we'll take it from here." Billy didn't budge. "I said you guys can go."

Ruth waved. "It's okay, Billy, really. You three head back. Sam will explain."

How'd she know that Sam would have anything more to say? He spun and squinted into the trees down the path. His friends and family often said that Billy had "quick eyes." He saw things others missed. They depended on him to spot street signs when they drove in the city, and lurking rabbits during hunting season. As to the latter, he was better than Buster, their beagle. When he scanned the trees down the pathway, he thought he saw movement. Maybe not. He looked more closely—nothing. An idea stirred in his head. It was too fantastic to be true, but it was the only explanation that made any sense at all, given what he'd seen so far. He headed to the cruiser.

"Okay, people, the service with the jurisdiction will take it from here." He turned back for a second. "You probably should check for some C4 residue or something like it around that propane tank. It didn't get over there under the floor by itself, but you probably already thought of that. Oh, and say 'Hi' to him for me."

He slid into the cruiser and drove off not sure if he should feel angry, cheated, or elated at what he believed he'd just figured out.

Holy cow, what if I'm right?

"Say 'Hi' to who?" Charlie Picket asked.

"Nobody. I was just having a go at the Feebs."

Holy cow!

Chapter Thirteen

When Billy and the two deputies disappeared around a bend in the road, Hitchens had Ruth climb into the SUV. He then drove down the pathway and into the trees. Ike stepped out from the shrubbery and climbed in. Hitchens reversed and regained the road.

"You don't look anything like FBI," Ike said.

"Don't need to. Your people just have to believe we are."

"They are not that slow, son. Next time try to look a little more rumpled. Where to now?"

"Mr. Garland will meet us at the Motel 6 down the road. I don't know what happens after that."

The ride to the Motel 6 "down the road" took two hours. Down the road meant somewhere around Mount Airy, North Carolina. Hitchens pulled into the parking lot and drove to its farthest end. He braked, hopped out, and knocked on a door. The door opened a crack; he mumbled something and came back to the car.

"End of the line, folks. Thank you for choosing Air America. Please do not tell your friends and neighbors about your trip."

Ike and Ruth stepped out of the SUV and approached the half-open door. The SUV disappeared in a cloud of North Carolina dust.

"Well, come in, you two. I don't think anybody followed you. Hitchens said you were clean, but why take a chance?"

"That's Charlie Garland, isn't it?" Ruth said. She did not look happy. She pushed the door the rest of the way open and she and Ike slipped in.

"Adjoining rooms," Charlie said. "One for you two and one for the rest of us for the time being, although I do not think we will be staying here very long. We need to get you two far, far away."

"That will be difficult," Ike said. "Ruth can't just drop off the map like that. People back in town will want to know why and then there is the follow-through on my death to set up."

"Follow through? What do you mean?" Charlie sat at a desk with a laptop open and glowing in its center.

"I'm dead, remember? Either I surface or there will have to be some public acknowledgement of it—a funeral—something."

"We can't have a funeral, Ike." Ruth sat and folded her hands in her lap. "A funeral is so…final. Something else, please."

"Well we don't have that many choices. But the point is, if Ruth disappears with no notice, more questions are going to be raised and the news media will be full of it. That could make hiding very difficult."

"Relax," Charlie said. "Are you hungry? I'll have some sandwiches sent over with a pitcher of something cold and we can figure this out. The important thing is, as far as whoever is behind this knows, you're dead and Ruth is pretty shook up. The bad guys will not be surprised if she attempts to go into hiding for a while. So we will set that up and while they chase around the country looking for her, we will triangulate on who they are."

"What? Ike, what did Garland just say?"

"I think he said they will leave a trail of credit card purchases here and there and see who is willing to chase after you. They can then be back-traced and if they get enough contacts, calculate the starting point. You, on the other hand will be somewhere else entirely."

"But won't they get suspicious when I seem to be in so many places?"

"You won't be in that many and there will be a logical sequence to them. They might wonder after a few days, but not right away."

"Okay, I see, but that still doesn't address the first part. What about the folks back in Picketsville?"

"The word out of the Sheriff's Department will be that the fire at the A-frame meant you had to move to a motel for a few days. Meanwhile, the DNA has confirmed the ID of Ike. You will release a message that the body, because of the fire and explosion and so on, had to be cremated and also, because of the timing and your state of mind, blah, blah, blah, you have decided to postpone any official memorial for a few days, maybe a week, and then there will be a service at the...what's the name of that church you don't attend?"

"Stonewall Jackson Memorial."

"Exactly, that one. Now, we need to plan on where to stash you while we unearth the bastard who started this."

"I have an idea," Ike said.

"Okay, I am all ears," Charlie said.

"After we eat. It's been a long day. Send for the sandwiches and instead of, or in addition to the pitcher of cooling liquid, could you order up a bottle of decent hooch? Oh, and get us a change of clothes or two. We'll talk after we eat. I need a little time to think it through."

>>>

Billy was hot. He slammed into the sheriff's office and stared hard at his brother. "When did you plan on telling me?"

Frank looked up from the photo-spread on his desk, eyebrows raised, and put a carefully constructed look of innocence on his face.

"Tell you what?"

"Now I know why you and Sam have been acting all strange like. He ain't dead, is he?"

"Billy—"

"Don't you go giving me no guff about how you don't know. Ike is alive and kicking somewhere and you knew it and didn't say anything. So, why? I'm your damned brother, Frank."

"Keep your voice down, dammit. Someone might hear you."

"Well, why not?"

"Why not what? Not let people hear you or why not tell you? Here's the why of both. If the people who tried to kill him knew they failed, they'd try again. The bomb they planted in that car was too big for just someone trying to kill a cop. There's got to be more. Then they take a run at Ruth, see? So, that's why we keep it on the down low. As to not telling you, Ike said if you knew too soon, you'd tell Essie and then everyone would know."

"Essie wouldn't tell anyone."

"She wouldn't have to. She'd light up like the Fourth of July and Christmas combined, and anyone who had eyes on us would figure it out."

"That's stupid."

"That's the truth and you know it. So, now that you know, you can't tell Essie. If you do, you have to send her away for a while. Billy, we all love your wife and would do anything for her, but she is as transparent as glass. Look, since they took a run at Ruth up there at that cabin, they must have known where she was. That means they have ears in here somehow. Get it?"

Billy sat down in a heap. Frank waited for him to cool down.

"You can't tell her, you know. Okay, what happened up on the mountain?"

"How am I not going to do that? Lord knows she's about as shook up as if her own daddy was dead. Frank, she could lose the baby if she don't come up out of that funk she's in."

"I don't know, Billy. Look, how about this? She isn't worth a bucket of spit around here lately anyway, so you tell her she's on baby-sitting duty for herself and Sam. Once she's okay with that, she can camp out at Ma's and then maybe tell her, but be careful with that. Even out and away…who knows? And for sure don't tell nobody else, got it? Not even Ma."

"She might buy that."

"She'll have to or you're both off the case and on vacation somewhere and I can't lose another man. So, you figure it out. Meanwhile, what about your run up to the cabin?"

Billy filled him in on what happened at Ike's house and how the FBI showed up and took Ruth away. He guessed Ike went with them. He did say he didn't like the looks of the men who said they were FBI, but Ruth seemed okay with them so he didn't say anything. Frank smiled and filled Billy in on who the men were and Charlie Garland's role in the transfer. Billy allowed as how he was okay with the spooks, he just didn't like the FBI, Karl Hedrick excepted, of course.

Frank couldn't tell him just then but it was the spooks, not the FBI, who were running the show at the moment.

Chapter Fourteen

"Idaho? Ike, have you gone completely nuts? Why in God's name should we go to Idaho? Isn't that where the radio tower thing is? Wouldn't that mean the people who want you dead are out there and could be breathing down our necks?" Ruth had nearly spilled her drink when Ike outlined his plan.

"Actually, it's not a bad plan," Charlie said. "Ruth, think a minute. Assuming they think Ike has gone to his reward, where is the last place they will be looking for you? Remember, you will be 'seen' in various venues on the East Coast for the next week. We will leave a trail that indicates you are headed north. My guess is they will assume you are headed to your cottage in Maine. That is where I would go if I were you and wanted to be alone."

"That is the fu…sorry, Ike. That is the absolute last place on this earth I would go to right now. Surely you haven't forgotten last May?"

"No, I have not. Will they know about that? They might. They seem to know everything else about your movements so far. But will they know that you might be concerned enough about that scuffle to stay away? I mean why would you make a connection like that? I don't think they will guess you are still discommoded about what happened up there."

"Did you just say, 'discommoded,' Charlie? Jesus, my old Granny used to say things like that. 'Discommoded and ker-fuffled.' Would I not be kerfuffled, too? But you're right. They probably won't. They would have to be deep inside my head to figure that out. So, okay, then what?"

"Then, this is how we will play it. We will assume they believe that you are headed there. They may have second thoughts and think it's a trick because it is the obvious place for you to go, but they dare not chance it. They will send people to check. We will be there first, waiting. In the meantime, they will have to deploy more people to track you *en route,* if for no other reason than to be certain it isn't a ruse. The more people they put in the field, the more chatter they will create and the easier it gets to trace the line back to the source."

"This sounds way too complicated to me."

"It is. That's the beauty of it. So, that's that. What do you need, Ike?"

"Okay. First we will need to be disguised a bit when we travel. Ruth, which would you like to be, a redhead or a blonde?"

"You're kidding. How do we do this? Are there CIA cosmetologists and hair stylists on tap, Charlie?"

"Well, now that you mention it, there are, but I think Ike is thinking wigs and appropriate clothing."

"I am. A gray ponytail for me and something nice in red or gold for you. Then, Charlie, I guess you already have or can acquire a safe house somewhere in that tower's broadcast area."

"I can."

"Wait." Ruth stood and leaned over Ike. "You're forgetting something. What about the rest of the family?"

"What?"

"Listen, the attempt to blow me into tiny bits means the game isn't just about you, right? So what about my mother? What about Darla? She is part of the equation, now, too."

"Oh."

"Not to interrupt this *tête á tête*, but what are you talking about and who is Darla?"

"I'm saying the people who seem intent on killing me off may not be satisfied with just the two of us. Doesn't it stand to reason that anyone with that much anger would not stop at the two of us? Wouldn't he or she or they also want to hurt the rest of my…our family, my mother, and Darla Smut? She is our ward, a reclamation project, if you will, but still family."

"Oh, right. I'd forgotten. We will scoop them up and whisk them away to someplace safe for the duration of this program. Where would they be most comfortable?"

"You're kidding. Comfortable? How is that possible under the circumstances?"

"Okay, ignore the last part. Where do you think they'd be least inconvenienced?"

"Chicago. My mother loves that city. Darla would see it as a great adventure."

"That, I doubt, but there is nothing for it. So okay, Charlie fix that up," Ike said. "Also, returning to the main plan, get both of us North Carolina driver's licenses, a rental car out of Lewiston, and a smallish plane. I will fly us out. It will take a couple of days. In the air or in some hotel near an FBO nobody will find us. If anyone asks, we'll be a couple of misguided realtors from Raleigh looking for investment property in Idaho. Once we're established in the safe house, you can send Sam to us with all her stuff. She can work as well out there as back here, and it will give us an extra gun, if we need it."

"Gun? Oh, no you don't, buster. I told you before, I am not playing Violette Szabo for you or anyone else ever again. I have seen enough mayhem to last a lifetime."

"It won't come to that, but if I have to leave, it would make me feel better if Sam was there. She has fewer scruples when it comes to pulling a trigger."

"We might set up another place close by with some of our people, too. A business, I think, would work. Real estate brokers? What do you think?" Charlie said. "So, okay, you need licenses, a plane, and a house. Give me a few hours. You can be on your way tomorrow."

"And appropriately awful clothes."

"That too. Short or long?"

"Short or long what?"

"Wigs. You want a short hair style or longish? Red or blond?'

"Surprise me."

⟩⟩⟩

The following morning, the Picketsville Sheriff's Office released a statement on behalf of the family of the late Ike Schwartz:

> *Mrs. Harris-Schwartz expresses her thanks to the com-*
> *munity for all their prayers and letters. There will be*
> *a memorial service a week from Friday to be held at*
> *the Stonewall Jackson Memorial Episcopal Church in*
> *Picketsville. Prior to the service Mrs. Harris-Schwartz*
> *will be traveling for a few days and has requested that*
> *they respect her need for privacy at this trying time.*

At about the same time and a hundred miles south and east, a King Air 400 piloted by a Mr. Marvin Gottlieb with his wife, June, sitting right seat, took off from a small airstrip outside Raleigh, North Carolina. They had filed a flight plan which would take them west to Idaho by way of New Orleans, El Paso, and Phoenix. Subsequent plans, filed along the route supported the original. In the meantime a woman answering the general description of Ruth Harris-Schwartz traveled north on her way, it seemed, to Maine. In three days she, and two other women, thought to be her cousins or close friends, alit on the scree at Scone Island and took up residence in her cottage. One or two of the island's permanent residents did not look too happy to hear that. There had been some talk back in the spring about a terrible helicopter accident on the island and its aftermath and some speculation that she and the man she had travelled to the island with were somehow involved in it. That's how rumors get started. Coincidentally, a group of businessmen from Manhattan rented the old Staley Place for a retreat, although how anyone would find that old wreck of a house a place to get any work done was a mystery, for sure.

⟩⟩⟩

Except for a brief foray to Scottsdale Fashion Square to buy more clothes, Ike and Ruth stayed in motels close to the stopovers when they put down for the night. Charlie had no concept of size and style. Ike had said awful. He'd complied. Three and a half days later, and enduring a very long leg from Scottsdale Airpark to Lewiston-Pierce Nez Airport, they put down and secured their rental car and disappeared. The clerk at the rental car counter told her friends that she didn't see how the marriage would ever make it.

"The man was, like all gray and old and, you know, like, grizzly and the woman was, like, this bleach blonde type, only red-haired."

"Trophy wife?" her friend asked.

"Prolly. Those ole geezers are, like, dirty old men. I hate 'em."

"Yeah, Doris, but I bet if one of them rich dudes offered you a house in the mountains and a diamond ring or two, you'd hop out of your panties in about a nanosecond."

How can you even think such a thing? I am in, like, a permanent relationship and you know it."

"Benny Stazic is a loser and the sooner you wake up to that the better. You ain't getting any younger, kid, and he ain't gonna take you nowhere but downhill. Hey, the old clock is ticking away. Tick tock, tick tock…"

"What do you know about Benny? You're just jealous because that check runner with the Beech Bonanza dumped you for Betsy Figs."

"He never. Besides, Figarelli is butch. And another thing, hotshot, did you know that your you'll-never-see-a-ring-from-me boyfriend is bonking Franny Nyquist?"

"Shut up, you're—"

Except for a brief mention on the Lewiston police blotter reporting a domestic disturbance at the Stazic residence, it is unclear how the ongoing affairs of Franny, Benny, Doris, and her friend concluded but the guessing was, not well.

〉〉〉

Sam knocked on the office doorjamb. "Frank, you asked if calls could be retrieved weeks after they're made and I told you in some special cases they might."

"You found a call made that night?"

"Not exactly. The transmission had been erased but I found a transcript of one from a burn phone that utilized a local tower at the right time. It could be our guy. Unfortunately, we can't identify the recipient or run a voice recognition scan."

"What's it say?"

Sam shoved a slip of paper across the desk. "You can read it yourself."

Voice 1: It's done.

Voice 2: Like we agreed? Schwartz and the mansion?

V 1: (pause) Right, like we agreed. I need a payday.

V 2: I can move the money tomorrow.

V 1: Not what we agreed. Tonight.

V 2: It's late and the banks don't open 'til…

V 1: Cut the crap. You don't need the banks to open and you know it. You have my bank number, move the money.

V 2: If I don't?

V 1: I just blew a cop to kingdom come. You think a big-shot business man wouldn't be easy?

V 2: Okay, I'll move it. Get off the line.

Both hang up.

"Well, I guess that's something, but not much. The phones?"

"Like I said a burn phone to the tower in Idaho. The first phone dialed a Bank in the Caymans right after that, an account ID and a password. I guess he was checking to see if the money was delivered."

"We already knew it was a hit and who did it. Damned shame we can't identify the second voice."

"Yeah. Maybe the FBI can retrieve the cash or the account it came from."

>>>

Ruth and Ike settled into their cabin late that night. Charlie's people had thoughtfully provided a meal and enough supplies to last a week. Ruth unpacked and headed for the bathroom.

"I need a soak, Marvin."

"Enjoy. Have I told you how sexy you look as a redhead?"

"Like, every three hours for the last three days. What is it with men and their wives in wigs? You know what I think? I think it makes men feel like they're cheating with another woman, but without the guilt."

"You are uncannily perceptive for a redhead. I will certainly recommend the practice to those whose marriages are flagging in that department. And come clean, don't you feel a little kinky too? You change your looks, and you can be someone different for a while."

"June Gottlieb, heiress to the Gottlieb Beer Pong fortune. Whoopee, and speaking of changed appearances, you look like a gone-to-seed Semitic Jesse Stone. Who'd want that in her bed?"

"Point taken. Speaking of Chief Stone, doesn't Tom Selleck have a ranch out here somewhere?"

"Is he a Republican?"

"No idea, why?"

"If he's a Republican, his ranch is in Idaho. If he's a Democrat, it will be in Nevada."

"And if he's an Independent?"

"Maine, obviously."

"Obviously? Oh, because that is where your cottage is. So, what about someone of my political persuasion?"

"I'm guessing Antarctica."

"I'm hurt."

"I calls 'em like I sees 'em."

Chapter Fifteen

Karl called Charlie with his personal iPhone. It wouldn't do to have his superiors know he was in communication with the CIA off the record and without authorization. Interagency cooperation is a concept that plays better at the top and in theory than in practice. What the FBI had uncovered about the radio repeater tower in Idaho, he said, was good news and bad news.

"Give me the good news first," Charlie said.

"The good news, if you can really call it that, is that the broadcast from the tower is generally directional. That is, it is beamed in a north by northwest direction and it only has any real strength for thirty miles or so. That could limit the search for the people we want somewhat."

"And the bad news?"

"There are two parts to that. First, all of the signals it transmits are encrypted or scrambled. My people say it is at a very sophisticated level. Second, it does not send a single signal. It seems that there may be as many as a dozen subscribers to the service on as many frequencies."

"Wait a minute. What do you mean subscribers?"

"The tower is owned and operated by a company registered as Dexiplex, Inc. We are trying to establish its corporate profile now, but the wonks in that department say they're being stonewalled for some reason. We do know it is a subsidiary of a larger media group. We haven't been able to uncover who. Dexiplex owns and operates several of these towers around the country in areas where a market has been created by folks who are paranoid and/or fear the intrusive practices of the NSA, which they are convinced are ongoing. Probably with some justification, if the news reports are right. And then, some of them are people who believe that the telephone equivalent of paparazzi are tapping into their private phone conversations or soon will be tapping. Since the Murdoch dust-up in Great Britain, that possibility seems increasingly real to them. That being the case, it's a fair assumption that at least one or two of the end users of the service are celebrities, movie stars of one sort or another, and their wannabes. Anyway, they have their calls routed through the tower and rendered undecipherable. They pay a pile for the privilege. The tower then sends the encoded message and the person buying the service receives a device that unscrambles it and is specific for his line only."

"That's interesting. Am I to assume that the encoding works in the reverse? If the owners of the system wanted to, they could be privy to all the calls. Is that right? When they purchase the service, they must have a high level of trust in the company."

"I suppose so, yeah."

"Hmmm...Okay, then if we want to find the one recipient of the calls we are sure were made to the person responsible for the two bombings, we will have to sort through...how many channels?"

"Hard to say for sure. If there are weekenders who only use the service occasionally, we wouldn't have picked them up yet, but on this tower I'm thinking fifteen or maybe twenty."

"That creates a problem on top of a problem. Okay, I hate to do this to you, Karl, but you're going to have to move up Sam's trip to Idaho. She can tap into some of the NSA programs that, as we all know, don't exist, and start breaking into those encrypted messages."

"Understood."

Charlie hung up and stared out the window which had been washed for a change. He could see the license plates on the bumpers of the cars parked in his section of the parking lot. That is if he looked up. Basement offices did not offer much in the way of aesthetics. On the other hand, no one coveted his office and he knew he'd keep it and all the odds and ends he'd accumulated over two decades. He thought a moment and then called Ike.

"Marvin Gottlieb, hello."

"Marvin," Charlie said. "How are you and June settling in? Not too much mountain air for you, I hope. Listen, you know that bit of real estate we talked about out there?"

"Good to hear from you too, Chuck. Are you speaking of the ranch house itself or the structure that may be connected to it?"

"Very good, you haven't lost your touch, Marv. The latter. Renovating it will be a tiny bit more complicated than we thought at first. I was wondering if we should send Sammy out to help with the deal. She knows more about the particular construction than any of us and also has access to the assets needed to untangle it."

"You think? Did you check with the spouse? Everybody okay with this?"

"Absolutely. Sammy'll be on the next plane. Say hello to June for me. I'm sending you an e-mail."

Charlie hung up. "He called me Chuck. Nobody calls me Chuck."

>>>

New Star Ranch spread across four hundred acres of pricy Idaho landscape. The entrance to it, as with nearly every other ranch in the West, seemed innocuous enough—two upright eight-by-ten-inch creosoted beams with a one-by-two-by-fifteen-foot crossbeam spanning the distance between them set at the Department of Transportation-recommended sixteen feet of vertical clearance. The word NEW and a large star had been burned into the crossbeam. They were the only indicators of what or who might lie beyond. Unseen but very much a part of the gateway was an array of surveillance equipment which would be triggered when the simple plank-and-truss gate opened. A car stop consisting of tire-puncturing spikes and hidden in the parallel pipes of a cattle guard could be deployed if the person or persons attempting to enter were deemed by the owner or his agent to be presenting threat. A quarter mile beyond the gate a copse of eucalyptus hid a large ranch house and a plethora of outbuildings. Persons seeking to enter this area by any means other than the driveway would find themselves confronted by at least two armed men with questions. The ranch owner was particular about who visited it.

Among the trees a second array of antennae fed a sophisticated communications room to one of the outbuildings. It enabled the ranch's residents to reach nearly any location in the world. Martin Pangborn did not like to be left in the dark on matters he felt to be important. Most, but not all, of the incoming signals were scrambled or encrypted in some way. He felt certain that the federal government was monitoring him. In a way, he was correct. Anyone with the connections he had with certain political and television figures would raise a few eyebrows in the Office of Homeland Security. So far, they had not done anything beyond placing his name on a watch list. The political connections were sufficiently important to maintain a "look but don't touch" stance. A change in the Administration could alter that, but for the moment, he was off-limits.

Another part of his surveillance network kept tabs on the arrivals and departures at the local airports and hotels. The arrival of Mr. and Mrs. Marvin Gottlieb had been noted and the routine Google search done. There was precious little to be found about the Gottliebs. Their brief bio stated only that they were recent entrants to the real estate investment business. Prior to that, they had a moderately successful beer-distributing business in the Raleigh area and another interest in two gas stations and a McDonald's. There didn't seem enough to launch a more complete background check beyond putting a general watch of their movements if and when they made inquiries about acreage in the immediate area. A wiretap was rejected for the moment.

The arrival the next day of their red-haired assistant with an inordinate amount of baggage was also noted.

On the other hand, the fact that the FBI had made inquiries about the repeater tower did raise a red flag. When told about it, Pangborn instructed his man in the Bureau to dig out who authorized the investigation. He was not pleased with the answer. He made calls to a few of his acquaintances in Washington. The special agent who requested the tower check, he discovered, had had run-ins with the hierarchy before. A deeper probe revealed he had been assigned to Picketsville as Agent in Place and worse, had been a friend of the late Ike Schwartz. Martin thought it might be time to put a crimp in Karl Hedrick's career with the FBI and said so to some people who could make that happen.

Chapter Sixteen

Ike had been pacing for an hour before the call from Charlie came through. Ruth thought if he didn't soon sit down or leave the room she'd clonk him on the head with a rolling pin. She said so.

"I'd worry if I believed for one minute you knew what a rolling pin looked like."

Ruth had a smart answer on the tip of her tongue when the phone rang. By the time Ike hung up she'd forgotten what she had started to say.

"So, what news from the genius? Has he found our killer?" she asked. She was not about to give up her enmity toward Charlie Garland just yet.

"The message we have been trying to track from the tower has some technical difficulties that only someone like Sam can unravel, it seems."

"So?"

"So, Sam and her NSA-borrowed software will be arriving tomorrow and she will set up shop here with us. She will have to unscramble the messages to isolate the ones we are after. Then, if we are lucky, we can somehow locate the position of the receiver."

"I see. I take it the honeymoon is over then? No more romping about in our underwear or other clothes-optional activities?"

"We still have tonight, but right now, I am going stir crazy. How about a walk?"

"A walk? You are not stir crazy. You are just plain crazy. You want to wander around in this area and risk someone sees you and all hell breaks loose? Ike, I've been there, done that. You stay put. Look, I'll even entertain one of those activities we just discussed." She reached for a button.

"A drive, then. Bewigged and wearing big sunglasses like tourists, and oddly mismatched clothes. Let's just drive around. Maybe we'll see someone or something. Ruth, I have been officially dead for about a week and have done nothing to get to the bottom of this. If I don't at least try, I will save the bad guys the bother and shoot myself. Sitting and waiting for someone else to solve my problem, well that just isn't me."

"How about lying down, clothes optional?"

"Tempting as your offer is…Come on, kid, help me out here. Grab your wig, Mrs. Gottlieb, we're going to look for properties. That's our cover, let's work it. Who knows, we might even find a secluded spot in the woods or hills where you can finish the suntan you began before somebody blew up our house."

"In my red hair wig?"

"Why not? Is that a problem?"

"Parts of me won't match."

❯❯◇

Ike had the car running and sat drumming his fingers on the steering wheel when Ruth finally exited the cabin.

"Sorry, in my hurry I started to put the thing on backward. I don't work as Cousin Itt."

"What?"

"It's a reference to a TV show you wouldn't know anything about. Where to, Sherlock?"

"Charlie said that Karl's agents believed the transmission is beamed roughly north by northwest. I have drawn it out on this map. He says it is a low-wattage broadcast, which means that during the daytime it will carry maybe ten or fifteen miles before the power will dissipate. That's a best estimate. I figure it will also spread in a rough triangular way, so, assuming the focus is pretty tight at fifteen miles, it would be fifteen miles across at the point where the power is weakening. That's this area here." He pointed at the map on which he'd marked out a triangle with a base and a height of fifteen miles.

"That's a lot of acreage, Ike. If I remember my geometry correctly the area of a triangle is, base times height. That means we have two hundred and twenty-five square miles to cover. How do you plan to do that?"

"You were a history major, right? So, math and you didn't get along?"

"What?"

"The formula is one half the base times the height, so that means we are looking at and area of about half that. Whoever said we never use math? Keep Geometry in the basic high school curriculum, is what I say. Now, look at the map. This is all relatively open space. There are only three roads large enough to warrant a blue line. Off from them are a variety of what must be dirt or private roads. We will cruise the main, marked roads and see what we can see."

"And then?"

"Then, we look for something out of place, something that doesn't belong."

"Like what?"

"I don't know. An array of antennae, an armored personnel-carrier parked in the front yard, Ronald McDonald noshing at a Burger King. Anything that seems a little or a lot off—unusual."

"This is Idaho, Ike. Unusual is the norm."

"Nevertheless, we look and then we wait for Sam to arrive and provide more specificity to the hunt. But this way, we may have a better idea where to go when she does."

"Roger that. That's what they say, right? Roger that? Who is Roger? Or is it the euphemism the Brits use in mixed company when they mean the F word?"

"Radio talk. Roger used to mean 'I understand.' So an operator responding to directions or something would say, 'Roger.' 'Wilco' meant will comply. Then they would say either 'Over,' which meant they were finished speaking, or 'Out' if they were signing off."

"Fascinating. The things you've stuffed into your brain over the years, Ike. So not the Brit meaning?"

"No, but it certainly has possibilities."

"Roger that."

They drove for an hour toward the tower, moving south and east along a county road. Periodically they passed an entrance to a ranch or estate and occasionally a cluster of large and recently constructed houses—McMansions, Ike called them—the mark of an entrepreneurial response to the celebrity *chic* attached to the area. They turned about a half mile short of the tower and were headed back, northwest, along a different secondary road when Ike pulled to the side and stopped.

"Why are you stopping? If this is about me taking in the sun, forget it. It is too cold in the first palace and there is no way I am joining a herd of…whatever they are…grazing in the field."

"Angus, and no that is not why I stopped. Did you notice the sign at the entrance to one of the ranches back about a half mile?"

"Which one? Ike, we've passed dozens of them."

"Yeah, I know, but this one didn't seem right."

"How, not right?"

"Well most of the entrances are pretty much the same. Fence and an entrance, some elaborate, some not so much, but almost all had tall upright posts with a crossbeam and the name of the ranch burned into or painted on it. Most of them were at least twelve feet, some a few feet higher. That is the clearance you need to safely accommodate the height of most trucks and a trailer behind a big rig."

"And?"

"The one I'm talking about had to be at least two to three feet higher, maybe more. Why would they do that?"

"Too lazy to saw off the uprights? Bragging? Little man has big uprights? I don't know, Ike. What's the difference?"

"I'm not sure. It's just one of those unexpected, out of place things I talked about. Not extraordinary, but a little off, that's all. Also, did you see the name on the crossbeam?"

"I gave up noticing those when I saw 'Dunrovin' and then 'KT' and the word 'Dor' with a bar over it. Cute but clearly not working ranches."

"The one I'm talking about read 'New' and had a big star next to it. I don't know why, but it triggered something in my memory. I can't figure out what."

"New Star Ranch? Probably a movie actor who just had his first hit or maybe an Oscar nomination. We could look it up."

"You're probably right, but why did it stir something in my memory bank? I don't follow movie actors born after nineteen fifty-five."

"Your loss. Moving on."

Ike stepped on the accelerator. "We'll go back and take a picture of it first. Then we can stop for lunch somewhere."

"In this wasteland? I didn't see any place to eat unless you plan on shooting one of those Anguses and frying us up some steaks. I'm all for it if you can get it done in the next half hour."

"I ain't rustling no cattle today, pardner. They hang varmits like that in these here parts. Besides, the GPS shows a restaurant about two miles this way."

"Roger that. Speaking of Rogers, were you trying to be Roy or Ginger just now? You need to work on your delivery."

"Gabby Hayes."

"Who? That's right, no stars born after fifty-five or did you say thirty-five? Honestly, Ike, join us in this century. So, lunch from the chuck wagon it is. Do you think they serve Kosher, Gottlieb?"

"Pictures, then we chow down. Is anguses even a word?"

"You want me to work out the declension for the cows? Anga, Angus, Angi, Angae...."

Chapter Seventeen

After two days of close monitoring by the agents occupying the Staley place, the Agency unraveled the coding used in the messages sent to the person alleged to have killed the sheriff of Picketsville, Virginia. Once done, they moved in to arrest them. The charges were vague, but as they were found with a substantial cache of C-4 and the messages they were sending, although in plain English, were obviously coded, they were picked up and arrested. Terrorism, whether domestic or foreign, the arresting officers explained to them, was still terrorism.

The men protested that they were patriots, not terrorists, to which the arresting officer retorted they should be happy then, because they were being charged under the terms of the Patriot Act. The men effectively disappeared. Sometimes, Charlie thought the Act had its uses. The three women in Ruth's cottage returned to Washington and resumed their duties; Ruth's doppelganger as the executive secretary to the director of the CIA, the other two to the "Farm" to train new Agency recruits in martial arts, among other things. The men moved from Staley's to Ruth's and assumed the task of forwarding plausible messages to the as-yet-unknown-but-presumed felonious recipient. The known word count of the set of transmissions provided a ready resource for Sam to eliminate many of the possible frequencies when she finally began to sort through all the signals emanating from the radio tower. Knowing the word count helped to eliminate well over half of them. Eventually, all of them save one. But Charlie insisted on knowing not just who was receiving, but what was said and who was saying it, which would take a few more days of fiddling with the encryption.

Down-Easters have a highly developed sense of privacy. Thus, most of the activity at the cottage went unnoticed by Scone Island's permanent residents. Vacationers, they knew, were peculiar people and after that big helicopter crash the previous year about which Trooper Stone didn't want to talk, they figured it was just one of those cycles when odd things happened, like the time the four lobster boats all had their bottoms stove in on Cooligan's reef in the same year, or when the tide didn't match the chart like it should have for three weeks. Caused some consternation, that did, eh-yah.

> > >

Buffalo burgers, among many offerings, were the specialty of Bert's Western Bar and Grill. Bert's also served a variety of sandwiches named after celebrities who had at one time been or were now residents of the area or who'd appeared in a film shot in Idaho. Sonja Henie and Marilyn Monroe both made the menu roll call. Ike said that was ironic. Ruth said she couldn't see why and before he explained, said that she didn't care. The back of the menu listed the eighty or so films made in the state over the years and a brief bio of Bert, the owner, and his career as an extra in two of Clint Eastwood's films.

"I thought the buffalo was an endangered species. How can this place serve them on a bun with," Ruth consulted the plastic laminate menu, "lettuce, tomato, pickle, and special BBQ sauce?"

"They were endangered. Some will insist they still are, but they have been domesticated for decades and the bison on your bun will be farm-bred and corn-fed."

"Someone in a ten-gallon Stetson didn't shoot him, you're saying."

"I don't think so, but I could be wrong. I think the government allows some limited hunting in the areas where the herds have grown too large on lands that are also leased to cattlemen."

"So, you don't know."

"Not sure."

"Then I'm having a chicken sandwich. I want to show my solidarity with the Plains Indians and a lost generation."

"I'm sure they will appreciate the gesture. Since when did you take up the cause of the Diminishing West?"

"It came with the red hair. Speaking of which, how are we to explain the arrival of Sam into our midst?"

"You just nailed it. She has red hair, if you recall. You have red hair. She is our daughter come for a visit."

"What? She isn't. Do you think I look old enough to be her mother? No way, Ike. You can be the dad, if you want, but there is precious little left of my youth and I don't plan on ceding it to that nonsense."

"Then your 'somewhat' younger sister. How's that?"

"Better. Here's our waitress. Order up and no buffalo burger if you want to continue sharing the connubial bed."

"Jesus, you're hard, June Gottlieb." Ike turned to the waitress whose badge announced that she was Marcie and 'Sure Glad to be serving Ya.' "Are these buffalo hunted or raised?"

Marcie seemed puzzled and allowed as how she didn't know but she'd ask Mr. Bert. Ike said it wasn't important and ordered two Francis Farmer chicken sandwiches and coffee. Sides and fries came with them Marcie explained, "Does the gennelmin 'n lady want swede potado or reglar fries?"

Ruth frowned and looked at Ike.

"Sweet potato for us both," he said. Marcie nodded and left to fill their order.

Ruth shook her head and turned her attention to the other diners. "How many of these people are 'all hat and no cattle'?" she asked.

Ike scanned the room. "All of them, I think. It's afternoon and I don't believe real cattlemen would waste daylight noshing on buffalo burgers in an obvious tourist trap like this. The real question is who, if any, of these people are connected with the folks we're looking for."

"You think they would be here?"

"I think it's possible. Anything is. If we are close to them, there is a reasonable chance one or more of these people would be on their way to or coming from the bad guys' lair."

Ruth swung her head around and asked, "Any candidates?"

"Well, just reading people, mind you, and with no real information as to why, I think the two guys in the too-new boots at the counter qualify."

"Reading people? So?"

"The tourists are scanning everybody else hoping to see a movie star. They, unlike the rest, are only interested in us. My guess is they will try to find out who we are and report back to somebody."

"What somebody?"

"Could be the local sheriff, or the bad guys, or the chamber of commerce. There is no telling just yet."

"How will they do it?"

"They will wait for us to leave and ask to see the credit card receipt we leave behind."

"So, we pay cash, right?"

"No, we pay with one of Charlie's fake credit cards. I want them to ID us now so they will leave us alone. We're the Gottliebs, remember?"

"And they will leave us alone?"

"Unless they are very anti-Semitic, I think so…well, maybe. It depends. If they are just plain folks, yes. If they are from the paranoid sector, no."

Their sandwiches arrived with two thick and lumpy pancakes on the side.

"What's this?" Ruth asked pointing to the pile. "They look like potato pancakes."

"Yes, ma'am, Swede potatoes," Marcie smiled and plunked a bottle of ketchup on the table. "Bonny appetite."

>>>

When the couple left, the woman, later identified as June Gottlieb, was heard haranguing her husband, Marvin, about what a waste it was to fly all the way out to this cowboy farm just to buy land when there was, like, lots of lots back in Carolina that they could have bought cheap, for crying out loud, and they could have saved the money. Her husband kept muttering something about movies and the latest trends in real estate investment. Idaho is hot, he said. Bruce Willis' name came up once or twice. They paid and exited.

Martin Pangborn did not need to concern himself with that pair. That is, he didn't unless they happened to stumble onto his property in their search for land to buy. Then, there might be a problem.

As it happened, it appeared one or two of his subordinates did have a problem. Mrs. Gottlieb was videotaped, camera in hand, taking a picture of the ranch gate. Why would a silly woman in that god-awful orange slacks suit from North Carolina want to take a picture of the ranch gate?

Chapter Eighteen

A second sedan parked in front of the cabin signaled that Samantha Hedrick had already arrived and set up shop in the cabin. She greeted them and reported she'd put her equipment in the bedroom next to theirs. She was planning on using the room at the end of the hall. It had its own bath, she said, and besides, she thought they might want a little privacy. She's blushed when she got to that part. People with naturally red hair blush easily—and obviously. Ruth smiled and yanked off her wig.

"That's nice of you. By the way, you are not my daughter," she said. "I don't know which sexist moron thought up that idea, but it has been vetoed. You are my sister, Beatrice Silver."

Sam stared wide eyed at Ruth. "Okay, I didn't know what I was supposed to be and…Right, I'm…Bea Silver. Anything else?"

"We always called you Trixie growing up. The boys in the neighborhood called you High-Ho Silver for obvious reasons. You were such a tramp."

"You did? They did what? Ms. Harris…?"

"Tell her, Marvin. We called her Trixie, didn't we?"

"It's okay, Sam. Ruth has had too many potato pancakes and is on a carbohydrate high. I warned her about ketchup too, but would she listen? Oh no. So, how are you, Sam? And welcome. Whatever arrangements you made are fine. Any news?"

"Thanks. Yes, two things. They put away two men who were tailing the fake Ruth to Maine. They had been monitoring their phone calls and when they figured out the code they used to call in their progress, they busted them. A second group has set up shop on your island and is still sending messages back here."

"What kind of messages?"

"Innocuous ones about the difficulties they have in finding the opportunity to get at the fake Ruth. Stuff like that. They also send them to me. I can use the word count to eliminate some, maybe all, of the other users transmitting to or from the tower. When I have them, I compare the count to the messages coming in and then focus on the one that matches. Then all I have to do apply the unscrambling software they're using and we got the bastards."

Ruth plunked down at the dining table and put her chin in the palm of her hand. "Scrambled signals. There's more than one kind, I assume."

"Oh, yeah. There's a lot of different ways to jumble or jam a signal. Do you want a history?"

"Do I? I am thinking, no. Just tell me the basics so I don't sound like an idiot when this is all over. That assumes we will survive, of course."

"The stuff they used to do back in the day has been pretty much replaced with digital voice distortion so it is closer to encryption than the old noise cloaking. Basically, there are two types. One introduces noise into the message that is filtered out at the receiving end. The second is a version of encryption where segments of the message are mixed up and the receiver has a program that reassembles the sequence."

"That's it?"

"Pretty much." Sam knew that she had left out ninety percent of the encryption explanation, but she doubted Ruth would want to hear it or remember it later anyway.

They spent the remainder of the afternoon organizing the equipment and settling Sam in.

〉〉〉

"So, now what? It's four in the afternoon. What comes next?"

"Next we gather data, listen to messages, fix on the location of the people we're after, and go get them.

"So you have a number count of some messages. No matter how they are fiddled with, you believe the count will stay the same. Then, when you have the right recipient, you unscramble the message and we know what they're up to and the cavalry arrives, rounds them up, and ships them off to Gitmo. Is that it in a nutshell?"

"Well, we'd need probable cause, but yeah."

"Did you know that CIA agents make terrible cops?" Ike said.

"This sounds like the opening of an insurance ad or one of your dumb cop jokes. Are you planning to go somewhere with this?" Ruth asked.

"Somewhere, yes. See, agents in the field do not have to bother themselves with things like probable cause. They form a plan and then either execute it or, if it happens to come apart along the way, they do not ask permission to revise and rethink. There is never time. Instead, they improvise something that will produce the same results. It is often a lot messier than the original, though. The *why* and the legalities of *what* and the ins and outs of *proper* procedure and protocol, and the difficulties that might create, are problems they will let someone else worry about."

"What did you just say?"

"It's like this. It has been a week since someone tried to blow me to bits, four days since they tried to do the same to you. That was a big mistake, by the way. So, if I am personally certain we have the bastard responsible for those two events in my crosshairs, I am not waiting with a warrant, for a judge to rule on probable cause, or a writ of this or that. I intend to hurt him, right then and there, period."

"Is it likely the person or persons who did the dirty work are the one giving the orders?"

"Not likely. So, they all go down. That is, the ones still upright and within range when I get ready to do it."

Ike delivered his statement in a flat, nonchalant tone, icily calm, in fact. He could have been ordering a celebrity sandwich at Bert's. He didn't slap the table, gnash his teeth, and he certainly did not raise his voice. There was an edge to it, but that was all.

Ruth sat up and stared. It was the first time she had witnessed what could only be described as cold fury. It puzzled her. She and Ike had been in tight spots before and yes, he had been angry, but mostly business-like. Doing a job he knew well. What had brought this on? If looks could kill, anyone who might have crossed Ike's path at that moment would have been vaporized. Then she understood. Her inclusion in someone's need to murder and maim made this encounter with really bad people different from previous ones. Before, only he had been at risk. He had been the target. Well, except for her car accident, but she'd been in the hospital and hadn't seen him. Maybe he had reacted the same way then. But this time she was present and awake.

She took a deep breath. That must be it. The last Boy Scout, a descriptor she once applied to him in the past, and not kindly she recalled, had made his position clear. Ike was almost too good to be true. Always there, always ready to act, and quick to disregard any danger aimed at him. Fearlessness tends to intimidate those who would do harm and Ike knew it. Because of his ability to brush aside fear, he always prevailed. But this time…this time things were different. Now the bad guys had put her in the frame.

To a man like Ike that was unacceptable. No one was going to hurt her because they wanted to get at him. That would be an act of ultimate cowardice. Ike was not just furious. Ike was close to homicidal in his anger and had the skills needed to act on that anger. Her "dutiful manager" was about to do his duty and God help anyone who tried to stop him. She realized that in that instant she loved him more than she had ever thought possible. She stared at this man who balked at using the F word, who watched old movies instead of television, who couldn't tell you who Bart Simpson or Duck Dynasty were if his life depended on it, and believed that the United States, though flawed in many ways, remained the world's best hope for the future. Her Boy Scout. She turned to Sam.

"Wonderful. That wraps it up, I guess. Wow. So, Sam," she said, "I don't want to spoil this reunion with having to fix a meal. Would you do us all a huge favor and run down to Bert's Western Bar and Grill and get us a stack of buffalo burgers to go? There's a map on the front seat of the SUV. Be sure to use one of the company credit cards. Thanks. Oh…and no need to hurry, okay?"

Sam seemed startled, blushed, and nodded. She collected her bag, the card, and the keys to her rental and left.

"What was that all about? I thought you were in solidarity with the 'Diminishing West' and we just ate, for crying out loud."

"Shut up and come with me." She grabbed his hand and headed toward their bedroom.

Chapter Nineteen

Jackson Shreve had committed to the cause early on and not just himself, but his wife and son as well. Belle hadn't liked it at first but once she'd heard Pangborn talk, she jumped right in. They were a Five One Star Family. All three were in residence, by God. That's commitment, right? Belle had done real good, better than him, actually, and worked in the Com Center. He didn't begrudge her that but he needed to step up, too. All he needed was the answer to the question that nagged at him: how could he make his mark with the top? Sitting in a room watching surveillance television screens was not what he'd envisioned when he joined. Should he call Pangborn directly with the news about the woman taking pictures of the gate? Pangborn was a long ways off and the local group leaders might not like that. Anyway, his partner, Buzz, said it probably didn't mean anything and if he had any smarts, he'd go through channels. Like, what were the chances someone like the top guy would want to talk to him? He said they found out that the woman was some old real estate person and maybe was cataloging local properties or something. Maybe she even thought New Star was for sale. They'd both laughed at that. But Jackson couldn't get it out of his mind.

It hadn't taken much urging to commit to this new way of life. He had succumbed to the antiestablishment ambiance of New Star Ranch and its organizational coda pounded into him with the other adherents to The Fifty-first Star in residence at the ranch. They, that is the people who did not share their particular view of the world, were out to destroy us. *Us* being the right-minded thinkers who believed as they did. So, even though a Mrs. Gottlieb from Raleigh, North Carolina, seemed an unlikely participant in the dark side's efforts to bring them down, he decided it wouldn't hurt to check. How he was to do it was less clear. Pangborn had people who were trained to make interventions like the one he contemplated. His job consisted of keeping an eye on the surveillance screens, one of which monitored the main gate, and that's all.

He knew he was capable of more. Hell, he'd been in Desert Storm. He had a medal to prove it. So, okay, he was a supply clerk in Stuttgart during the fighting, but he'd served, done his part, would have pounded sand if he'd been asked. It wasn't his fault he had to drop out of Spec Forces. Lots of people get shin splints. Anyway, he would have to think about what he would do about the Gottlieb woman and then he'd deliver big-time for the boss.

His cell phone buzzed and he struggled to retrieve it from his pants pocket. He tossed his keys, a wad of Kleenex, and pocket knife on the counter. The knife skittered across its surface. The Kleenex didn't make it and fell on the floor. The keys landed on the button that, when depressed, opened the main gate.

> > >

Sam overshot the turnoff that would have taken her to Bert's. She was several miles down the road before she realized it. She slowed, and seeing an open gateway with a driveway extending off into a pasture beyond, pulled in. There did not seem to be a ditch on either side of the roadway so she decided to make a U-turn by driving on through and then swinging the car in a wide loop and exit the way she entered. She ignored the challenge on the loud speaker since she believed she'd be long gone before anyone noticed or cared. Besides, it wasn't like she intended to drive on in. It was when she had rumbled over the cattle guard and started her turn that the tires blew. All four. The car skittered left and thump-a-thumped to a stop.

She stepped out of the car and stared in amazement at the wheels. One tire, she could change, but four? She reached for her phone and called Ike. No answer. Of course not. She searched her apps for the number of the nearest towing service. She called it and then redialed Ike and left a message. She sat on the hood and waited. A minute later, a truck looking more like a military assault vehicle than a ranch pickup tore down the road toward her. Help had arrived, thank goodness.

〉〉〉

"Not that I'm ungrateful, but can you tell me what that was all about?" Ike said. He sat half propped in bed, Ruth's head on his shoulder.

"You really don't know, do you? Okay, let's just say I had an epiphany and let it go at that."

"You're okay?"

"I am now. You will never let anyone hurt me, will you?" But it wasn't really a question. "It's in your DNA to be fiercely loyal, and brave, and steady, and never say fuck."

"Well, the last part is true. I don't know about the rest. What's this all about?"

"Ike, if Holloway had not jumped in the wrong car, you'd be dead. If that were so, I wouldn't have been in the A-frame away from the crowds and more or less incognito, but out in the open and in the clear. I'd be maimed, broken, or dead by now, too. I just realized how paper thin life can be and how we are never guaranteed anything from one day to the next, and that being the case, I need to make sure to use every minute of every hour being grateful and enjoying what I have."

"That's it?"

"No, but the rest is mostly about me and what I have been missing. You know it's all well and good to sail through life with snappy dialog and athletic sex. For a lot of people seeing us, they would say, 'Wow, there goes a pair. I wish I could be like them.' But it's more than that. It has to be. Listening to you a while ago when you were saying what you'd do, it was like a bucket of ice water had been tossed on me, a wake-up call, and made me realize that we are not just Nick and Nora sailing through an adventurous life together. We are locked in a life that seems more dangerous at times than normal, but the rest is 'business as usual' and I don't want to take it for granted anymore, that's all."

"I see, I guess."

"That's why I sent Sam for more lunch. I needed to nail it down before I said something stupid in an attempt to be witty."

"Okay. Well, thank you for that. Shouldn't she be back by now?"

"I told her not to hurry."

Ike cocked an eyebrow. "Okay. But still…"

"She would have called if she was in trouble."

"The phone is in the other room and on vibrate."

"On vibrate? Why?"

"I don't like the ring tone."

"So, the sheriff is picky about his music. Fair enough. Maybe she's back already and on tiptoe so as not to disturb us."

"One of us should check."

"Better she sees me half naked than you. No offense."

"None taken. Off you go."

"I'm off. Hey, you do know you can change the ring tone."

"Really?"

Ruth wrapped up in a robe and left. Ike heard her rummaging around, but no voices. Apparently Sam had not sneaked back.

"You have a missed call and a voice message," Ruth shouted. "It's from Sam. She had a flat tire. No, she had four flat tires. How is that possible? Anyway, she said she's called a tow truck, but needs us to come fetch her. She's at that ranch with the too-high entrance."

Ruth began to dress. "Four flat tires is not normal under any circumstance, is it? Get some clothes on. I think we are about to encounter the strange and unusual once again. Jesus, married to you is one continuous party."

"With some 'business as usual' thrown in between."

"Not much of that lately."

>>>

"Your name is Silver?" The man facing Sam could have been the model for a GI Joe action figure. He wore camo, aviator sunglasses, and had an M 16 look-alike swung over his shoulder, barrel down and a side arm hung on a duty belt, its keeper unlatched.

"Yes."

Sam paused. She had not spent much time memorizing her cover story and scoured her brain for possible answers to questions she thought she might be asked. She thought her time would be spent indoors and so had given the script Charlie Garland had prepared for her only a cursory glance. Ruth had changed some parts anyway. She segued into a routine she'd developed years before when she had wanted to get rid of an undesirable suitor or avoid a speeding ticket. She became that which she could never be in real life, an airhead of the first order. Assuming there are orders of airheads. "Baffle them with bullshit," some wise politician is alleged to have said. She could do that. She hoped she could anyway.

She smiled happily at the men. "Beatrice Silver."

"Silver? They call you Bea?"

"Oh, sometimes, yeah, Bea, or Beatie, Beetricks, Trish, Trista—"

"I got it."

"Trixie, Tra—"

"I said, I got it."

"Got it? Right. Trixie, mostly. Say, do you and your friends need to point those guns at me? They make me nervous. I hate guns."

"They do. Well, then, Trixie, what were you doing in the pasture?"

"Um, so I was, like, making a U-turn, you know, because I missed the turnoff that goes to Bert's Western Bar and Grill where I was, like, sent by my sister, June, to get some lunch, but she really wanted to be alone with her husband, that would be Marvin, because she has the hots for him at the moment, only I don't get what she sees in him, the big jerk, so, like, I—"

"Right. You could have made a three-point in the pull-off back there. Why here and how'd you get through the gate??"

"There's a gate? I guess there is…it was, like, open so… Umm, so I just went on through and, well a three-point turn is…that's the hard one where you pull in, and around, and in and…like that. So, there really isn't any reason to not turn back there, you know. I mean, I just saw the gate open and said to myself, I said, 'Trixie, you don't need to do a three-point turn, which you are very bad at, because that gate is wide open and there's a field where you could, like, pull in and turn this car right around and get on to Bert's and get those burgers because June should be pretty well done bonking Marvin by now,' you know? See, he's not much in the sack, June said, so, like quick. So, I just turned in here and something must have been in the field out there because all four of the tires blew. How the heck do you explain that, I'm asking myself? Is that gun loaded? I hope not because I had an uncle once who shot himself in the foot one Wednesday afternoon when—"

"Stop!" The action figure shook his head and waved in the tow truck which at that moment had arrived.

"Get this airhead and her car out of here. And, ma'am, just stay the hell off our turf in the future."

◇◇◇

Earl's Garage had the car on the rollback and was pulling onto the road when Ike and Ruth arrived.

"Sis," Sam yelled. "You won't believe what happened to me. Four flat tires. Oh, and I didn't get the burgers. Sorry."

"Get in. Ike, get us the hell out of here," Ruth hissed.

"You should wave goodbye and smile at GI Joe," Sam said. "Lord knows we don't want to upset him. Will you look at all that artillery?"

"I guess they weren't exactly expecting company."

Chapter Twenty

"What did you tell them?" Ike kept his eyes alternately on the road and the rearview mirror.

"Nothing. I was Doris the Ditz. I had the lead in *Born Yesterday* in college and I just played Billie Dawn with a lot of Valley Girl thrown in. I think the goon with the wannabe shades bought it. Sorry, but I'm afraid he has a pretty low opinion of you two now."

"Low? How low?" Ruth asked.

"June, like, you're a slut. That low. And Marvin, you're so totally a jerk. Sorry, but I was improvising."

"Works for me," Ike said. "I would never say it to you myself, June, but your sister has you pegged."

"She didn't miss much about you either, hotshot."

"Did you two have a nice nap?" Sam asked and, in spite of her efforts not to, blushed.

"You were always Mom's favorite. She spoiled you rotten, Trixie, and just look at you now." Ruth said.

"Moving on. Sam, what did you learn about that place?" Ike knew Sam and he knew she would take in as much as she could. She'd been a cop before she became a NSA snoop.

"Well, the goons were all armed with military grade weapons, not US, though. AR 15s or AK 10s, I think. One or two had a side arm, maybe Glocks, judging by the butts, as well as the rifles. As near as I could tell, all the safeties were off on the long guns. You can guess where that might go if one of those drugstore warriors got excited. Apparently the gate was not supposed to be open, so somebody screwed up there big-time. The camo on most, but not all, looked new and store-bought, you know, like they did their shopping at Cabela's or the Bass Pro Shop. Not US military-issue, at any rate. The guy who was hassling me had an insignia on his jacket. It looked like a star with a number in it."

"What number?"

"I'm not sure. He kept moving around and I was too busy trying to remember who I was supposed to be."

"The ranch is called New Star. Could it have not been a number, but a word? Could it have said, *New*?" Ruth asked.

"Oh, well maybe. Like I said, he moved and it wasn't very big."

"It was the number fifty-one." Ike said.

"How can you possibly know that?" Ruth stared at Ike.

"Because I've seen it before but I can't think where. I think that's why the name, 'New Star,' on the crossbeam jogged my memory yesterday. A new star on the flag would be number fifty-one, you see? Star fifty-one has to mean something more than the ranch name. When we get back to the cabin, Sam, link us up to a satellite and go digging for anything about a star with the number fifty-one inside it, or similar notations. Now, earlier you said 'two things.' What else?"

"Oh, yeah, someone has hacked the Sheriff's Office back home. No surprise there. So Frank has to be careful what he posts and what he doesn't. I wasn't able to locate the source before I was called out here, but the best guess is it is the same people who went after you two."

"They are good, I'll give them that. There ought to be some way we can use that information to our advantage."

"What about dinner?" Ruth said. "Trixie, here, never made it to Bert's."

"I said I was sorry, Sis."

"Shut up, you two. We'll go back to Bert's and do takeout. Then we go back to the cabin, search for a satellite link, and then tackle the five one-star."

"Take my advice, Trixie, don't order the Swede potatoes."

"But I like sweet potatoes."

"Not these, you won't."

〉〉〉

Jackson Shreve had a very bad moment when he retrieved his keys and saw that he'd inadvertently opened the main gate. He spent the next twenty minutes going over in his mind the different ways it could have happened that didn't involve him or his keys. The best he could do involved supposing a mysterious power surge had overloaded the circuit and caused the gate to swing open. He was refining that scenario in his mind when he was ordered from the room and back to the barracks until further notice. His attempts to describe how startled he'd been when the lights dimmed and then got very bright fell on deaf ears. He was on the next plane to Wyoming where the Fifty-first Star had an auxiliary camp for retraining. So much for "delivering big-time for the boss."

When Shreve had cleared the room, the four men who'd made the intercept at the gate sat and dialed up the Section Commander. The screen brightened and the image of a man who could have been the twin of the one who accosted Sam appeared.

"What the hell happened out there?" he said.

"Screw up big-time by a Probationer. Won't happen again. No harm, no foul. We sent him back to base camp."

"Who?"

"Shreve. You know, the nerdy guy with the Fu Manchu."

"What about his wife?"

"She stays."

"Pangborn…?"

"You know how it goes. So, one or two questions raised at the gate, however."

"Questions? What kind of questions? Do I want to hear them?"

"Maybe. You remember that man and his wife who pulled in here two days ago. Their name is Gottlieb, Marvin and June Gottlieb. She was seen taking a picture of the gate. We didn't think too much of that. Tourists and people new to the area take a lot of dopey pictures."

"So?"

"Well, the woman who trespassed was the wife's sister, she says. The phone intercept we listened to the day before indicated the person coming out here was pretty bright. It seemed the Gottliebs were looking at something with a problem in an outbuilding. The caller, Chuck somebody, seemed to think she could solve a problem that needed some kind of special, I don't know, skills or something."

"Why is that odd?"

"The woman might be that person."

"So, she came out to fix whatever they wanted fixed, right?"

"Yeah right. Here's the thing. If she's the one, I'm thinking she is the biggest airhead this side of Washington. I mean if she has any skill set, I didn't see it. She sounded like a complete moron."

"And she's the sister, or whatever, of the woman who took a picture of the gate?"

"Right."

"Okay, maybe she isn't the person who was talked about in the call and maybe she is. I think I need to kick this up to the top. In the meantime, put a team on them...all of them. Find out everything you can. Where they come from, who they know— everything. If they don't come up squeaky clean, get back to me. We will be working the same databases back here. Good work."

"Thanks. Say hi to Jack for me."

The screen blinked off.

"You heard the man. Tomorrow, find a way to get in and toss their house. Get some pictures for a facial recognition scan, fingerprints, financials, the works. Oh, and put a tail on them twenty-four seven. I want to know what they're up to."

>>>

Ike surveyed the cabin and the room Sam had set up as her work space. "Sam, you need to make all this equipment look as inconspicuous as possible. Anyone coming in here would know we are snooping."

"Well, we are."

"I know that, but I don't want anyone else to know that. This place should look like the digs of some real estate speculators, not the eastern Idaho annex of NSA. Can you program the computers so that whoever opens them will see real estate websites—here and in Raleigh, North Carolina? You'll need to block any access to their browsing history, too. Oh, and when we leave, scatter the laptops around to other spaces so it looks like we're just land brokers looking for bargains."

"What about the big screen we use?"

"Set it up to run as a TV when we're not around. Any heavy equipment, shove behind the washer/dryer."

"And we're doing this because…?" Ruth asked.

"Because Sam had a run-in with some not-your-usual cowboys at a ranch with a name that is producing bad memory vibes for me. Those guys qualified as sufficiently out of the ordinary to warrant extreme caution in the future."

"That's it? Sam plays dumb with some macho idiots and you want to shut down the camp?"

"Not just because of that. I am certain the goon in the shades will want to have a look at our cabin and unless it slipped your mind, someone tried to kill the two of us and isn't done. Also, please remember that we are in the bad guys' backyard and I want to avoid having them ask embarrassing question when I am tied to a chair and they practice unlicensed orthodontistry and facial massage on me."

"So we use a fake credit card on purpose and we stage the house on the assumption it will be searched. Don't you think you're being just a little paranoid, Ike?"

"Yes, I am. Being intentionally paranoid is the reason I survived as long as I did in the field. It's like this, no matter how smart you think you are and how cleverly you plan. Staying alive usually means that you are prepared for the opposite—that you are stupid and careless. That way, you'll be ready for the unexpected, the bizarre, the screw-up. I failed at this once and it cost the life of someone close to me. I won't let that happen again.

Ruth began to respond, recognized the cloud that crossed his eyes and the determined set to his jaw, and changed the subject.

"Okay, Sheriff, we stage the house for showing, but first, can we eat the burgers that got us in this mess in the first place?"

They sat, opened the bag of enormous burgers with the packets of fries Ike bought from Bert's. Ike passed mustard, pickles, ketchup, and bottles of beer. They ate in silence. Ruth started and shivered.

"The hair on the back of my neck just stood up," Ruth said. "What do you suppose that means?"

Sam swallowed a mouthful of bison and washed it down with beer. "My Aunt Camille would say it means trouble is coming."

"Yeah? So what else is new?"

Chapter Twenty-one

The next morning the three made a show of leaving the cabin and driving away. Anyone observing their behavior from, say, the nearby shrubbery, would have seen the two women, the sisters, bickering, and the older man, resplendent in a large pattern green-and-white houndstooth sport coat barking at them, "Shut up and get the hell in the car." It should have been convincing. They drove away, and after a pause, two men emerged from the shrubbery and approached the house. A third man stepped into the driveway farther along and spoke into a shoulder-mounted radio. The men stopped at the front door, acknowledged the call, picked the lock, and were inside in less than thirty seconds. Motion-detectors planted in several places responded and recorded their visit with the cameras placed in every room. They stayed for thirty minutes and left, leaving, they believed, no trace of having been there.

At the same time, another duo stopped by Bert's and made copies of the surveillance footage taken the previous day. The tapes were taken to the New Star Ranch where a team of men ran them through facial recognition programs. The process took several hours and resourced every database available to them but no identities were made or confirmed. To more sophisticated reviewers, that should have been a red flag. By this time, in the country's terrorist-obsessed culture, nearly everyone had been photographed and cataloged. Between NSA, Homeland Security, the FBI, CIA, and the remaining alphabet soup of acronymous security services there were precious few people over the age of twelve who were not resident in one registry or another. But these three were nowhere to be found. Had the scan been done a day later, it would have identified Beatrice Silver, June Gottlieb (nee Silver), and Marvin Gottlieb, all from Raleigh, North Carolina, but Charlie Garland had been busy with debriefing the agents ensconced in Ruth's cottage in Maine. He did hear that the scan had been done and hoped that the persons looking at the Gottliebs would not notice their absence in the files. He certainly would have.

> > >

The director of the FBI was a career agent. Unlike his recent predecessors, he had actually served in the field as a special agent. Over the twenty-five years he'd been an agent, he'd worked his way up through the ranks and the president, at the time torn between two conflicting loyalties each vying to have their choice appointed to the directorship, had solved his dilemma by appointing a career man instead, thus satisfying no one, but not offending anyone either. The *New York Times* called it a "bold, nonpartisan move for which the President should be commended."

The director studied the pink memo on his desk with disgust. He did not like political interference in the operation of the Bureau and especially not the sort that emanated from the Congress. He thought that Congress and its members, past and present, had enough skeletons in their collective closet to suggest they give the Bureau a wide berth, not stir up questions by seeking political favors. But politicians are not known for their introspection, and so the requests for special consideration landed on his desk nearly daily. Anyone who knew him also knew he was not stupid and realized that bending in the wind would sometimes prevent breaking. Occasionally allowances had to be made.

The matter of Karl Hedrick's continued employment in the Bureau hit his desk that morning. He did not understand why a senator would presume to question the effectiveness of an agent he'd never met and about whom he knew nothing. It bothered him. Obviously, Hedrick had stepped on someone's toes and they did not like it. On the other hand, he thought a few of the boys on the Hill could use a looking into and toyed with the idea of opening the file on the person making the request. He was pretty sure the Bureau had one. He shook his head, sighed, smoothed his patterned silk tie, a birthday gift from his wife—he hated it—and passed the request on to a senior deputy with more ambition than scruples. The deputy, in turn, scanned Karl's file and noted the adverse entries already in it. He ignored the exonerating documents accompanying those entries and pulled Karl out of Picketsville and back to his desk in the Hoover building.

⟩⟩⟩

Karl's removal from the case, while serving as a blow to the work underway at the site, did provide another bit of information for Charlie to work with. Who had enough pull at the top to initiate a request like that and, more importantly, whose pocket was he in?

"We are triangulating," he announced to Alice. She smiled an acknowledgement but had no idea what he was thinking. She didn't ask. She knew from experience that to do so would interrupt the process he referred to as "problem solving."

⟩⟩⟩

When they were well away from the cabin, Ike turned to Sam in the backseat. "We're set with surveillance?"

"Done and done. I have motion-activated cameras all over the place. When we get back, we can download the footage and see who visited us and what they were doing."

Ruth twisted in her seat. "Won't they see them? I mean, if they are breaking and entering, isn't it a fair assumption they will be looking for cameras?"

"That depends on whether they think we might not be who we say we are. Then they might. But I don't think they will. Not this time, anyway."

"There will be another time?"

Ike grinned. "Oh, yeah. If they are professionals, there will be. People with suspicious minds like theirs will always repeat a search on the assumption that we are as suspicious of them as they are of us and assume we staged the house for a search, but are not smart enough to anticipate a follow-up. They might guess that we will hide things and then, having been searched, get careless and leave stuff lying about. So, to be sure, they will come back in a day or two."

Sam leaned forward and handed Ruth a picture of a clothes hook. "What do you think?"

"Very minimalist. Are you and Karl doing your closets in black and white?"

"No. This is a picture of one of the cameras, Ruth. It looks like a coat hook but it isn't. My only concern is that the people in there will wonder at the number and placement of clothes hooks in the house."

"This is all very Edgar Allan Poe."

"Poe? How?"

"C. Auguste Dupin in 'The Purloined Letter.'"

"Ruth is being professorial," Ike said. "It's a story about a missing letter and it is hidden in plain sight, in a letterpress with other letters. Your hooks work because they look like they belong where they are"

"Sorry, Sam, Ike is right, couldn't resist showing off a little. With all you spooks, snoops, spies, and cops, I never get a chance to play in your sandbox and have to take what I can get. So, how many hooks?"

"Twelve in all. Then, there are three alarm clocks, and four electrical outlets all with built-in cameras. I hope they don't try to plug anything in. They are electrically dead."

"Why would they? Just as a matter of general information, how many of those things are in my bedroom, and when were they installed?"

"Just two—no, three, and this morning. Don't worry, your sex life is not about to go public."

"You're sure?"

Sam grinned wickedly. "Why would I lie?"

Ruth slumped back in her seat, not mollified. "Ike, when we return to normal, you are to shoot Sam. Maybe I will. It would be self-defense."

"Only after I've seen the videos. If I remember rightly, they just might have some commercial value. Think of all the *nouveau célébrités* who have launched their dubious careers with a tape like that. Who knows? You could be the next Kardashian."

"Do that and I will save your enemies the trouble and shoot you myself."

"Gotcha. No naughty tapes. You hear that, Sam? We switch off after we review what happened today."

"I planned to, although I must say, from what I've heard about you, June Gottlieb, I'm surprised you'd be finicky about a measly sex tape. The boys back in the old neighborhood said they have stuff on you that would start a fire, already."

"Shut up, High-Ho, or you're walking home."

Chapter Twenty-two

Billy stepped into Ike's office, now Frank's temporary one, and dropped into a chair. He did not look happy. Frank peered over his reading glasses and waited.

"So, I got bad news and some maybe-okay news," Billy said and dusted the brim of his Stetson against his knee.

"Bad and okay. That doesn't sound like a very promising start for the day. So, the bad news is?"

"They pulled Karl off the case. Something about him being too personally involved and 'not objective enough.' Lot of bullshit, if you ask me."

"Yeah, maybe, but you're right. Maybe he was getting too close to something, but it wasn't Ike. Hell, I don't know. I mean he's an FBI agent. That's all, and an agent who knows Ike, but he doesn't work here or anything. Somebody must have a special interest in this case and is someplace up high. Jesus, listen to me. I am beginning to sound like some conspiracy theory addict. You're right, that's definitely not good news. What's the okay news?"

"Well, you wanted us to check out all the places where the assassin might have installed the arming device or the bomb in the car. Remember we figured it must have been rigged to go off when a certain mileage point was reached? That way it had to be put in place or set to working pretty close to where it went off. We were thinking Ike must have stopped for gas, or coffee, or something before that. So, anyway, we picked up surveillance footage from every donut shop, filling station, and convenience store within a twenty-mile radius of Picketsville."

"I'm guessing your okay news is that you found a piece of tape that needs another look."

"Yeah, you could say that. We found one where he makes a stop that night about fifteen miles up the road. So, if the bomb was planted there, we'd have it on this tape. I don't know if he made any stops further up, you know, so this might be the one and it might not. I wish Sam was here and not off to wherever Garland the Spook sent her. What's with that guy, anyway? I mean he's CIA. He can't tell us what to do."

"No, he can't but since he's at least four steps ahead of us, and since he has the resources to do stuff that we can't, he's taken point and I'm good with that. If he thinks Sam needs to be somewhere else, so be it. What's on the tape that you think is important?"

"I ain't that sure. It's only that Ike stopped long enough for a device to be put on his car. It's the last place he stops before the last place and we know the thing wasn't put on there. That makes this one the best bet. The trouble is, I can't think it's where it happened because there's a county cop there at the same time."

"There's a cop in the picture? What does he do?"

"That's it. He don't do nothing. Ike drives in, gets out, and goes into this, like, 7-Eleven store. Another car pulls in and parks next to him. Right behind that guy, a Rockbridge County Sheriff's car pulls in and parks crosswise in front of Ike's car. So, now Ike is, like, blocked in. The deputy gets out of his car and follows Ike into the store. Okay, so far, so good. So then we fast-forward. He and Ike come out together and chat. The cop seems like he's apologizing for blocking Ike. They talk and then the cop leaves. Ike leaves."

What do you mean, 'fast-forward'?"

"We hit the fast-forward button. You know, nothing was happening so we sort of zipped through the middle part."

"Nothing? You're sure there was nothing? I want to see that tape, especially the middle part you skipped."

〉〉〉

Nothing is ever simple. You order a hit. You pay good money. You have people in place and then the milk goes sour. The hit man needs a cover and so we give him a one of ours and not just anybody. This guy is a policeman who is to provide it for him. So what happens? The bomber gets picked up by the Feds at the airport. What doesn't a trained killer know about explosive residue and there're dogs at airports trained to detect it? Idiot. We have to send people to take care of him. Then, the cop whose only job was to stall the Jew sheriff connects the dots and starts acting goosey. He says, "I didn't sign up for killings." You provide cover for a guy to plant a bomb and you don't think somebody is going to be killed? What doesn't he understand about collateral damage and the greater good? Another idiot. Where do these people come from? Martin Pangborn picked up the phone and punched in a Philadelphia area code and number.

"Bratton, just listen. Don't talk. You know the public servant we employed to monitor the fireworks display we scheduled last week? Well, he's not feeling well. You might want to drop in on him to see if he can't be given some attention. Am I clear?"

The other end went dead. Pangborn relaxed. Problem solved.

〉〉〉

Frank had the surveillance booted up and running. Four deputies sat in a semicircle watching snowy black-and-white footage roll across the monitor. Someone had left the coffee on too long and the aroma added to the nervous tension in the room.

"There, you see that? The County Sheriff's Department cruiser is not only blocking Ike's car, it also blocks the line of sight to it. That's important. Watch closely down in the corner of the screen. Remember, Ike and the county cop are still inside. Okay, now, we don't fast-forward this time. So, pay attention to what else is happening with the cars parked side by side. There, you can just make out that the door on the car next to Ike's opens. See, someone, all hunched over, slips to the driver's side of Ike's car, uses a slim Jim to open the door. Wait a second and there, the hood pops. I figure now he goes to work under the dash and then the front seat. He's pretty quick, like he's done this before. Now look at the front door of the store. What's going on?"

"Ike comes out with the cop. They have a chat. Probably apologizing for blocking Ike in."

"You think that is what the deputy is doing?"

"What else?"

"Come on. What just happened to the car? Don't you see? He's stalling Ike. Okay, now the hood on Ike's car comes down. The guy who's doing the job on his car slides back in his own car…click, his door closes. He scrunches down in the front seat. Meanwhile, Ike is trying to get to his car but like you said, the county car is in his way. The cop apologizes, blah, blah, blah. The cop gets in his car and drives off. Next, Ike gets in his car and drives off and right after that, the third car drives off, probably following Ike. There you go. Too bad we don't get a good look at the bomb-planter's face."

"Wouldn't help. It's pretty sure to be the guy the FBI had and lost."

"Better them than us."

"We need to have a chat with the county cop. Do you have an ID?"

"We have a time stamp, a location, and a car number. Someone will know who was driving that thing."

◇◇◇

"Where to now?" Ruth had the backseat of the car all to herself and was busy scanning the digital images on her camera she'd taken earlier. "Please, no more bison burgers. Isn't there somewhere we can get a salad?"

"We will head to that little town we passed yesterday. There has to be a restaurant, even a franchise fast food would do. What I want is a chance to look at an aerial view of this general area."

"I brought my laptop," Sam said. "We'll do Google Earth or something. If that doesn't work we'll try Zillow or one of the more sophisticated programs I can access. What are you looking for?"

"I can't get that New Star Ranch out of my head. Something there is not kosher. I want to see what lurks behind the gate they are so careful to protect."

"Look at this," Ruth said and passed the camera up to Sam. "Does that look like a normal cow bell to you?"

"Cowbell? On a steer? They don't bell steers. That's a dairy farm thing."

"Tell me, Sheriff, just how would you know that?"

"My father has a farm, remember?"

"But he doesn't work it. He rents it out. So, how?"

"I get around. I read, I—"

"You mean you watch old movies. That's how you know, or think you know. *Ma and Pa Kettle Down on the Farm*, or something with Marjorie Main, anyway," Ruth said.

"What do you know about Marjorie Main?"

"I peeked at your Classic DVD collection, that's what. Among other titles she played Ma Kettle."

"She did. Sequel to *The Egg and I*, if memory serves."

"You're kidding. The egg and…what?"

"Whatever," Sam said. "Moving on, this thing on the cow's, sorry, *steer*'s neck looks vaguely like a bell, but I'd bet my next-born that it is a surveillance device of some sort."

"A surveillance device in a bell?"

"Like my coat hooks or your Poe letter. Who'd suspect? It will record a day's grazing or whatever time is built into it. The owner stops and downloads the video, checks the batteries, and sends Bossie off on her or his way. They'd have a record of anything or anybody who happened to come by or who trespassed. More important, they could track frequent visitors."

"Sheesh, we are living in George Orwell's world."

"Have been for years," Ike said. "The question is, what the hell is going on at the New Star Ranch that requires that level of security, and why do I think I should know something about it?"

"I need a salad and you two can visit Google Earth and maybe we'll find out," Ruth said and flopped back in her seat.

❖❖❖

From the *Richmond Times Dispatch:*

Rockbridge County Sheriff's Deputy Thomas J. (Tommy) Frieze, a Marine Corps veteran with three tours in Iraq, a Bronze Star, and two Sheriff's Commendation Citations, was killed in a roadside shooting this afternoon. State Police Commander Colonel Jason Scarlett, speaking for the Governor, stated that Deputy Frieze was in the process of making a routine stop for a minor traffic violation when he was senselessly shot. The assailant fired his pistol for no apparent reason and fled the scene. As yet, State Police have no leads and no suspects. Deputy Frieze is survived by his wife, Jannetta, two children, ages 10 and 13, and his parents, all of Lexington.

County police have yet to determine a motive and an investigation is ongoing.

Chapter Twenty-three

"Our funny cop is dead. I heard it on the radio just now. They said that someone shot the deputy we know was at the 7- Eleven that night. He was gunned down this afternoon during a routine 10-38 outside Buena Vista out east on Route 60 past the town line." Billy scratched his head.

"That don't make sense."

Frank swiveled around in his chair. "He pulled over to have a chat with someone driving suspiciously and the guy just shot him? Wait a minute. Is there dash cam footage?"

"Don't know. You want me to make a call?"

"Yeah. No. Wait a minute. If we call, they will want to know why and I'm not ready to speculate on whether he was involved in the installation of that bomb."

"Not ready. Jesus, Frank, what more do you need? You said yourself that he must have been the guy."

"I did and I do believe it. I just don't want to go public with it yet. We need some background on him and if we start asking questions now, everybody will have their nose out of joint about people slinging mud at a hero. You know how it goes. Someone dies LOD and then another person says, 'Yes, but…' and the cops all clam up and people write angry Letters to the Editor, and…let's wait. Give Karl a shot at this. LEOs expect Feebs to act like horses' asses. When that happens, we will have a better shot at getting what we want. We'll be sympathetic listeners."

"Karl's off the case, remember."

"I do. He's riding a desk in DC. He has access to all kinds of stuff up there and nobody to question why he's in the file room or whatever they do to access files.

"I gotta say it, Frank. You are sounding more and more like Ike every day. That's supposed to be a good thing, by the way."

"I'm flattered. All I have been doing this last week is asking myself, what would Ike do? How would Ike react? I tell you, Billy, it isn't easy. He makes it look easy, but it's not. Maybe for him it is, but I am worn out trying to stay ahead of events."

"I reckon Ike might say the same thing if he was asked. "

"Maybe. So, what else have you learned watching Ike over the years?"

"Ike taught me there is nothing wrong about sleepovers with the right woman."

"Jesus, Billy, that's it?"

"Naw, but come on Frank, you need to relax a little here."

"Yeah, so okay, now what do we do? Our best lead is dead. We can't hassle his family. What?"

"If the county sheriff runs his outfit like any other cop shop, someone in it did not like…What's his name?

"Tommy Frieze."

"We need to find who didn't like Frieze and do some digging. Can you handle that?"

"Yeah, maybe. Frank, I ain't told Essie about Ike being alive yet. If I keep it off the table, can Essie help me out? She is going batshit crazy out at Ma's with them kids. She needs to do something. She feels really left out."

"You really haven't told her yet?"

"No. I got to thinking how she'd react and all the 'what ifs' that are hanging over our heads, and decided not to say anything just yet. It ain't been easy, for sure. So can she?"

"Do you think you can keep the Ike thing quiet?"

"I have so far."

"Okay, then you and Essie find an excuse to talk to some of those county guys, go pay your condolences at the Rockbridge

Sheriff's Office or something. Ask if there's going to be a caval-
cade, if so, when…stuff like that, and poke around. See what
you can find out. Talk to his friends and his not-so friends.
Everybody has something on them, good or bad, that people
want to talk about. Whatever it is, it could lead somewhere. But,
hey, be careful. The last thing we need is for people to find out
Ike is alive. Got it?"

"Got it. Essie will be happy."

> > >

The Gottleibs, that is to say, Ruth, Ike, and Sam, found a coffee
shop with delusions of grandeur signaled by a sign over the
door which announced it as: One Step Up (From St*rb*cks).
Whether they thought the asterisks protected them from copyright infringement lawsuits or they were just being cute wasn't
clear. What did seem certain was that the real St*rb*cks had
nothing to worry about. They ordered coffees and settled in
a booth across from four young men whose eyes strayed from
their laptops only long enough to sip at their coffee or drag on
something that looked like an old-fashioned cigarette holder
held in their teeth but didn't seem to have a cigarette inserted in
the end. On cue from somewhere out in the ether, they exhaled
a cloud of what looked like smoke. There was no tobacco odor
in the room, however.

"Somebody tell me what they're doing." Ike said.

Ruth turned her head to look. "Googling and vapeing, I'd
say."

"Say what?"

"Come on, Ike. Where have you been? People who can't give
up smoking, buy those electronic things that produce a nicotine-
loaded vapor. They inhale it and blow it out. Vapeing."

"I'm glad I'm dead."

A young man with a scraggly beard and a nine-millimeter
pistol strapped to his hip stepped up to the order station and
asked for a caramel-mocha frappuccino with extra whip.

"Can someone tell me what is it with men and open-carry
guns?" Ruth said.

"It is about their sense of sexual insecurity," Sam said as she rummaged through her rucksack. "It's debilitating to the point of emasculation. Psychologically, the gun is like a new set of balls."

"You're not being just a tiny bit judgmental there, Trixie."

"I call 'em as I see 'em." Sam found what she was looking for and plunked a thin file on the table. "Here's what I got on something called the Fifty-first Star. I think this must be the connection you're looking for."

"In three sentences, what's it say?"

"Three? You're joking, right? Okay, here goes. They are one of those militant, 'patriot' militias. They are on the NSA watch list as a possible domestic terrorist group but at the same time have political connections that keep them insulated from close scrutiny. Their ostensible leader is someone called Drexel Franks, who is a longtime crank caller of note to nearly every newspaper and politician in the country, and they have deep pockets. That's three. You need to read this. Do you know a corporate big shot named Martin Pangborn?"

"Who? Maybe…I don't think so. Why do you ask?"

"He's listed as a major player. Like I said, you should read this."

"I'll read it later. What else have you got?"

"That's what NSA has on them. Since we all were folded into Homeland Security, the boundary between domestic and foreign has sort of evaporated. Nobody is happy with that so we are careful to change our metaphorical hat when we cross it. Anyway, as I said, the Fifty-first Star has been looked at from time to time. It is classified as 'Militant Survivalist.' I think some of the analysts wanted to up the ante but the word from the top was to leave them alone."

"Word from the top? What does that mean?" Ruth asked.

"Whoever runs it has some friends on the Hill at the very least. There were whisperings about some of their activities, that's all. Anyway, nothing beyond that. The Bureau might have more. We could get Karl to snoop around. Now, look at this."

Sam pulled up Google Earth on her laptop and zoomed in on Idaho and then their portion of it. New Star Ranch stood out from the others because of the number of its outbuildings. The total seemed unusually large, but more importantly, they seemed different from the buildings on nearby properties, a few of which also had a large number of buildings.

"What are we looking at?" Ruth said and made a face after her fist sip of a skinny latte. "This is terrible coffee. Do you think they do a better job with chai tea?"

"If you insist on drinking trendy coffee, you get what you deserve. Plain coffee in a cup is good enough. It looks to me like an unusual number of buildings and all alike," Ike said, and tried to enlarge the image. "Maybe they can put it in one of those electronic gizmos and you can vape the chai thing."

"This from the man who thinks K-cups qualify as gourmet fare. Besides, I am sure that vape is not a word and neither is vapeing. God, what has happened to us? Okay, so what's so important about the buildings?"

"Look at the other ranches. Some of them have almost as many buildings, but they're all different sizes and shapes. New Star's buildings are all the same and lined up like a camp or something. I bet if you looked at a military installation, maybe not a new one, but one from the forties and fifties, it would look just like that. Barracks, that's what those buildings are or I'll eat my hat."

"Could it have been an old Army installation that the owner bought in a surplus sale?" Sam said.

"We can find out, but I doubt it. They look new. I wish they had caught people in the picture. I wonder if Charlie could arrange a drone."

"You want the CIA, which is in enough hot water over their use of drones overseas, to institute domestic surveillance? You're not serious?"

"I didn't say I wanted the CIA to send a drone. They won't do it. I said, 'I wonder if Charlie could arrange a drone.' There's a qualitative difference."

"A what? Charlie Garland has a private fleet of drones?"

"No, of course not, but other people do. Jeff Bezos has lots of them. And corporations, police, even private citizens do, too."

"Jeff Bezos?"

"Amazon.com. He says he wants to deliver packages with them. Drones are everywhere. The last catalog I received from someone wanting me to shop for Christmas in July had one with surveillance capability equivalent to the early Predators. They wanted thirteen hundred bucks for it."

"Maybe we should get one of those and leave the CIA out of it."

"It won't do. It's big and clunky and obviously a spy-in-the-sky. Those fake New Star warriors might be politically obtuse, but they're quick enough to spot it in a minute and paranoid enough to shoot it down in the next. Anyway, most drone manufacturers are falling all over themselves right, left, and center, to land a fat contract with a police department, a government agency, or some big commercial enterprise like Amazon. So, I will ask Charlie to suggest, only suggest mind you, that he would like a demonstration of someone's product, one with eye-in-the-sky technology and able to work relatively unseen. He's CIA, but he doesn't have to say he's not a procurement officer, just hint, flash his creds, and see what happens. Some hungry entrepreneur with a drone equipped with good TV surveillance system will happily offer to demonstrate it."

"Over Idaho?"

"Where better? If they were to do it over the East Coast, too many people would know, questions would be raised, competitors would wonder, but out here? Wide open spaces with nothing but buffalo."

"You are a very bad man, Ike Schwartz."

Sam's face lit up. "Do you think he'll go for it?"

"We can ask. I'll make the call. Can you get me a secure line on that thing or must we wait until the dopes have finished searching our place and go home?"

"We need to wait."

"Then, let's look at real estate in town. Charlie said we should look for a location to set up a satellite office in Idaho. Gottlieb Realtors, only we won't call it that."

"We are? Really?" Ike nodded. "Why?"

"I'm pretty sure we will need more boots on the ground soon. The office will be our cover."

"Okay, but why not Gottlieb Realtors?" Ruth asked.

"Too obvious. If you were in the realty business and were expanding into someone else's territory, you'd pick a generic name, something that sounded local."

"I don't understand."

"Okay, let's say you are looking for property in this part of Idaho. Are you going to go to Gottlieb, Gottlieb, and Silver, Real Estate Brokers, or Western Sky Realty?"

"Oh. You don't think a company with that name already exists?"

"I'd be surprised if one didn't. We'll think up another or we'll use it. People will assume we're a branch office. Anyway, are you done drinking your brown water?"

"Done. Let's go find an office. I take it you are okay with the locals knowing that Western Sky or whatever is really the Marvin and June Gottlieb and Trixie Silver deal?"

"I am. By the way, Sam, what's a chai tea?"

"It's a fancy meal where they serve little cakes and things at four o'clock in Chicago."

"Shut up, you two."

Chapter Twenty-four

Charlie Garland spent the day on the phone with contacts in various agencies. He had to call in a few favors and needed the director to call his counterpart in the Federal Bureau of Investigation to get what he wanted, but he finally had a name. Oswald Connors, junior senator from Idaho, had made the request to have Karl Hedrick removed from the Picketsville bombing case. Idaho. Of course, another Idaho association. Now all Charlie needed to discover was who made the call to Senator Connors and he'd have his man. He hoped.

The director of the FBI, in turn had to wonder why the director of the CIA was interested in a local, and only remotely possible, terrorist strike in Virginia. That agency did not stick its nose in for no reason. They wanted to know who sent the request. That meant they must know something about him. He scratched his ear and then ordered his people to pull any files they had on the junior senator from Idaho.

Karl Hedrick's friend in records thought Karl had been given a raw deal when he was assigned a desk. He called Karl and told him so. Karl thanked him and, as an afterthought, asked if he would send a copy of what the director had asked for. That's when he discovered the rumor about Senator Connors.

The senator, it was alleged, liked boys. Not as in he supported the Boy Scouts of America, or Big Brother, but as in the sixth-century BC Greek-sense. No reports of pederasty had been confirmed, nor had there been any accusations made—only rumors and gossip. Whether there was substance to them had not been determined. The file noted: evidence or not, the rumors should be taken seriously. The senator served on an oversight committee that had both the CIA and the FBI under its purview and, therefore, had access to sensitive classified material. Analysts at the Bureau felt because of that, he could be an easy target for possible blackmail and subsequently a threat to National Security. What all this had to do with his request to pull Karl from the case, he did not know, but he passed the information along to Charlie anyway.

> > >

For his part, Charlie did not like coincidences. He knew that they happened naturally and often. Much of Russian fiction was predicated on them. What were the chances that Lara would be domiciled in the same town in the middle of central Russia where Zhivago rode in to borrow a book? Or was it to buy a loaf of bread? Charlie couldn't remember. This business with the attempt on Ike's and Ruth's lives seemed riddled with too many coincidences. The mysterious repeater tower was in Idaho. The junior senator with a penchant for interfering with investigations (and possibly young boys) also hailed from Idaho. And that ranch, mustn't forget the ranch with the familiar-sounding name. The Idaho connection seemed too much a coincidence to dismiss.

So, two questions: if the FBI had files on the allegations about Connors' behavior, who else knew? It would be fair to guess someone else did. Was it another Idaho link that would close the loop and encircle our master bad guy? That would certainly explain a lot. Charlie called a contact he knew and trusted at the *New York Times* and fed him just enough to set him on the hunt. Then, he had Alice run up a list of all of the senator's contributors, both the ones declared on the disclosure forms and the darker ones buried in PACs. Somewhere in the list of righteous political movers and shakers lurked a very nasty piece of goods and Charlie wanted him. As soon as he had that information, he would set the dial under the pot to boil and that should make someone jump.

>>>

At first glance, the tape from the dash cam that recorded the shooting outside Buena Vista didn't show much. The deputy approaches the car and as he leans in, he is shot point blank, and the car speeds off. The assailant's license plates were missing. That, Frieze's supervisor assumed, was the reason the deputy had pulled the car over in the first place. There were some other small irregularities regarding operating procedure used on approaching a suspicious vehicle. If the result had been anything other than lethal, Frieze might have had a "sit down" with the sheriff's administrative assistant. But Frieze was dead and calling his sloppy technique into question at this point would be beating a dead horse. The PR person who made that statement had blushed and muttered something about there being no pun intended.

Before Frank could task Charlie Garland to secure the dash cam footage, the Rockbridge Sheriff's Office, as a courtesy, sent a copy to Picketsville. A few eyebrows were raised at the time. What did the Picketsville Sheriff's Office needed with it, anyway? It wasn't in their jurisdiction and did not involve any of their people. They shrugged and reminded themselves that even hick cops got the courtesy nod once in a while. The chief was funny that way.

As he had done with the previous surveillance tape taken at the site of the bomb-planting, Frank called in as many deputies as were available to scan this new footage.

"What's wrong with this picture?' Frank asked them.

Charlie Picket scratched his grizzled head and asked, "What do you mean?"

"All of you went through the academy. Sometime or another you called in a 10-38 and made a stop like this one. What's not right?"

"One correction, Frank," Billy said. "The word I get from the County is he never called it in. He just made the stop, which is why they didn't know about the shooting for, like, two hours after it happened."

"Okay, I'm guessing that's real important, by the way. So, with that in mind, what else is wrong with this picture?"

"Umm, I'm not sure but shouldn't he have readied for a confrontation? Like, he doesn't unsnap the strap holding his piece on its holster," the new kid said.

"Exactly. That's drilled into us all the time. If you pull someone over, your never know what you are about to run into. You always have you gun free and safety off, right?"

The men murmured their assent.

"Next?"

"Crap, he's got his hands in his pockets when he steps up to the driver's side door."

"Anyone like to guess what that means?"

"It means he knew the guy he pulled over," three said at once.

"So we have a murder, yes, but not a random shooting. This was premeditated. Whoever was in that car knew our deputy and lured him to his death. So, who has a motive to shoot our fellow officer?"

"Oh shit," said Billy. "He's the cop at the 7-Eleven when Ike went in and the bomb was planted, so that means he, for sure, had to be implicated. He wasn't just there by chance. He must have followed Ike there. So, it looks like someone in charge decided he couldn't be trusted to keep his mouth shut and had him erased. Whoever these guys are, they sure play rough. Jesus, Frank, that raises another question."

"Which is?"

"What if they know we've seen the tape? What if this guy was rubbed because someone found out we pulled the surveillance tape from the store and they were afraid we'd make the connection and get to him? If that, is it possible they, whoever they are, might be after us, too?"

"How do you figure?"

"We know what it means. Like, if somebody has eyes or ears on us, doesn't it follow they know that and could come down here to make sure the rest of us don't pass on what we know? Maybe punch one of us out to intimidate the rest into not saying anything?"

"I hadn't thought of that. It's a stretch but I guess it could be. So, everybody, if what Billy thinks is the connection, there's a cop killer out there and one or two of us could have a target on our backs. All of you stay sharp. We don't need any more of us going down."

"Frank, you think that's possible?" One of older deputies had a worried look. When the first of his six children arrived, he'd transferred in from the Baltimore Police Department because he believed Picketsville was not a high-crime duty station. Now, he wasn't so sure.

"You're good, Bob. First of all, you haven't seen the tape and, second, for all practical purposes, aren't tight with the investigation. No worries."

Bob didn't seem convinced. He had less than five years to his twenty and pension and he wanted to be on the right side of the sod when he got there.

◇◇◇

"You want a what?" Charlie had received some bizarre requests from Ike in his time but his insistence he needed a drone fly-over in the middle of nowhere took the cake. "Where? Idaho. Yes, of course, Idaho. That's where you are and you want this because? Suspicious buildings? Ike, I love you like a brother, but if you think I am going to be responsible for the internecine warfare that will erupt when the other branches find out the Agency is doing domestic surveillance on the hotbed of conservative America, you are nuts."

"Not the Agency, Charlie. A private contractor eager to demonstrate his wares to an unidentified government agency alleged to be in the market for a hi-res TV surveillance drone."

"I see. And we need this why?"

"There is a ranch out here with too many men in full military attire who're resident and some of whom are, even as we speak, searching our cabin. I may have footage for you to run some facial recognition scans in a few hours. At any rate, all of this activity is too much to dismiss as suspicious human nature. The place is called New Star, like fifty-one star, for God's sake. Worse, since we arrived here we have been scrutinized, followed, photographed, and now our belongings are being searched. It is way over the top, Charlie. I want a peek into that ranch and the military arrangements of their buildings. So, can you fix it?"

"Why can't you ever ask me for something easy, like a small nuclear device or the original Enigma Machine? Why don't you just buy one from Radio Shack or something?"

"They are too obvious, have limited capability and wouldn't last five minutes in the sky. I want one of those sneaky ones you told me about."

"Sneaky? Like the thing that looks like an eagle? It's just a rumor, Ike. Maybe you'd like an armored personnel carrier, too? They are real and available to every police department and sheriff's office in the land. Why don't you ever ask for something easy?"

"If the armored car looks like a buffalo, I'll take it."

"Yeah, yeah. Okay, give me some time. By the way, we have a development at this end. Karl has been told to stand down. I have been pursuing who made the request and why. You might find it interesting to know it was Senator Connors."

"The senator from Idaho. I'm not crazy about that being a coincidence, Charlie. Stay on that and get me some satellite pictures of the New Star Ranch. Sam will send you the GPS coordinates. Oh, and who is Martin Pangborn?"

Ike tapped off and turned to the two women. "Well that's interesting."

"What's interesting?"

"Sam, your husband is in the doghouse again. He's off the case. Before you ask, I don't know why, but it's hard not to believe it has something to do with the three of us."

"Someone up there doesn't like him. I'll call and find out why. Do we get our drone?"

"Maybe. Charlie is not happy, but he's working on it."

Chapter Twenty-five

The deputies operating out of the Rockbridge Sheriff's Office spent their off-duty time in two places. The more abstemious ones were to be found at a diner on old Route 60. Those more likely to require liquid support before or after work would be found at Benny's Sport Bar and Grille, AKA the Cop Stop, a few clicks east. Billy and Essie assumed that Frieze would probably frequent the latter and that is where they headed.

They left Picketsville toward evening and the twenty-minute drive from the office to and through Buena Vista went by in frosty silence.

Billy plastered a smile on his face. "So, is that new perfume? You smell nice."

Essie riding shotgun, stared straight ahead. "It's soap…Dove bar."

Billy realized he needed to deal with the chill in the air. He also knew this wasn't normal coming from the usually voluble Essie, and therefore, it could not be good. "Oh. Well, it's um… nice. Say, what's eating you, Babe?"

"When were you going to tell me?"

"Tell you what?"

"That Ike ain't dead."

Billy made an effort to rearrange his face into something resembling incredulity. Billy had never been good at covering his emotions, which explained why he was such a bad poker player. He failed at this as well. "What makes you think…wait a minute, why you asking something like that?"

"Look, Ma didn't need help watching them babies. You and Frank talking about everything else 'cept Ike, and everyone acting so smug and cheery. There're only two possible reasons for that. First, you don't care he's dead and for sure that ain't the case, so second, he ain't dead. You all thought that if I knew about him being alive I'd tip it to anyone who mighta been watching. Am I right?"

"Well, yeah, but you have to understand—"

"I don't have to understand anything. You all treated me like…Listen, I'm part of the office, right? We're a team. So teammates trust each other. If they have a problem, they hash it out. They don't go jumping to conclusions like you and Frank did."

"Essie, I'm sorry, but it was so important that nobody know. Not then. Not now. So—"

"So…okay, at first I would have, you know, tipped off anybody who could have been sent to check, I mean, but now I had time to think about it, I wouldn't have. I am not stupid, you know. So, how about I come back to work full-time? I'm going crazy out at Ma's."

"Yeah, Okay, I guess. Talk to Frank. Here we are. Jesus, what a dive. Okay, remember, we are just being cool. If we're asked, we just want to share our sympathies about a fallen brother and all that. Otherwise, we're grabbing a quick beer on our way to work."

"Got it, but I ain't done with this."

The bar was crowded with off-duty cops, firemen, truckers, and the town layabouts. There is an aroma that identifies bars where desperate men drink—somewhere between stale beer and fear. Well not fear, exactly. Something that signals danger anticipated and/or avoided. Whether going on duty or coming off, there was an exhalation of that distinctive scent—cop pheromone. Essie excused herself and cut through it on her way to the restroom. It was a "lady thing," she said. Billy found a high-top near a pair of cops and ordered two beers. Essie emerged from the restroom and a man whose moustache suggested he was a devotee of *American Chopper* sidled up to her and offered to buy her a drink.

"You got plans for tonight, honey?" he asked.

"Sure do. How 'bout you, sugar?"

The guy hitched up his jeans to show off the horseshoe-sized rodeo buckle. "Mebee we could do some of that planning together."

"You think? Well, here's the thing. I got two little kids to home. I got number three in the oven, you could say. I ain't got rid of the belly fat from the second and there's a road map of stretch marks the whole way round. And, oh I forgot, my husband is mean as a snake and packs a .357 Magnum. You okay with all that?"

Moustache drifted away. Essie pulled up to the high-top.

"What was that all about?" Billy said.

"He wanted to know if I wanted to romp in his playpen. Then he changed his mind."

"Yeah?"

"I told him you packed a .357 and were the jealous type. That caught his attention and he asked to be excused."

"Wow. You still got it, Babe."

"And don't you forget it. What did you learn so far?"

"Not much. The two dudes at the next table were sort of friends with Frieze, not real close, though. They thought he was weird. They said he belonged to some right-wing survivalist thing and kept at them to sign up. I kinda think that might be important, but I don't know why."

"We should buy them a drink, don't you think?"

〉〉〉

Charlie Garland finished his call to the drone vendor and hung up the phone. He shuffled the papers on his desk and drummed his fingers. Martin Pangborn. His eyebrows converged. He knew that name from somewhere. Where or when? Not recently, but not that long ago. He yelled for Alice to come in. He needed her to run a complete scan on Martin Pangborn.

"Give me everything, Alice, his birth, siblings, where he went to school, girlfriends, boyfriends, imaginary or real, I don't care. I want it all."

〉〉〉

"So, what was the name of that organization he was pushing you to join up with?" Essie asked.

When Billy was on duty, as opposed to relaxing with friends, he had one of those faces that defied reading, try as you might. If he chose to and unless he was very angry or in pain, one look at him and you would think there was absolutely nothing behind those brown eyes. "The lights were on, but nobody is home," the expression goes. It wasn't true, but it had always served him well.

Billy let Essie do the talking while he relaxed his expression into amiable stupidity and studied the two men at the other hi-top through the bottom of his beer glass. Essie opened her fringed leather vest, batted her blue eyes, and flashed her hundred-watt smile. She had a way of extracting information from men that was way different from his. At the moment, her way seemed to be working the best. Three beers and that smile would to do it. Essie was not another blond airhead, but she could convince anyone she was, if so moved. The two county cops were dazzled. That the beers were taking effect and they were a little tight made Essie's job a whole lot easier.

"Shit, lady, I don't know. It had something with a star in it, I think," the first cop said. "So, who do you all work for again?"

Before she could answer, the second cop blurted, "There was a number in it, but it didn't make sense. Like, something-star, twenty-one…no, bigger number, I can't remember."

"Fifty-one," the first one said. "Yeah, that was it. He was a member of the Star Fifty-one. No, that's not right. It was the Fifty-first Star. I thought it was a Masonic thing at first, you know. A lot of them lodges have a star in their name, so that's why I thought that, but he said no way, it was a patriotic organization that had true patriots for members. I remember saying, 'Well, of course it does.' On account of, well duh, if was a patriotic gang, wouldn't that be who'd be in it? I mean, it stands to reason."

The other cop nodded. "Frieze was a nerdy kinda guy and I don't think he was wrapped too tight either. Anyway he said things like, 'There is patriots and then there is true patriots. True patriots respect the Constitution of the U. S. of A. and the others just wave flags but don't do nothing when their country is under attack.' I asked him who was doing the attacking and he listed a whole bunch of people and, you know, organizations and such. Didn't any of it make much sense to me so I stopped listening. He was an okay guy, though, except for that. I mean nobody should take a bullet in the face like that. No way. Son of a bitch."

"No, they shouldn't. Cops put their lives on the line and deserve better. Right, Billy?"

"Right, they do. Son of a bitch."

"Damned straight," the second cop said. "Umm. Come to think about it, that group there, it was like a survivalist thing, only military. Like, they went off in the woods out west somewhere and lived off the land, took target practice, stuff like that. You'd think mandatory range duty here would be enough, but he said he needed time with automatic weapons and the big stuff."

"Big stuff?"

"Yeah. I don't know what he meant by that, I figured he was just blowing smoke."

◇◇◇

Sam removed the memory chips from the various surveillance devices she'd set around their cabin, loaded their images into her computer, and arranged them into a slideshow.

"That's one of the guys at the gate," she said and tapped the screen. "He seemed to be in charge. The rest were mostly spear carriers, you know—stood around fingering their weapons and looking fierce. Oh, and I think that one was too, but I can't be sure."

"Send that array to Charlie and ask him if he can put names to faces. Do you think any of these guys copied or took anything with them when they left?"

"Keyboard logger says no. They might have bypassed it by taking pictures of the screens but I doubt it."

"We should be good for a day or two and then they'll be back. I wonder what we should leave behind for them to find that might knock over a domino."

Ruth sat up. "Say what? You want them to suspect something? We don't have enough trouble already?"

"The fact that they felt a need to search this place means they are suspicious. What I want to do is satisfy their curiosity and confirm their suspicions, but send them in a different direction. I'm thinking of something that will divert them. Look, our cover story is pretty thin, right? I mean what is the likelihood the Gottliebs from North Carolina would come all the way out here to buy ranch land? Even if it were the truth, who'd believe that? It doesn't smell right. Now, suppose we were to leave brochures and a prospectus about mineral rights and fracking lying around. Now, our 'secret' will be revealed. They will congratulate themselves for being suspicious in the first place and then smart enough to figure out what we were really here for. Since they know that we are not likely to do anything more than talk and poke around, they will leave us alone."

"That is very devious."

"My middle name. And then, because we are not really a threat to them, they will make allowances for our behavior which they might not otherwise do."

Chapter Twenty-six

Charlie turned his attention to the picture array Sam sent him. He forwarded it to the desk that handled facial recognition and e-mailed what he was doing to his opposite numbers in the FBI and Homeland Security. He didn't need an interagency kerfuffle over what could be perceived as the CIA meddling in domestic affairs. Possible terrorists with ISIS connections, he'd noted on the transmittal. That would give them pause but shouldn't upset anyone. Most of the people working national security issues were willing to cut the sister services a little slack now and again. It's just that they did not like surprises.

E-mails sent, he went back to scouring the databases available to him that might reveal anything that seemed off-kilter in Idaho. A second message from Ike sidetracked that search. He spent the next hour with the Agency task force responsible for real estate transactions and safe houses. Shortly thereafter, Western Sky Realty or whatever Ike decided to call it, had office space in Idaho. A packet of brochures and prospectuses outlining the oil exploration processes connected with fracking were shipped out on the next flight to the state as well. He left for a late lunch and returned to find he'd missed a call from NuFlyte Industries. They would be pleased to demonstrate their drone and when would Mr. Garland like to see the product? Charlie set up a meeting for the next morning and no, he didn't need to see it fly, he only need to know its capabilities and if the company would release one in his custody. He was told that even though it was an unusual request, considering the source, they would be happy to oblige. He sent out a requisition for field agents to assume duties at their fake real estate business, two women and two men ought to do it, he thought. As an afterthought, he asked for Karl Hedrick to be seconded from the FBI and added to the list. All their faces were erased from the databases used for facial recognition. Alice stuck her head in the door to announce that she had completed the task he'd given her. It had taken most of the afternoon and early evening. She dumped a thick stack of printouts on Charlie's desk.

"It's late and I'm going home. After reading all that, I need a stiff drink and long soak. Until I clock-in tomorrow, you'll have to get your own coffee. Good evening, Charlie."

Charlie hefted the papers and shook his head. He began reading. After an hour, he remembered where he had run across Martin Pangborn before and, more importantly, the circumstances. It seemed unthinkable that that run-in had prompted all that had transpired since. He read on, dug into the scant history available about the businessman's childhood, the more detailed data about his business dealings, the havoc they'd caused countless families, and concluded that it was, indeed, possible.

He needed to warn Ike to be careful. If Pangborn ever figured out that his plan had failed, things could get very sticky, very fast. Charlie sat back and considered what or who else might be on Pangborn's agenda, or in his crosshairs, to be more exact. That's when he realized that, among others, he might be on the man's hit list, too. It was an interesting thought and one, if true, he might be able to use to his advantage. That assumed, of course, that Pangborn didn't know that he, Charlie, had stumbled onto him. A risky assumption.

Frank Sutherlin called to tell him that he and the deputies in Picketsville had teased out the where and how of the bomb-planting and who might have been involved. Unfortunately, the cop who'd been involved was dead, he said, and did Charlie know anything about a group called the Fifty-one or Fifty-first Star?

Charlie said he did now, but not enough. The last he'd seen of that logo was on a burned-out helicopter on an island in Maine. He'd put somebody on it in the morning and complimented Frank and all the people in the sheriff's office for work well done. Did he need anything else? Not right now but told them to keep digging. Was anyone else in the Rockbridge Sheriff's Office a member? Could he track the car driven by the cop killer? Frank said they were trying but there wasn't much to go on. Just the dash cam image. Charlie said to send it to him. He'd put his people on it.

It had been a slow process but things were starting to come into focus. He felt the tingle in the back of his neck. He was onto something. He turned his attention back to the printout of Martin Pangborn. Mr. Pangborn, it seemed, had himself connected all the way up to the former President of the United States. He was a consummate wheeler-dealer, a confidante to celebrities, a would-be kingmaker, and judging by some of the practices he'd employed in the course of acquiring his wealth, a nasty piece of business.

It was a little after midnight when Charlie believed he might have stumbled onto the connection between Pangborn and Senator Connors. It was pretty thin and he'd want to think about it before he said anything. Ike should probably know, but no one else. Something that explosive needed to be verified, rock solid. Martin Pangborn had friends and money in high places and would not roll over easily, even if he was a blackmailer.

He packed up and went home. He made sure no one followed him. Tomorrow, things should pick up.

◇◇◇

The sun had been down and what passed for dinner consumed. Sam was occupied with the messages coming in over the encrypted airwaves. She felt pretty sure she had isolated the receiver they were looking for. All she needed was to connect a place to the messages. Which ranch, mansion, or motel harbored the recipient? She thought she'd need to drive around with a tracker and triangulate before she did. Tomorrow she'd request the fake bad guys to up the radio traffic.

Ruth listened with half an ear, her eyes on Ike. Ike was pacing. She recognized the behavior and knew that nothing in her bag of tricks would make him stop. She'd tried once and felt like a fool when Ike smiled absently and paced on by as she, wearing a lacy nightgown which was more lace than gown, attempted to lure him away. Even her feeble attempt at a hip thrust went unremarked. Ike apologized later and said he didn't remember anything. She'd found that hard to believe.

"Are you sure? I mean I know that thing that you don't wear often enough and if you had been in it and…did you say thrust? I would remember that."

"I did and you didn't, Sheriff. Your loss. That is not something I do on a regular basis and after that rebuff, I might never again. It was cold."

"That part, I remember."

Ruth sighed at the memory and watched as Ike reached the end of his ambit and started back. She poured two fresh cups of coffee and offered Ike one as he walked by. "What do you need?" she said, hoping it would be something in her power to deliver, but certain it wouldn't.

He took the cup and sipped. "Movement."

"Movement?"

"We are stuck. I need to move forward, sideways, even backwards if it will get us out of this rut."

There wasn't much she could do about that. It was only after the crate arrived and its contents revealed the next day that Ike had what he needed to get back on track.

Chapter Twenty-seven

The UPS truck gnashed its gears, reversed, and drove away leaving the crate and several packages on the porch. Ike hauled them indoors and opened the largest one, the crate.

"Unless I missed something," Ike said, "this is our drone."

Sam shook her head. "It looks like a big model airplane. My brother used to put them together only his were made out of balsa wood and some of them had a rubber band motor. Is that Styrofoam?"

"It is, among other things."

"So, we ask for a drone to put eyes on the ranch and this is the best that Garland can do?"

"You didn't think he was going to commandeer a Predator, did you?"

"I hoped. So what do we do with this Cracker Jack toy?"

"Give me an hour with the manual and I will let you know. In the meantime, why don't you locate the source of the chatter? Five will get you ten it is the New Star Ranch."

Sam packed up her gear and drove off after assuring Ruth and Ike she would be back for lunch, so if they had plans that required complete privacy, they should act accordingly. Ruth told her to shut up.

"She has a point, though, Ike."

"What. You want to romp? Now?"

"No…yes, but that's not what I meant. What the heck was Charlie thinking and how can that flimsy thing possibly solve your problem?"

"Patience. According to the book this is a technological marvel. Why don't you unpack the rest of the boxes? I gather we have real estate in town and agents on their way to help us. We will need to get them settled when they arrive and by then I hope we will have something for them to do besides pretend to be looking for fracking sites."

Ruth tackled the rest of the boxes and Ike studied the drone manual. After an hour he'd unpacked all of the components and began to assemble it. Completed, it appeared much larger than either thought. Sam returned with her map and an expression that indicated she'd been successful.

"You were right. The signals are coming from and going to the New Star Ranch. Where did that thing come from?"

"Good. That 'thing' came out of the crate. Not much of a toy now, is it?"

In fact the assembled aircraft did not look like what any of them had imagined. It had a wingspan of nearly five feet and with its propulsion unit mounted high on its dorsal surface, it resembled a flying shark as much as it did a plane.

"You're going to launch that over the ranch? They'll see it in a minute and probably shoot it down."

"Wait, wait for it…." Ike opened what appeared to be a brief-case but which revealed a panel that looked like the binnacle of an airplane cockpit. He flipped a few switches and the whole underside of the aircraft changed color. More than color, it seemed to sprout feathers. "Behold the wonders of nanotechnology."

"Where did they come from?"

"This stuff is not my long suit but apparently the underside of the unit is covered with an ultrafine network of micro filaments or tubes which can respond to signals sent to them somehow. During the day, the underside of the thing looks for all the world like a large turkey vulture. That's its name, by the way, the Vulture. The Air Force and the CIA have the Predator, we have the Vulture."

"Should I be impressed?"

"Yes, you should. Not only that, but it is programmed to circle like one of those birds. The problem with the earlier models of this kind of drone was that they looked like a bird, but that's all. They simply flew in circles. It wasn't long before the people on the ground caught on. This one banks and sails like a real bird. If you watch it through binoculars, for example, even the feathers seem to flutter in the air current and when it banks, according to the book, they flare as they would with a bird. Now watch."

Ike flipped another switch and the feathers disappeared and the underside turned sky blue. "If you were watching it with binoculars, it just disappeared from view."

"And at night?"

Ike flipped another toggle and the drone turned matte black.

"Holy crap. I want one of those," said Sam.

"I'm impressed. Wow, think of the possibilities," Ruth said. "You could have a dress made with that stuff. Someone comes to your party in the same outfit, you flip a switch and you have completely new dress."

"Umm, yeah, I guess that could work."

"Or you could change the color of your car to match your shoes. The applications are limitless."

"Now you're being sarcastic."

"You noticed. But, you heard it here first, that will be but a few of the civilian applications that some guy with perfect teeth and hair will flog on TV and sell a million dresses, cars, hats, you name it. It is a brave new world we are entering, kiddies."

Sam grinned. "Okay. So what kind of payload can it carry and for how long?"

"It says here it can carry a HiDef TV camera and transmitter and at night, a night vision unit. It can fly around for eight hours before it needs refueling. Charlie says if we need really close-in stuff, they will reposition a satellite for us, but there would be a ginormous hassle to do that so we're not to ask unless we have something really big."

"There is more space in there."

"Yeah. The manual says it can carry a small explosive charge. I guess it would be rigged to go if it were to fall into the hands of the wrong people."

"Or a small bomb?"

"That, too, I guess."

"So now what?" Ruth asked.

"Now we fuel this bird up, set it to Vulture mode, enter the geographic coordinates and launch. Later this evening we can bring it back and reconfigure it for a night run."

"One problem," Ruth said. "What about our nosey oafs? Mightn't they be watching? And won't seeing this thing buzz off the property give them the heebie-jeebies, not to mention a very bad impression of who we are?"

"Point taken. We need to secure the perimeter. Charlie sent us some cameras and a monitor in that box over there. Let's take a walk."

> > >

Ike studied the monitor. It had taken him a few minutes to adjust to its relatively small size. The camera in the bird, now circling the New Star Ranch a few miles away, held steady and in focus irrespective of the maneuvers the "bird" made. Ike guessed there were servos that kept the camera pointed and focused as the platform shifted its position in the sky.

"What did you expect to see?" Ruth had fixed sandwiches and passed one to Ike.

"Anything from a herd of cattle to a battalion of tanks. I don't know, really. The place is just too odd not to study. I would love to search one of those barrack-like buildings."

"Could the Vulture swoop down for a closer look?"

"It could, but I don't want to draw attention to it just now. Up close only an idiot would think it's a big bird."

"So you got nothing."

"Not nothing, but what I do have, I don't know how to interpret. There are men down there. They move around like they have things to do. You know, working and so on. Then there seem to be some young people there as well. A fair number. It's like a camp. But boys only."

"Any women?"

"Oh, yeah. No girls, though."

"Hey…"

"I mean there are women, a number of them. Not as many as the men, but they are there. What I meant was, there don't seem to be any female children."

"And?"

"And…I don't know. Why boys and no girls? I don't like asymmetry."

"If I had any idea what that meant, I'd be impressed. What does it mean, anyway?"

"Look, you have men. You have women. Normal arrangement only more of the former than the latter. That would be an acceptable ratio on a ranch. Okay, you have children. One expects a similar ratio of boys and girls. Not true here. I don't see any young girls at the ranch, just boys. I want to know why."

"Okay, here's a flash, Sheriff. At the distance you are scanning, you couldn't distinguish boys, young males, from girls. Not if they are in jeans and checked shirts, have short hair, and wear Nikes. I know you think you can but you can't. Those things that obsess men, the bumps and curves, don't appear until later. You could have all girls, for all you know."

"You might be right and you might not. If I am correct and there's even a disproportionate number of boys to girls, I bet it's important."

"You have a very suspicious mind. Okay, let's say you're right. How about they are running a boys' camp?"

Sam looked up from studying the screen. "I thought I read that the militia group there had a young people's subunit called the pioneers…something…Young Pioneers. That could be them."

"There you go, Sherlock, the Mystery of the Too Many Boys solved

"Okay, that would explain it. And yes, I do—have a suspicious mind, that is. Hand me a beer, will you?"

"Here you go. Okay, enough with the gender issues, real and imagined. I've been thinking about my nano dress."

"Your what?"

"The dress that is made with those micro fiber things that can change color and do stuff like make the Vulture disappear, that nano dress."

"Okay, the theoretical dress. What about it?"

"How would it work if it disappeared, you know, went blank? Is it like Harry Potter's Cloak of Invisibility? Would I disappear too? That would certainly be convenient at times. Or would I be standing there in my panties? Or just wearing a dull white dress?"

"And you need to know this why?"

"It would make a difference if and how much I spend on underwear, that's why."

"Eat your sandwich."

Chapter Twenty-eight

Charlie added the six pages of single-spaced notes the reporter from the *New York Times* had sent him to the growing pile on his desk. It told him more about Senator Connors than he really wanted to know and added little to his growing corpus of intel relating to Ike's attempted assassination. Still, you never knew. Things connected in odd ways sometimes. "Everything is connected to everything else." An eco guru told Charlie that once. He couldn't remember where or when exactly, only that he thought at the time the guy was a complete phony. The swami had the circle of life or something like that sort of thing in mind, but in Charlie's experience, connectedness between people and events meant something different and frequently sinister.

Sam reported that she had pinpointed the receiver at the ranch, so Ike's instincts were still sharp. In any event, it meant the operation in Maine could be shut down. When the calls ceased, something should happen at the ranch. They would worry. They would want to know what happened. Back in Maine, attorneys would appear out of the woodwork to protect their clients' right to remain silent. Not that they'd need them. The men they'd picked up had not uttered a word in the days they'd been stashed in a pre-Guantanamo holding facility. So far no one had thought to provide them with their phone call, so no lawyers yet. Assuming everything is connected the way it seemed to be, two of their men in the hands of the authorities had to produce a reaction. Some of the activity should ripple up the chain to whoever was behind this. The *whoever*, Charlie felt certain, would be the same Martin Pangborn whose bios, news clips, confidential assessments, and intelligence constituted two-thirds of the pile on his desk. Releasing them didn't necessarily mean turning them loose on the public, however. They might get lost in the system. Charlie loved that phrase. It covered all sorts of incompetence at so many levels.

The problem with men like Pangborn stemmed from their ability to surround themselves with multiple layers of deniability. Charlie knew that no matter how deep they probed, they would never find any direct or admissible evidence implicating Pangborn to Ike's attempted assassination, to Ruth's, or to the cop in Virginia. At most, he would be an anonymous voice on the phone or, if he were to be in direct contact with someone, that person would be fiercely loyal like the goons they'd picked up in Maine or, like the bomber the FBI lost, be eliminated before they could talk. He made a call and the Maine operation ceased. He would wait and see what popped.

◇◇◇

Sam noted a flurry of activity on the ranch communication channel. She had not heard back from the cryptographers yet, so she could not know what was being said, but clearly, something happened to stir up the troops.

Ike," she yelled down the hall, "are you seeing anything? The phone lines to the ranch just lit up like a Christmas tree."

"Some people hot-footing to one of the buildings. I can't tell if what you have and this are related."

"Charlie just sent this," Ruth said and slipped beside Ike on his bench.

"What's it say?"

"Umm…They shut down the transmissions in Maine. That's one thing. He also says the two of you need to talk. Just you two? I'm hurt. And finally the Fifty-first Star is the key to the whole puzzle. Goody. Now, just what or who is Martin Pangborn?"

Ike stared at the screen as the Vulture made another east-west pass across the center of the ranch and then banked north to start a north-south sweep.

"Ruth, do you remember Maine?"

"The slogan that started the Spanish-American War? Before my time. Or do you mean our vacation gone sour last year when you accidently blew up a helicopter?"

"A fortuitous accident, as you recall. Those people had murder and mayhem in their hearts. Yes, that Maine memory. The incinerated chopper and its occupants belonged to Martin Pangborn. I gather he is still upset about it."

"I thought it was covered up by the Agency's clean-up crew."

"As did I."

"I guess you and the ubiquitous Charlie will have to have your chat. That can't bode well."

"Why would you say that?"

"Every time you and your spook buddy have a sit-down, all hell breaks loose and people get hurt, as in dead."

"Not always."

"Often enough. Listen, Ike, I know we have to see this through and if it means things might be bloody, well okay. I get all that. But I have to tell you that I am not happy going through life in some nut's crosshairs and it has to end. This is not normal living. I came to Picketsville to take a job at the college. That's all I wanted to do. College presidents are supposed to face down sit-ins, angry parents, thick-headed board members, and insolent faculty, not be shot at, blown up, and maimed. You need to find a new line of work or I need body armor."

"Maybe made with nano technology so you could change its color? Or disappear?"

"I'm serious, Ike."

"I know you are. The problem is, most of the really bad things that come my way have to do with who, or more precisely, what I was, not what I am now. The sheriff of a small town has his moments, but nothing like this."

"You're right. Maybe you need a nano tech past that we can make disappear."

"I know you are being facetious, but the truth is, that is more of a possibility than you might think."

"What?"

"I need to talk to Charlie. Let's get this mess settled and then I will find a way to throw a switch and my past, like our Vulture, will disappear from view."

> > >

Martin Pangborn expected a phone call. He would wait. Meanwhile, he watched the rush hour traffic stop-start its way eastward toward Whacker Drive. Worker bees on their way home from dead-end jobs and wasted lives, he thought and smirked. If they only knew what he knew, but then, if they did, where would he be? Success, he believed required a ratio of something like a thousand to one, losers to winners and he was definitely one of the winners.

Pangborn stood just under five feet ten inches. His height did not make him a short person as it is generally understood. But he didn't qualify as a tall one either and that was a constant source of annoyance. As a teenager he'd longed to be at least six feet tall. All the popular boys were. Through no fault of his own he'd failed at that, but it might have been the last thing he would fail at. Well, except for the hair. Most of his hair deserted him in his early thirties, though the beginning of male pattern baldness could be seen in his high school yearbook. Like many men, he was in denial about it and sported a comb-over that began just above his left ear and streaked to his right. By now, precious little remained to comb, but he stayed with the practice even after the meager strands on his pate looked as if they had been drawn there with an eye liner. "More comb than over," one of his employees had said. Unfortunately he didn't know Pangborn had come up behind him and he had joined the ranks of the unemployed the next day.

He glanced at the phone willing it to ring. Martin Pangborn did not panic. He had assets he had not yet deployed. That's how he put it to Jack Bratton, Colonel Jack Bratton. Jack had risen to an E-7 rating in the Navy, no mean achievement, but Colonel was a reach. He'd achieved a small bit of notoriety as bodyguard to a series of bratty rock stars and wannabees. Currently, that is when he wasn't cleaning up after Pangborn, he spent his time providing security, muscle, for concerts and off-the-grid sporting events. The latter had caught the eye of several local police departments but nothing had ever been laid at his doorstep. Nevertheless, in the inverted world of the Fifty-first Star, Colonel had been his landing place. Pangborn had taken to him and had seen to his advancement primarily because Bratton did not seem to have any sensibilities. He was the sort of man who matures from the boy who tortured the cat, pulled the wings off butterflies, or bullied those weaker and more vulnerable than he. There were half a hundred men and an equal number of women who would happily stand idly by and watch Brattan drown, fall over a cliff, or die of thirst while they sat on a case of Perrier. None had yet screwed up the courage or had the opportunity to do anything like that and probably never would. The Brattans of this world appear immune to the limits imposed on the rest of us.

The phone chirped. Pangborn let it continue through five cycles and then picked up. "Go."

"Yes, sir. You want me to have a face-to-face with the guys so that they get their stories straight before they meet the lawyers, right?"

"I wouldn't say that. I am only concerned about the welfare of some acquaintances. You know that. We have people in the federal prison system and the local Maine constabulary. Find them and see if you can determine what, if anything they need."

"Yes, sir. Message received."

Pangborn frowned and tapped off. He liked Jack in many ways and in others he didn't. People had their uses and then they didn't. Among other things, Bratton lacked discretion. His time in the useful category might be reaching its limit, he thought.

The phone line hummed in his ear. He hung up and muttered.

"I will have to do something about him before too long. He's too eager. But first things first. This means the woman is still out there. We need to find out where and finish what we started. People need to know that it is not a good thing to cross me. What else does that mean? Damn, they know something. How much? If they knew to set up that blind, did they know about the tower? No, how could they? Still…time to call in a few IOUs."

He picked up the phone again and dialed a series of numbers with Washington, DC area codes.

>>>

It promised to be a long night for several people who would have to search their consciences and weigh their political and financial futures, their survival, against assuming some of the responsibility for the certain destruction of one or more people they'd never met. In the end, personal survival would win, but in fairness to one or two of them, there were a few qualms before the storm.

The next morning, phones began to ring across Foggy Bottom—in senator's offices, the FBI, NSA, and the White House. Charlie received a heads-up from the director.

"I don't know who you pissed off, Charlie, but the proverbial fertilizer is about to hit the fan. I hope your pals are tucked away someplace safe."

Chapter Twenty-nine

Ike's Vulture nearly flew into the rotors of the approaching helicopter. The drone's guidance system was capable of challenges
of all sorts, wind shear, rain, even lightning, while doing things
bird-like, but to spot an aircraft and avoid it was not one of
them. Fortunately, prop turbulence knocked it to one side and
into a dive. Its programming recognized that the craft was off
course and losing altitude. It recalculated its flight path and the
adjustments the bird's software needed to reset. Within seconds,
it had wheeled about, regained altitude, and returned to its preprogrammed vector. People on the ground who happened to
witness the near collision, laughed and wondered aloud what, if
the bird hadn't dropped when it did, would "chopped buzzard"
have looked like splattered all over Mr. Pangborn's new toy?

The tiny five-by-seven-inch screen restricted Ike's view of
what happened. He had a sudden sinking feeling that he'd lost
his bird and then what he might have to say to Charlie. Charlie
told him he needed the drone back and in one piece in three
days' time. What he would say if Ike shipped him a crate full of
diced Styrofoam? Nothing repeatable in church, certainly. In the
next instant he recognized that the drone had righted itself and
cleared the chopper's path. He breathed a sigh of relief when
the drone leveled out and resumed its preprogrammed course.
He made it wheel away and "disappear" for a few minutes and
then had it return following a different flight pattern.

"Something big is happening," Sam shouted. Her voice traffic had escalated quickly in the last few minutes.

"I've got it," Ike shouted. "A helicopter just flew in and landed. I have our bird changing its altitude and flight pattern. I want a peek at the passengers. Any idea what the chatter on the phone lines is about?"

"Software is still installing. Another couple of minutes and we can listen in, but right now, I have nothing."

"Why'd it take so long for the spooks to release it? Never mind. I can guess."

"From my experience at NSA, they are not good at sharing. Charlie can do only so much."

"Right."

Ike checked to make sure the Vulture was recording and resumed squinting at the screen. With any luck they would be able to grab a few usable face shots and run them through facial recognition programs. He reckoned he already knew who it would be, who he hoped it would be. If they could get the author of all this craziness on the ground and close, he could end it. Ike did not think he'd bother to wait for an arrest warrant if that were the case. All this assumed, of course, that the dots, when correctly connected, led to Martin Pangborn.

"Software is up and running. I will have some transcripts from the earlier calls for you in fifteen minutes." Sam sounded excited. Then Ike remembered that she had always sounded that way when some new techno-goodie arrived for her to play with. She piped in the live conversations.

"Star Two is on the ground," the digitalized voice reported.

"Star Two? Assuming that is the tag for whoever just landed, who or where is Star One?"

"Remember when I looked at the analysis of the Fifty-first Star? Someone named Drexel Franks was described as the head of it. I didn't see his name anywhere else in the material, though."

"You sound disappointed, Ike," Ruth said. She had come into the room when the shouting started.

"If I assume Star Two is the second in command, Star One must be the Mister Big I'm after and the guy I'm interested in. I hoped he was the one who got out of that chopper, that's all."

"Well, perhaps this is the advance party."

"Maybe, but I doubt it. From what Sam just said I'm thinking it's more likely the real brain behind all this is smart enough to put a patsy in as titular head. That would be this Franks character. Then if there were any serious breakdown, people would naturally go after him, that is Franks, not the actual manipulator of the organization. He, in turn, would glide away into the miasma and disappear."

"He?…Miasma?"

"I'm assuming the person behind all of this is male and Star Two is our friend Pangborn. I could be wrong. It could be the Dragon Lady, or Meryl Streep having a bad hair day, or Drexel Franks, but my money is on Pangborn. Miasma…fog, mist with an ominous or foreboding valence. Miasma."

"My ass to you, too. Don't go all English as a Second Language on me, Schwartz."

"Sorry, Doc. But you see what I mean. If we are going to bring this thing to a close in this decade, we need the players correctly identified and located where we can get at them, not lost in a fog by any other name."

"And if they all show up here, what will you do?"

"Take care of business. I will make sure they know that I know and that there are always consequences for seriously screwing around with me and mine."

"Bravely spoken, sir. There is just one problem with that. You have no hard evidence that Pangborn or Meryl Streep, if your second guess is correct—"

"She was a joke."

"I got it. If he/she is in fact in play, you got nothing to justify going all Rambo."

"Evidence is a vague sort of concept, don't you think?"

"You went to law school. You tell me. Or does your sense of righteous outrage trump due process?"

"What's up with you? You said you wanted to put an end to this. You said you understood that bad things might happen, but you were tired of having a target on your back. You know me by now. So what is the problem?"

"I said all those things and I meant them, and I do, indeed know you. That is the problem. I also said a lot of other things over the years, some of it on reflection I am not proud of and would take back if I could. Other stuff…well. Now I am saying this to you, Ike. I do not want justice at the expense of losing you. I've already come too close to that, if you recall. Whether from friendly fire, bad guys getting off a lucky shot, or more likely a judge who has little or no patience with vigilantism putting you away for twenty to life, I will not accept losing you because you can do what you do. I want these monsters brought down the right way. That's all."

"Wow. Well, at least you didn't drop the F bomb. I'm proud of you."

"I was tempted. If ever there was an occasion."

"Okay, I hear you."

"Hearing isn't enough. I want a promise that you won't go all Lone Ranger on me and ruin what we have just to drop one slimeball."

"The Lone Ranger was the good guy."

"You know what I mean."

"You do understand that if we play straight arrow, we might never get this guy. If the source of this continuing nightmare is who we suspect, he will not be easy to nail. People like him have layers around them like an onion on steroids, to prevent anyone from getting close. And he is connected to all sorts of powerful people."

"Ike…"

"Let me finish. Do you remember when the financial collapse hit a while back and banks had to be bailed out and General Motors teetered on the verge of bankruptcy? Some were considered 'too big to fail' so the bozos who engineered that fiasco not only got a pass, but to add insult to injury, gave themselves performance bonuses for their monumental incompetence. Some of what they did was clearly criminal yet, they were too big to go to jail. So, it appears there are some people in this society who are permitted to skate on moral thin ice because they are just that—too big, too important, too connected, or too rich, to bring down. They will have alibis, fall guys, high-priced lawyers, and friends in high places who will grease the skids for them. Or enough money to flee the country to a venue with which we have no extradition treaty and, by the way, take their money with them. This guy is one of those people. He might be impossible to bring down the right way."

"So, you will do it your way?"

Ike sighed and said nothing. What could he say? Any answer he gave would be a lie—to himself or to Ruth. There was no middle ground here.

"Okay, then. I have a pot of stew on the burner. You and Sam need to eat. You can plot and scheme with Dinty Moore. I'm going to settle for a tall scotch and water and leave you to it. Just this, I don't like it."

Chapter Thirty

Pangborn Enterprises occupied a suite of offices in mid-town Chicago. More prestigious addresses were available, but Pangborn thought a status address rarely justified its cost. Business started early, as much of the company's competition was located on the east coast, and in consideration of the west coast business, it ended late for the same reason. Starting at five in the morning, the hunter/gatherers that made up his staff busied themselves on their telephones and computer screens. There appeared to be no evidence that the news about the men who'd been assigned to track down and dispatch Ruth Harris-Schwartz and had now dropped out of sight had set off alarms.

Pangborn made a point to keep his business separate from his involvement with the Fifty-first Star. Thus, the company's flinty eyed employees, handpicked by Pangborn personally, continued their planned rape and pillage of the economically vulnerable commercial sector.

Three struggling companies were targeted for the next round of acquisitions. Two companies, currently on the books, were methodically dismembered and their viable parts sold off at an enormous profit, the marginal units dumped on the scrap heap of American capitalism. Previous owners took what they were offered, happy to have avoided ruin while their employees, who'd been persuaded to take pay cuts so that the company could keep going, now found themselves on the street without warning and wondering where they would find a job, the cash to make their next mortgage payment, and how to explain to their families what had just happened. Few, if any could have identified the source of their personal disaster. One or two would try.

His flight department was the only exception to the separation of the corporate body and the Fifty-first Star. He kept a Global Explorer hangered at Teeterboro and a small fleet of Bell helicopters in varying configurations at the FBO at Martin State in Maryland. Their fuselages were all marked with a star with the number fifty-one in its center. The Explorer and the helos he leased through a subsidiary, Fifty-One Sky Star. He also kept an executive Bell at Chicago's Midway for his personal use. It was the latter that had carried him to the ranch. He'd left the offices that morning because he did not want to be available when the obvious questions were raised by the recipients of the calls made the night before to people who owed him their allegiance or who, for one reason or another, feared him.

He arrived at the New Star Ranch in the late afternoon and retired to his personal residence. From the outside it looked like the all the other buildings which were arrayed in two rows on the site. Inside there was a remarkable difference. Whereas the others were spartan in their appointments, some even configured like army barracks with rows of cots and lockers, his residence was sumptuous. He and his guest settled in and called for brandy and an update. He would listen to his chiefs for the remainder of the afternoon, have dinner, and then he and Senator Connors would amuse themselves in a more commodious way. It was his word, commodious. Some would say, rhymes with odious. But to do so would be judgmental.

Neither he, nor any of his men or women domiciled on the ranch had spotted Ike's drone, except, of course the two or three who'd believed it was the buzzard they thought had nearly decorated the helicopter. They could not know that it had returned, equipped with infrared sensors, and in its alternate coloration or lack thereof. Matte black, it noiselessly circled the ranch buildings, recording everything that occurred on the ground for the next eight hours.

❭❭❭

Charlie Garland had had a busy day, considering the fact that ostensibly neither he nor the CIA had anything to do with the investigation into the apparent death of Sheriff Schwartz, late of Picketsville, Virginia. Facial recognition identified the men at the gates of New Star Ranch as former Army or Marine enlisted men. Three of the four had less than honorable discharges. One was a person of interest in an open case in Nevada involving a missing child. The second batch of images verified that Martin Pangborn had taken up residence at the ranch along with Senator Oswald Connors. The men taken into custody in Maine had still not said anything, insisting they had a right to an attorney and they wished to exercise it. The FBI, which would be brought in later would agree and then, as Charlie would report to Ike, "When the lawyers show up and eventually find their clients, the cat will be out of the bag." As it happened, there would be some annoying delays before the attorneys latched onto their clients. They might get lost in the system and didn't Ike just love that expression?

In the meantime, he suggested Ike should consider dropping deeper into the dark. Ike thought he'd had enough playing at being someone else and if even the slightest hint linking Pangborn to his situation was verified, he would end it. Charlie worried how that might play out. It was one thing to erase a low level spy, a compromised diplomat, even a decorated military figure with alternate views of the Constitution. Taking on someone with Pangborn's connections and backing was another thing entirely.

The analysts finished their examination of the dash cam images and reported that they were able to reconstruct a scrap of a bumper sticker on the car carrying the shooter to positively identify it as a rental. They would have more in a few hours. Charlie sent that off to Frank Sutherlin in Picketsville. Ike's deputies were feeling frustrated at being left out of the hunt. It would give them something to work on. As an afterthought, he also sent the names of the men identified by facial recognition from the various sweeps and scans the Agency had done.

Charlie managed to get Ike on a secure line and they talked for two hours about what they knew. Most of the time was spent discussing the possible connection between Connors and Pangborn, beyond the obvious, political one. Now, little doubt remained in either of their minds that the impetus for the bomb came from Pangborn. It appeared equally clear that the chance of making that case before a Grand Jury were slim to none. What that left them with Charlie couldn't say.

"Ruth says I am not to act alone on this."

"She's right, Ike. There is no way anyone can protect you from what will happen if you're caught and, given the obvious linkages you and he now have, you will not be able to avoid some smart prosecutor from nailing your hide to the wall if you so much as cause him to break a nail."

"Yeah, yeah. You need to tell me again what you think the connection is, or what you think Pangborn has on Connors."

"I will, but first tell me how the drone is working. The VP for sales has been on the phone every couple of hours for an update."

"It is a thing of beauty, Charlie. You should buy some. At the moment it is circling the ranch in night mode. From vulture to bat, you could say, and recording whatever is going on down there. I will look at the tape tomorrow and give you an update."

"Good. Please try not to break it. The Agency does not know they are on the hook for it. Okay, repeating, this is what I think might, emphasis on 'might' be the thing that binds Pangborn to Connors. It could be nothing but coincidence but the FBI file marks it as a possible problem at the National Security level."

Charlie discussed the allegations Karl had uncovered in the FBI file on Connors, speculated the possible ramifications and how it could impact Ike's situation. Ike listened, asked a few questions and finally wanted to know when the people recruited to staff the fake real-estate agency would arrive.

"You should have them early tomorrow. Are we done here?"

"Are we? I don't know. We have a possible blackmailer and... let me think a minute. No, not quite finished. Charlie, what do you know about health and safety regulations as they apply to privately run retreat centers, specifically in the state of Idaho?"

"Absolutely nothing."

"Neither do I. Could you have one of those smart people you're sending to me come prepared to play expert in that area?"

"Health requirements for community housing and/or camps? Sure. What are you thinking?"

"A couple of things. I need eyes on the ground. The Vulture is great, but the perspective is wrong. I want to know how the ground is laid out. I might need...no, I will need to know the points of access into that compound and my guess is that night would be the best time to slip in there, if at all. The other is a hunch. Either way, I will need some fake IDs made on short order."

"That's it?"

"For now, yes. I have to look at the tape from our drone."

Chapter Thirty-one

It would be unfair to describe Frank Sutherlin as resentful. He wasn't, but the fact that the Picketsville Sheriff's Department was not actively engaged in the search for the man or woman who had engineered the attempt on Ike's life rankled. "Out of the loop," Billy had said. So, it was a sense of mild annoyance that Frank studied the scraps Charlie Garland had tossed the sheriff's department. It was to be expected, he knew, but still, you'd think Garland would be more alert to the sheriff's office's need to be active in the search for Ike's presumptive killer, especially since he knew how the attack had affected them. After all, they uncovered both when and where the bomb had been planted in Ike's car.

He called in the new kid and told him to see what he could do with the enhanced dash cam images they'd been sent. The kid nodded and dashed off to the computer room as eager as a new puppy chasing a tennis ball. Frank didn't expect much, but he hoped. Too bad Sam had been called away. If anybody could scrape something off that tape, she could. He spread the lists of names across his desk. Maybe, just maybe one would jump out at him. One did. Now what to do about that?

Billy dropped into a chair and whacked his Stetson against his knee. "I'm getting tired of all this here chasing our tails, Frank. Everybody else seems to be hot on the trail of something and we're just sitting here picking our teeth. We got nothing."

"You and Essie checked to see if any of Frieze's fellow officers were in that Fifty-first Star thing?"

"We did and came up empty. If there's anybody else in, they ain't admitting it."

Frank turned the sheet of paper around on his desk the put a finger on a name. "What about this guy?"

"Whoa. He's one of them?"

"That's what they're saying."

"Well, I think we should just haul his butt in for a chat. Do we have anything heavy enough to go after him?"

"Maybe. The county ME sent me a surveillance tape of a guy posing as an FBI agent. It's pretty grainy, but I'll eat my hat if it's not him. I think we need to do some more digging, but we do have that piece, if we need it. In the meantime, go through this list and see if you or anybody else recognizes a name."

"Why don't we grab him right now and bounce him around a little?"

"Not yet. We will eventually, but bouncing or not, I don't think he'd say anything right now. He has backup, or thinks he does. Maybe later we will when we have a full deck to play with. Meantime, get me something."

"On it." Billy scooped up the sheets and banged his way into the squad room to tackle anyone coming in or heading out.

〉〉〉

Three agents arrived as promised and took up their positions at the newly constituted Silver Gulch Realty office. Karl had been sent separately to Spokane where he was to hire a car and drive in. Too many people arriving at the same place at the same a time could raise some eyebrows. Besides, Ike thought he might need to keep Karl separate from the others for a while. The Agency people and the Bureau's had a spiky relationship at best and these new arrivals did not know about Karl and his past. They didn't need to.

"So, you decided against Western Sky for our name, I see. Where exactly is the Silver Gulch?" Ruth asked.

"Ask your sister, Trixie."

"You're bad, Marvin. Speaking of Sam, where is she, by the way?"

"Karl is driving in from Spokane. She's going to meet him. I don't expect to see her the rest of the day. That's too bad because we're going to be busy and I really would like to know what they're talking about over there."

The four new arrivals cleared the security area. Ike introduced himself and suggested they move to the parking lot before saying anything else. Once there, the woman who seemed to be in charge held out her hand, "Mary Jean," she said.

"Last name?"

"Spencer. I was a Lynch but that went away. There were a whole bunch of us growing up, cousins, uncles, and aunts. We were known as the Lynch Mob. It was funny then. Not so much now."

"Political correctness will be the death of civilization as we know it. Which one of you is the public health expert?"

"That would be me," a pert brunette who looked more like a high school cheerleader than a trained agent said. "Cristy Clemmons. And this is Josh Daniels and Mark Sipowitz."

Josh could have passed for the fullback on Cristy the cheerleader's team, Mark the right tackle. If Ike needed muscle, he had it.

"Okay, we need to talk, all of us. In the meantime I have some tape to show you and we need to get caught up with what Charlie Garland thinks he knows."

"Mr. Garland said to ask you the same thing and he wants to know how much longer you intend to keep his drone."

"One more pass over the ranch at night and after we set something in place and then he can have it back."

Ike filled them in on the backstory they were to use to cover their presence. He told them that they would be checked out very carefully and would most likely have the office and their motel rooms searched. They were to leave "evidence" of their secret mission conspicuously hidden."

"Isn't that an oxymoron?"

"Yes it is. What I mean is you should hide it like an amateur, not an agent, so that if they are any good at what they do—and I think they are—they will find it. They must buy into the idea that we are here to destroy the local water table with fracking. They need to be convinced that is why we are so circumspect in what we do. Then when we do what we do, they will leave us alone."

"And what is it we are doing?"

"For them, real estate speculation. For us, that is where the health inspector IDs come in."

〉〉〉

As it happened, the FBI did not have the men Pangborn had assigned to finding Ruth Harris-Schwartz in custody. As Charlie had predicted, they were "lost."

Jack Brattan called Pangborn to tell him that and to ask for direction. Pangborn slammed his fist on the table.

"What do you mean, they're lost? They were arrested and taken into custody. Either the Maine cops have them or the FBI does."

"No, sir. Look, our people inside the Bureau are as confused as we are. They checked with the Maine cops, the local LEOs, everyone. The cops in Maine are under the impression the Feds have them, the Feds say no, the Maine police must."

"Goddamit, Brattan, find them and get the lawyers to them. If they talk, remember it's your ass that's on the line, not mine."

"Yes, sir." A chastised and shaken Brattan hung up and, Pangborn guessed, screamed at his underlings. He might have also considered turning on Pangborn, but that wouldn't happen. Brattan knew that one shaky moment on his part and he'd be gone. That was the trouble with bullies. They were useful when it came to shoving weak people around, but useless when it came to planning and execution or someone bigger and meaner shoved back. What Martin Pangborn needed at that moment was the latter. Jack, he decided would be surplus baggage when this was over.

Senator Connors lifted his gaze over the rim of his reading glasses. "Problems?" he asked. The two of them were having a late breakfast. It had been a long night.

"Who do you know that you can squeeze on the National Security Committee?"

"What do you need?"

"Some of my people were picked up by the police and they have disappeared. I need to know where they disappeared to and I need to get my lawyers to them pronto. The FBI claims they don't have them, the local police, ditto. So who has them and why are they where they are?"

"What were they doing that got them arrested?"

Pangborn swung his head around and graced the junior senator from Idaho with a stare that would be described by a witness, had there been one, as ten miles of ice.

"Okay, I don't need to know. I guess I don't want to know. So, in the wind, are they? That smells of CIA. Would the Agency have an interest in what they were up to?"

"I don't see how, but it's a thought. I'll put someone on it."

He picked up his phone and tapped in a private number, explained his problem, said that there would be the usual compensation for the information and hung up.

"I should know tomorrow. Maybe you could make a call or two for me."

"I don't know…"

"Just do it."

Connors reached for the phone, frowned, looked at Pangborn, shook his head and made the calls. As Pangborn reminded him almost daily, he owned him and Connors knew it. Of course, if he thought about it for a minute, he had Pangborn over a barrel as well. But the senator's reputation did not include much in the way of deep thinking. That could change if the situation warranted. Connors might be considered slow, but he wasn't stupid and he had a few friends in high places as well.

Sam transcribed the calls. If there had been any doubt about Pangborn's involvement before, it evaporated at that moment.

Chapter Thirty-two

The new kid tapped on Frank's door. He was either about to explode or he had developed a severe rash in that place where no one wants one.

"Come on in. Steady, son. What's on your mind?"

The words poured out of the young man. Spewed, you might say, like lava from a B volcano movie except, as everyone outside Hollywood knows, lava generally flows slowly, inexorably, destroying everything in its path. The kid said he had managed to tap into some of the more sophisticated software installed years before by Sam before she left for NSA. He'd been able to enhance the residue left from the damaged bumper sticker. He said he discovered where the car had been leased. He had checked with the rental car agency and they gave him the name of the person who'd rented it the afternoon Frieze was shot. As he spoke he shifted from one foot to another. Pranced would be a better descriptor.

"That's good work." Frank held up his hand to slow or stop the rush of words. He glanced at the slips of paper on his desk. "The name, was it this one?" Frank tapped one of them and slid it across the desk. The kid read it and his face fell.

"Yes, sir, him."

"Don't look unhappy, kid. You just cracked the egg. We needed a solid reason to haul this guy in here. You found it."

"I did?"

"You did and I'm not sure anyone else would or could, so chalk up one for you. Now, go tell Essie to call in Billy and then tell them both to meet me here ASAP."

"Yes. Sir. Ah…who is this guy?"

"Big-time bully, braggart, and small-time thug. And it appears he just made a big mistake."

"Sir?"

"You don't have to call me sir. This guy? His mistake was to use his real name. What kind of idiot on his way to commit murder does that? Anyway, who is he? He's a man who hires steroid-pumped misfits to provide security at rock concerts and things like that. Where his people work, there is always trouble. Sometimes I think his roidheads pick the fights themselves. Luckily, there haven't been that many events in the area lately, but when there are, all the cops within fifty miles are put on notice. I've always wondered where people like him got their money. Now I know. It looks like he's muscle for someone bigger. That's good work, kid."

"Thanks. So how come you needed this? I mean, what else did we have on him that finding this helped clinch the deal?"

"He showed up on some security footage as the probable guy posing as an FBI special agent over at the ME's office. We couldn't be sure, though. The image wasn't so hot. Now we have something solid. The important thing here is, if we pick up someone like him, and if we can get him to talk, we might get at the top. Nobody believes he's working alone. With a little persuasion he just might crack a door wide enough to give us a chance at ending this mess. One way or another, I think we have the first piece to put together a case for murder one and put one more skell away for good."

Frank put out a BOLO for Jack Brattan, wanted as a suspect in the murder of a police officer. He should be considered armed and dangerous.

〉〉〉

Ike had launched the Vulture early and the tape of that flight was running on the screen in front of the group. Everyone squeezed together and stared at the diminutive screen on the Vulture's monitor.

"You see these people? They're going and coming from this one building. They are carrying towels and small bags or something similar in their hand. That building is the bathhouse or I'm crazy."

"If you say so, Ike. Why is that important?" Ruth asked.

"Okay, wait a second while I boot up last night's recorded run." He switched the settings and fast-forwarded the recording to a spot he'd apparently marked earlier. "Now, here is a night view at…" He checked the time stamp. "Eleven thirty-two. Watch this house and then that one."

Against the dark background, greenish silhouettes moved across the space between the two buildings.

"This one is the location where I believe Pangborn and his guest are staying. So, out come two people. By the stride and relative size, I'm saying they are adults. Connors and Pangborn, most likely."

"So?"

"So, I don't know. It's just nags at me. They go to that one which I am sure is the bathhouse."

"Okay. So what? Sure, it's little late for a shower, but lots of people do that before going to bed."

"Indeed. If that's what's happening. Pangborn doesn't have a private bath? You think? The interesting part is what happens next. Watch."

They watched as a single figure entered a second building and a few moments later two others emerged and went to the presumed bathhouse. What might have been the first returned to his original destination.

"What do you see?"

"No idea. People going to the bath place. Potty break?"

"I don't know. I need eyes on the ground. The drone is nifty, but at an elevation of one hundred feet or even at fifty, we are missing too much. Spencer, where are those IDs? Your gang has work to do. Where's Sam? Time is wasting."

"You're in a hurry?"

"Have you forgotten? There's a memorial service for me any day now. I don't want to miss it."

"In a mahogany box or an urn, which? Never mind, what happens next?"

"You up for some acting?"

"I am the president of a moderately good university and I have chaired at least three dozen board meetings. Does that qualify? Also I am married to you and if that doesn't take a creative spirit, I don't know what does."

"That last is not quite the role I had in mind. But the first...I need a bitchy bureaucrat."

"I can do bitchy."

"I know."

＞＞＜＞

Martin Pangborn was not happy. No one could tell him anything about the missing agents he'd sent to track the woman. If that weren't bad enough, his source at the FBI reported that the Picketsville Sheriff's Department had issued a BOLO for Jack Brattan. They had him identified as the prime suspect in the killing of a Rockbridge County deputy. The source suggested it would be a good idea to find Brattan before cops did. Pangborn told him that that would be his job. The voice on the other end of the line stammered a few words and then said he'd see what he could do.

Oswald Connors studied Pangborn with the look that one will sometimes see on a man eyeing his wife while considering whether to have an affair with another woman. Pangborn did not miss it.

"I own you, Senator. Don't you forget it."

"Yes, as you so frequently remind me. I think you have bigger problems to deal with than what I might or might not do, don't you think, Martin? You're right, I can't turn on you. That would be like playing Russian roulette with a fully loaded revolver. But the thought crossed my mind that you might be better served in the short run by putting some distance between us. The last thing you need is for both of us to be together if people start asking embarrassing questions."

"There will be no questions asked of me, embarrassing or otherwise, I assure you."

"Of course not. You are insulated, I know that. I merely thought that for both our sakes it might be prudent for us to be in different places for a while."

"You have a point. Okay, tomorrow, you're out of here. We still have a little business to transact tonight."

"Tomorrow, then." Connors looked relieved.

〉〉〉

Frank Sutherlin glared at Special Agent O'Rourke. The sun had been up less than an hour when the Feds in the person of O'Rourke, had arrived in town and begun pushing. Interference by Federal agents was nothing new. Local police expected it. The attitude in Washington seemed to be that anything occurring outside the Washington beltway must be hopelessly inept and uninformed and in dire need of a guiding hand. He knew that, but why was this officious Bureau wonk sitting in Ike's office telling him that the FBI would assume the total responsibility for the search and apprehension of Jack Brattan?

"It's way out of your jurisdiction, O'Rourke, and since when did a BOLO, become limited to one agency's enforcement?"

"It's Special Agent O'Rourke, Deputy. Technically speaking, interstate is our jurisdiction. It is out of yours. The dead cop was shot over near Buena Vista. That's not even close to Picketsville."

"It's close enough. Okay, you're right about who owns the perp when he is finally caught, but we popped the lead. We want to follow it. It's our BOLO, after all. Every law enforcement operation can and should pursue and arrest. So what's your interest that makes it so special? This is local, right?"

"It was a cop killing. The Bureau has launched a new program. We are concerned with the rise in attacks on police and other law enforcement personnel. We have made it our business."

"That a fact? Is the FBI telling every other police department this? I'm just asking because that seems a big undertaking. There are something like fifteen thousand taxing districts in the USA and I reckon each one of them has a police department in one form or another as part of it. Hell, I ain't even counting the federal units, the armed services, and you guys. How in the name of everything holy do you figure to keep them in line, O'Rourke? I don't want to believe we are the only one you're going to be talking to. We aren't, right? Okay, now I am committed to inter-agency cooperation and all that. Always have been, unlike some of my colleagues. See, I'm your friend in this." O'Rourke sat back and frowned. "But what you're forking out here is bullshit and there is no way I am going to have you horn in on this. You pull whatever strings you have and try and stop me, but we're going after Brattan and if we are there first, he'll be ours."

O'Rourke stopped smiling. "You'll regret this."

"Yeah, maybe. See you around, Special Agent O'Rourke."

When the main door to the offices slammed shut behind O'Rourke, Frank had Essie call the FBI and then get Billy on the line. He wanted to know all about the new program directed at investigating attacks on law enforcement personnel from the Feds and alert Billy of this new wrinkle.

The race was on. They had to find Brattan before the Feds did and started a game of hide and seek with their killer. And who the hell was Special Agent O'Rourke, anyway?

Chapter Thirty-three

Charlie put down the phone and shook his head. He felt like a marionette master whose puppets had gotten their strings crossed. Or maybe he had it wrong and he had never had them in hand to begin with or maybe they were the handler and he was the puppet. Frank's news that Jack Brattan had been identified as the probable driver of the car used in the cop killing came as a surprise. Not that the driver was Brattan, but that the Picketsville Sheriff's Office had managed to make the identification. His people had used every bit of computer wizardry they had on the dash cam tape and come up empty. Frank's people had it in an hour. Then, if that wasn't enough, Frank had jumped the gun and issued the BOLO before checking with him. That didn't sit well either. Too many agencies rabbiting around could only lead to confusion and a possible screw up. Then there was someone who claimed to be an FBI agent horning in on the BOLO. The way Frank described their meeting didn't sound right either. The puppets were not behaving. He put a flag on the wire. If Special Agent O'Rourke was real and bent, they'd find out soon enough.

The director called and said that all kinds of horseshit had arrived on his desk and continued to do so and what the hell was Charlie up to?

"I thought you told me the Agency's presence in this mess would be so thin it wouldn't even cast a shadow. What's going on?"

"I think the problem you're about to have to deal with may have to do with the goons put on Ruth Harris-Schwartz's trail. We picked up that pair of rotten eggs and put them on ice in a Gitmo holding facility. Their boss just discovered they've been busted and is annoyed he can't find them. He's probing, that's all. If his contacts in the FBI say they don't have them and the several Maine LEOs say they don't, he figured we must."

"Do we?"

"Director, deniability is the key to longevity in your position."

"That's horse hockey, Charlie, and I don't like it. It puts us in the frame and we can't be. You can play with this thing all you want to, but you can't get caught doing it. Cut them loose or find a better solution. If the word gets out, I'm toast. If I'm toast, you can guess what you are, Charlie."

The director rang off before Charlie could answer. Just as well. What would be worse than toast in that metaphor anyway? Burnt toast? Hot buttered toast? French toast?

He called Ike and told him he didn't have much time and if they had anything on Pangborn, they had better move fast. Ike replied, "Today is the day and tonight is the night." Charlie said he had no idea what that meant, but the last part sounded like the punch line from an old joke. Ike said he was close and hung up. Charlie turned his attention to the chart Alice had drawn with the players and personnel of the Fifty-first Star, as far as they had been, or could be, identified. Charlie called her in.

"Alice, good work. Excellent, in fact. Now, what I really want to know is who isn't on this chart but has enough drag to heat up the phone lines to the Agency and the Bureau. Can you get someone on that?"

"I can after I have my coffee, Charlie. Deprive me of my coffee and I turn into the equivalent of the Hulk with PMS."

"The Hulk is a man."

"If you say so. Coffee first, then I'll start turning over rocks."

Melba toast?

❯❯❯

Sam arrived and was told she had half an hour to collect and dismount the surveillance clothes hooks scattered around the cottage, convert them from record/retrieve to record/transmit and set up the monitors to capture the transmissions.

"You're not asking for much, are you? Do you want to tell me why?"

Ike explained what he had in mind.

"You're serious? You're going to go into the ranch and plant them?"

"Not me, you and these fine folks on loan from Charlie's farm, and yes, that's the general idea."

"I won't ask how you think you can breach that security system. But why?"

"There are two things I believe we need and we need right away. The first is access to the ranch. Obviously, daylight is out. There are way too many yahoos out there with guns to make a daylight appearance. However, the nighttime video shows that it is quiet, very quiet, at night. I want eyes in there so I can map an entry."

"And the second reason?" The man called Josh appeared nervous.

"Something is just not kosher over there and I think I have an idea what that is, but can't be sure until I see for myself."

"That's all of it?"

"For now, it is. Okay, your faces have been erased from any facial recognition programs that we know of. I suppose it is possible that these people have assembled one of their own, but I doubt it. It is also possible they have somehow already connected you to Silver Gulch. Again, I don't think so but you never know, so when you go in, change your appearance if you can. Nothing obvious, but glasses, wigs, things like that."

"Okay, you're the boss. Do you want to tell us why and where?"

"I want you to be County Health inspectors and go scour that ranch and plant surveillance equipment and bugs wherever possible. Since you have a role to play, start in the kitchen. Health inspectors always do the kitchen, right?"

"Right."

"Also the bathhouse and, if you can, spot some near Pangborn's door."

"Because?"

"I want to hear what he has to say. I doubt you can get in the house, but you might try. Anything is better than always guessing."

"It's a long shot, Ike, but we'll try."

"Bitchy bureaucrat might get away with it," Ruth said.

"You be careful with that. They will raise hell when you push in there, you know. Pangborn will insist the ranch is private and above regulation. I am certain they all believe it to be and they will insist it is so, even if they know the opposite. They are rabid anti-governmental types and will get their noses out of joint at the thought a government official of any sort has invaded their space. Nevertheless, you are to flash your credentials, badges, whatever, and bull your way in. You should have enough time to plant some hardware before they bring enough pressure to get you out of their hair."

"You're sure about this?" Mary Jean asked.

"I am about as sure as I am about anything, given the amorphous nature of the situation we find ourselves in. Okay, Ruth, switch to a blond wig and purple lipstick or something equally distracting. Wear those horn-rimmed spectacles, too. You will be the annoying and officious chief inspector. The rest of you head to the kitchen, the hallways, bathhouse, wherever, and plant the hooks and cameras in as many places as you can and where the view is the widest."

Karl walked in and reported that a BOLO had gone out for the suspected killer of the cop and that Frank had issued it. He also said that there were other players in the game including at least one from the Bureau and that it didn't look good.

Charlie called back and said that they had identified the loose cannon in the Agency and he was now being fed misinformation, which should keep Pangborn guessing for a few more days. He hoped the Bureau would turn up one or two as well. Pangborn had deep pockets and a long reach. He said he also worried that the BOLO on Brattan might spook their guy. Ike said he hoped not, but what was done was done.

"Maybe it will force him to make more calls, which we can trace. So far we know he's having a double duck fit over what's happened and Sam can give you a half dozen phone numbers and the content of the calls that he and Senator Connors made. You might want to put them in the FBI's inbox. It's looking like a lock on Pangborn. I'm not sure how deep Senator Connors is into this."

The four "employees" of the Silver Gulch Realty Company were called in. When they and Sam, Ruth, and Karl were ready, he sent the "health inspectors" off to New Star Ranch. The government was about to meddle in the affairs of private citizens and the residents of the ranch would not be pleased. Ike just hoped that he had it right and that the hooks would be located in places that would give him what he wanted.

Of course, they had to avoid the tire spikes at the entrance, but he assumed their credentials and a little bullying would do the trick.

It did.

>>>

Pangborn's phone woke him from a post-breakfast nap. He was told that somehow, people claiming to be county health inspectors had managed to talk their way through the security at the gate and were crawling all over the place. He told them to deal with it. A knock at the door revealed a particularly disagreeable woman leaning against his doorframe and who insisted she need to inspect his kitchen.

"Who the hell are you?"

"Angie Pederakis, County Health Department, is who. Are you the owner of the ranch?"

"Yes, now get off my property."

"You are operating an institution and as such, all health regulations must be kept. I need to inspect your kitchen."

"Not in this lifetime, woman. Now get out of here."

"Very well, but you realize your refusal to cooperate with our inspection will be in my report."

Before he could respond, the woman wheeled about and stalked away. He called his security people and told them to get the damned busybodies the hell off his ranch. Half an hour later, they confirmed that all the intruders had been escorted off the premises. One woman, who seemed to be in charge threatened to come back with the local police. She was, the reporter said, "a five-dollar bitch." Pangborn said they'd met, thanked him, and sat back wondering who he should call.

"Connors," he yelled, "you're the senator for this goddam state, who do you know who can keep these idiots off my place?"

"What idiots would that be?"

"One of your county suits decided I was running a camp or something out here and sent in the Health Department to snoop around."

"What? People are inspecting the buildings?"

"Kitchens, bathhouse, and some of the bunkhouses. They think because we have some kids here we're running a camp."

"Well in the first place, this county does not have a health department. You must mean the state."

"I'm sure that awful woman said county, and so did the man at the gate."

"An easy mistake to make. I'll call some people. You don't have to worry. Even if they find something, we can make it go away. By the way, by bringing your Young Pioneers here for 'educational purposes,' which you insist is the reason they're here, means you are running a camp and, therefore, you may be liable for Health Department regulation. I thought I warned you about that."

"Maybe you did and maybe you didn't. It's my property and they are trespassers. It's another example of government over-reach, by God, and something I expect you to do something about next term. Call whoever is in charge and make sure they don't come back. I don't like people wandering in here and I especially don't like having pushy women on the premises. I don't want anyone I haven't personally invited here on any day and definitely not state bureaucrats. I don't want anyone in here who doesn't belong, dammit."

"Come on, Martin. No biggie. Calm down. I'll make a call. No probs."

Martin Pangborn had a list of expressions he wanted erased from the language. High on the list was, "no probs," which was closely followed by "no biggie."

Chapter Thirty-four

Jack Brattan had a friend in the Philadelphia Police Department, Jocko Mulloy. Actually, *friend* didn't quite cover it. An "acquaintance who shared mutual interests" would be closer. Neither man could be said to have a relationship with anyone that would qualify as a friendship as the term is normally understood. Mulloy joined the Fifty-first Star after two horrific tours in Iraq which involved several near-misses with IED and later a chance meeting with Jack in a local pub. Jack had explained to him that the best way to exorcize his simmering PTSD demons would be to associate with others who, like him, were "going to do something about it." What exactly "it" or the "something they were going to do" was never surfaced, but it resonated with Mulloy's muddled mindset at the time. In addition, his continued tenure as a cop had become tenuous following several Internal Affairs investigations which looked into his alleged use of excessive force on three occasions, a suspicious shooting, and moonlighting as muscle at local concerts and other events. The moonlighting was not deemed to be counter to police regulations, but the particular events he'd worked caused some concern higher up. Jack's security company provided the needed manpower for all of the events in question.

Out of misplaced concern, or a response to a kindred spirit, Mulloy called Jack and that's how he found out about the BOLO. Also, that was how he managed to drop out of sight so quickly and well before the most local LEOs were even aware of it and could close in.

It had not been easy, but Jack had the instincts of a hyena and he knew that if the cops wanted him for murder, there was a better than even chance that Pangborn would be after him as well. He'd had a hand in the elimination of Felix Chambers and Jack reasoned that Pangborn might react similarly to him if he took it into his head that Jack might plea bargain his way off death row by giving up the name of the person who'd called in the hit. Would he? Maybe, maybe not.

He cashed out five Fifty-one Star credit cards at as many different banks for the maximum allowable withdrawal and then gave the cards to five homeless men he met on the street. He told them they were twenty-five-dollar debit cards and that they should get themselves something to eat and a place to stay. He was certain the recipients would try to maximize the card's utility by cashing them and then passing them along to others. Whether sold or discarded, they would circulate for days as they passed from one homeless guy to another. He knew that if they had the numbers, the police would track the cards. So would Pangborn the instant he learned about the BOLO. The cards should keep the trail cold for days, weeks even. He retrieved some clothes and one additional credit card he kept in the name of his ex brother-in-law, one Pangborn did not know about. He'd need to have some means to survive after the cash was gone and before he could come up with a long-term plan. His final stop was to his office where he cleaned out his safe and picked up a fake ID left over from an operation that had been cancelled a year ago and which he hoped no one would remember.

Later that afternoon he stole license plates from an Escalade parked in a suburban shopping mall, being careful to replace the stolen ones with his own. They weren't vanity tags so, unless the housewife who owned the Cadillac ran a red light or had an accident, it could be months before anyone would notice the switch. He headed south. He knew the BOLO originated from Virginia and was stunned when he discovered it came from

Picketsville. How did those hick cops manage to find him? Of course they would still be pretty hot over losing their boss. In spite of that, heading south still seemed his best bet. The first place the cops would look would be Philadelphia and then either Idaho or Montana. They would stake out Pangborn's operation in Chicago as well and maybe the Wichita area where he grew up. No way would he head home. There were people there who'd be more than happy to save Pangborn and the cops the trouble of taking him in.

The last place they'd look would be somewhere close to them. That was his reasoning at any rate. The trick was to find a place where strangers are the rule, not the exception. Tourist attractions would be best. Did he have time to reach Orlando or New Orleans? Probably not. Williamsburg was close and might work, but the crowds there were thin this time of year and especially on weekdays. A man alone would be noticeable and he didn't have time to find a family. Virginia Beach and Norfolk were close by. Those places would be crawling with Navy, coming and going. His chief's uniform still fit. With a little planning and some good ID, he could disappear into the Norfolk area and no one would ever find him. He headed south on I-95 and cut east, south of DC.

◇◇◇

As if the Health Department pushing their way in wasn't bad enough, his man in the hunt reported that nobody could locate Jack Brattan. He had dropped off the grid, they'd said. A trace on the credit cards he'd been issued had ended in Philadelphia. They were still in use, but by street people. The accounts had been shut down, of course. They had bounced the bums around a little and none of them knew except that the cards had been circulating in the homeless community for a while and no one remembered where they came from in the first place. He said they'd also tossed Brattan's apartment and had come up empty. Brattan had cleared out. No one knew where he'd disappeared to. The last thing his secretary heard was that he'd been searching for the guys that got busted in Maine. Pangborn asked if anyone had contacted the Philadelphia cop. He couldn't remember his name. After some consultation, someone remembered Mulloy. They checked out Jocko. When they found him, He'd been drunk and uncooperative and grinning at them like a crazy man. It took three men to put him out of commission and then only after he had caused some serious damage to two of their kneecaps with a baseball bat. He said he didn't know anything. He said he'd been dismissed by the Philly PD and had been drinking for days. By the look of him, he had. They'd get back to him, they said, when he sobered up. If he ever did.

Pangborn forgot his own directive and began bellowing on the phone, overriding his institutionalized paranoia that his phones might be tapped. Perhaps he was careless. Perhaps he believed the encryption would be unbreakable even if the lines were tapped. Either way, he made a mistake. It would not be enough to put him away, but would add to the growing pile of evidence that might.

"Keep looking," he screamed. "I want that idiot found before the police get him. Who knows him? Anyone? Dig through his file. There has to be something in there that will lead you to him. Where would he go? Where do people go when they have no good options?"

"He may have built himself a bolt-hole, boss. He was that kind of a guy."

"Maybe, but I doubt it. People like Brattan do not plan or believe they will be caught. It is their fatal flaw. Dig in the file and call me back when you have something."

〉〉〉

Frank understood Garland's annoyance at his issuing the BOLO without checking with him. He didn't care. The Agency, he'd said, had the capability to do many things far beyond that of the Sheriff's Department in Picketsville, Virginia. Frank agreed but reminded him that he was limited in that the Agency couldn't operate in the open. Furthermore, and more importantly, it didn't have the same psychological need Frank's people had to be engaged. Frank tried to explain to Charlie that his deputies needed to be doing something—anything. After all, they had traced the rental car to Brattan and it should be obvious to Charlie that the next logical thing for them to do would be to circulate a BOLO and go after the suspect their investigation produced. Not to do so would raise more questions than he cared to answer.

"Mr. Garland, we have an investment in this that we believe is as great as or greater than yours. With respect, sir, for us not to proceed with what we had would make no sense to them. Their response, if you were to ask them to stand down would be, to think you're saying, 'Sorry, hick cops, but this is a job for the big boys.' My people wouldn't buy it."

"That's not what I'm saying, Frank. You know that. It's just that by putting the BOLO out so soon alerted Brattan and his handlers. Now they know that we know something and it's just that we didn't want them to know it yet. Sorry, that's a little convoluted. Look, it's just that now they are as likely to pick up Brattan as we are. If they do, he will either have an airtight alibi and a phalanx of expensive lawyers, or he will disappear forever. Remember the bomb-planter? We need him to make a case. Worse, we have to scour the countryside. They don't. They know where to look. We needed a head start."

"Okay, that makes sense, but just let me ask you this, WWID?"

"WWID? You mean WWJD, don't you? Not being a religious man, I have no idea what Jesus would do, Frank."

"No. WWID…what would Ike do, or more properly, have done?"

"Oh. Ike. Got it. He wouldn't wait for me. In fact…never mind. Good luck."

"We will keep in touch and, Charlie, we aren't a bunch of hillbillies, you know. Us all jes talk like 'em."

"Okay, okay, I know. Never said you were. Listen, I'll send you what we have on Brattan. Maybe you can see what we're missing, like you did on the dash cam."

Chapter Thirty-five

Brattan arrived in Norfolk early in the afternoon and negotiated a week-to-week lease at a motel frequented by Navy personnel between assignments. He told the landlady he was TDY while waiting for reassignment to a ship. It was a story she'd heard many times before. She took his money, jotted down the name he gave her, and handed him his key. She didn't bother to ask where he was assigned TDY. She didn't care. As far as she was concerned, if you've seen one beached sailor, you've seen them all and he paid cash. Brattan thanked her and made his way to his room.

The motel had been built decades before and clearly on the cheap. He liked that. His unit stood well to the rear of the second story. He liked that, too. Ten minutes inside convinced him that the non-support walls had been built with twenty-four inches between the studs. Cheap and convenient. He went into the bathroom and removed the medicine cabinet by backing out the two screws that held it in place on one side only and wrestling it free from its inset in the bathroom wall. As he suspected, the hole created by the builders to accept the cabinet had been cut along one stud and the opposite side contained only insulation. Even that came as a mild surprise. Truly cheap would have left out the insulation. He had his place to hide the cash and weapons he'd brought with him. After a half an hour and with the judicious use of Velcro and some flat Tupperware, he'd concealed everything that might get him into trouble. If someone, well anyone but an expert that is, were to search his room they'd find nothing.

All the cash, guns, ammunition, and miscellaneous papers had been safely stowed between the walls in the space conveniently provided by a builder maximizing his profit. Battan thought that Pangborn would have been impressed. The medicine cabinet he replaced snug back in the wall, but with Velcro to hold it in place, not screws. Next he turned his attention to his car. He'd need a new set of tags.

The parking lot two blocks away had several vehicles covered with dust. He guessed their owners would be deployed at sea, maybe for a good while yet. He switched his tags again, but only after searching for a Pennsylvania car on the assumption that this owner, like the housewife in Philly, would not notice the switch right away. That done, he drove to the local Goodwill store and purchased more appropriate clothing. Then he used his old Navy ID to enter the Naval base and the PX. One hour after that he had uniforms, a new name plate with his ex-brother-in-law's name engraved on it. He could comfortably use the credit card now. He dug out his old ribbons, remembered that SEALS and sailors with combat experience usually wore only the "top three." That evening he was in uniform and having a beer at the CPO Club. During his shopping, he'd realized that more than a few years had gone by since he last wore the uniform and a chief petty officer his obvious age might raise an eyebrow or two. He decided he had better give himself a promotion to senior chief. That wouldn't earn him much in the club, but around town, it might produce a little deference.

One of the advantages he'd enjoyed while still in Martin Pangborn's good graces was that the latter did not like to get his hands dirty. What that meant, in practical terms, was Pangborn did not want to know where "the bodies were buried," as he'd put it. As importantly, he didn't want to know where things used in transacting his business came from, like, who supplied what, or how things got done. "Deniability," he'd said. "I want results, Jack, just results. I don't need to know the details. What I don't know can't hurt me, right?"

Certain it would be safe, Brattan called on one of his contacts to make him fake IDs and a set of phony orders indicating when and where he was to report for duty. A phone call, a cash transfer and an address and the job was done. So, because Pangborn had scruples, he knew that Pangborn would never be able to trace him. It might be true that what Pangborn didn't know could not hurt him, but in this case what he didn't know couldn't help him either.

He intended to settle into an ersatz Navy life for a long time. Well, as long as it took for the heat to be off and he could make his way to South America and visit some of Pangborn's money he had stashed away over the years. What kind of idiot trusts numbered accounts with their employees?

〉〉〉

Frank had Brattan's file copied and distributed to the five men he thought would have the best insight respecting its contents. Since he also believed the new kid would benefit from observing the process, he included him in the distribution. He called them into his office.

"Read this through. Take your time. We need to find Jack Brattan before anyone else. See if you can come up with any ideas where he might have gone to ground from the report."

After they'd had a chance to read and think about it he cleared his throat. "Okay, what do we have?"

"All I see is a guy who needs to be tuned up," Billy said. "We need to bust this guy's balls."

"Yes, we know that, Billy, but that is not what I'm asking. What do you see that might make finding him easier?"

"I got nothing."

Charlie Picket cleared his throat and gave him an "Um-er-ah."

"Charlie, what are you thinking?"

"Okay, I don't know if this is what you were asking for or not, but if it was me looking to disappear, I would naturally head off to someplace where I would, you know, blend. See, if I needed to drop off the map, I would get on down to Atlanta or maybe head out to the southside of Chicago and get me a cheap room in the ghetto. Okay, we don't call it that no more, but you know what I mean. There is bound to be a brother in a place like that who could set me up with a job and cover. It might not last too long. Man on the run usually have a price on his head and probably somebody'd want to cash in on that, but maybe not. Anyway, that was what I was thinking."

"I'd head to some big college town," the kid said. "I have a cousin out in Arizona. He goes to Arizona State and that town out there where it's at has so many kids my age, I would never be found. I'd grow a beard and—"

"Not this year you wouldn't, Peach." Billy said.

"Okay, so anyway I could sit around a coffee shop with a laptop all day and nobody would notice."

"How'd you live?"

"Pizza places don't ask for ID or if they do, don't look too hard. You just need a car and a driver's license. Work a full shift in the right neighborhood, like the suburbs, and you can get by on the tips plus what they pay for part time."

Billy raised an eyebrow. "Sounds like you done that a time or two. I don't see none of them options open to me, though. I been a cop all my life. I don't reckon hiding out with other cops is much of a choice."

"Not quite, Billy. You did a hitch in the Army, too. Now, this guy was Navy once," Frank said. "With apologies to Charlie, here, but that's a little like being a minority. You know, you put on a uniform and who's going to question you?"

"Hey, that's right, Frank. I mean, look at all the 'stolen valor' postings. Wannabes working the malls for dates, meals, drinks, and other shit. People don't ask questions, whether the uniform is real or not. They just assume you are what you seem to be."

"Okay, so, if he thinks like Picket or the kid—"

"You all know I have a name," the kid said and then realized he may have pushed too soon.

"Of course you do. Sorry, kid. Where was I? Oh, right. So, where would he go? This report says his last location was somewhere in Philadelphia. I'm guessing he's headed to a Navy yard."

"For God's sake. Frank, there's, like, one of them in every port on both coasts, the Gulf, and most lakes—big ones, at least."

"Yeah, yeah, but where is there one that's really big and full of sailors coming and going?"

"Wait a minute. We got no evidence he's done any of this. He's a crook, too. So why wouldn't he just dive into the underworld? That'd be a whole lot easier that playing sailor."

"First, he wouldn't be playing at it. He's ex-Navy. He knows the drill. Second, because, like Charlie, here, said, he'd have a price on his head. He can't risk some snitch hoping for an AG to reduce a charge or go easy on him, or a payoff from one of his playmates afraid he'll sing. He'd never know if someone would maybe rat him out. Hey, I grant that this is a long shot, but here's the thing, we got nothing else. Every police department in the country has the BOLO. If he's in plain sight, if he's in the expected places, they will grab him. So, what do we do? See, I've been trying to think like Ike. Ike would play a hunch, wouldn't he?"

"Ike's hunches are on the money. I seen you play poker, brother, and yours suck."

"Okay, they do, but trust me on this. We can sit back and hope this dirt bag happens to drive through Picketsville and we pick him up running a stop sign, or we try something. I am open to any other suggestions, but for my money, this is our shot. I'm saying he headed straight to the nearest, for him, version of the 'ghetto' and I'm guessing that will be Norfolk Naval Station or thereabouts. Billy, how about you drive over there and have a look? You could bunk in with Danny over at Little Creek and check out the whole area. I'll notify all the other bases just in case. Hell, it's worth a try."

"Who's Danny?" The kid asked.

"Our brother. He's in the SEALs and stationed at Little Creek, Virginia, kid. Sorry, um…Ken."

"Oh."

"This is crazy."

"What else have we got?"

"Okay, I'll call Danny. You're going to owe me big-time, Frank."

"Only if I'm wrong."

Chapter Thirty-six

Analysts at the FBI received a heads-up by their sister service in Langley suggesting that Jack Brattan might be posing as a naval NCO on one of the East Coast bases. They did not act on that information. They believed that there were too many naval installations and they preferred not to squander scarce resources to cover them all. They passed the information on to the local LEOs and turned their attention to other, more pressing matters. Charlie assumed they would. He dispatched a few agents, between deployments and getting bored with desk duty, to Norfolk and Philadelphia on the off chance he'd guessed right about what Brattan would do. There were other ports with active naval personnel he knew, but if one were looking for Jack Brattan, he figured those two would be his most likely landing places.

At the same time, Billy Sutherlin drove his pickup to Norfolk and connected with his brother Danny at his apartment outside Little Creek. Danny was happy to see him until he heard why he's come.

"Billy, you have to be nuts. Do you have any idea how many sailors there are in this part of the world?"

"Nope, don't care."

"You should care. There are something like eighty thousand men and women on active duty. Then there is a hundred thousand plus family members with them and maybe thirty thousand civilian employees spread out all over the area. I ain't counting all the retired Navy guys, who by the way can still wear their uniform under certain circumstances. Finding one chief petty officer, real or fake, in that mix is like finding a needle in a haystack. I take that back, it's like finding a nickel-plated needle in a stack of stainless steel needles. It's impossible."

"Right, and a really big stack of needles, I bet. I believe you. So, with that in mind, if you were going to look for the nickel-plated one anyway, where would you start?"

"You're serious?"

"Danny, this guy shot a cop in cold blood. He's connected to the bomb that...that blew up Ike's car. He's a certifiable bad ass. He can lead us to the people that have been after Ike and Ruth, and God only knows who else, come to think of it. We need to nail him, and do it before the Feds or some other police department does. If they find him first, we miss our chance to interrogate him. It's real important that don't happen. If he's here, I want him."

"You mean beat the crap out of him 'til he talks?"

"No. Come on. I just want the chance to remind him what could happen if someone else gets to him first if I was to cut him loose. If he thinks about it, he will want to deal. The other thing is, cops aren't the only folks looking for him. He's got himself some hard people who are for sure going to shut him up permanent because they know if he talks some real important people is going down and they won't want to let that happen. They get him first and he'll disappear. Danny, this is real important. If I can, I need to find him and put him away. Will you help me or not?"

"Okay, but it's a waste of time."

"A waste of time? Suppose your SEAL team was assigned to go into some raggedy-ass place and take out a terrorist. Do you calculate the odds and decide it's 'a waste of time' or do you go in and get the summabitch?"

"Okay, okay. Tell me more about this guy. Maybe if we can narrow the target area a little we might get lucky."

Billy showed him the file. Danny read it and sat for ten minutes drumming his fingers on his kitchen table. He sighed and called in a half dozen of his teammates. They arrived and debated, then asked their lieutenant for a few days to run an "undercover exercise" on the base. The object, they said, would be to see if they could infiltrate various restricted locations without being detected. They said they needed to keep their "escape and evasion" skills sharp. The lieutenant gave them a "who do you think you're bullshitting" look and said "Okay." They didn't mention that the locations they intended to infiltrate were motels, service men's clubs, massage parlors, bars, and brothels. They didn't have to. The lieutenant was not born yesterday.

❯❯❯

Ike had the Vulture disassembled and ready to ship back to Charlie. Sam watched him fit the pieces into the crate. She did not appear pleased.

"Do we really have to give it back?"

"We do. Get your stuff together, too, Sam. When we pull out of here I don't want any loose ends. Ms. Silver and the Gottleibs need to be in the wind as soon as we bust those guys. When the smoke clears, there will be nothing to prove we were ever here. Not a scrap of paper, a bar of soap, and certainly not this great lump of a fake bird."

"Because?"

"Because we owe it to Charlie to make sure there are no CIA fingerprints on this operation. He's done a lot for us. We can't let him take a beating from some Congressional oversight committee for it. We disappear and resurface as ourselves as if we just spent a week at the beach."

"What about the surveillance equipment we planted around the ranch?"

"Well, I hope no one will ever notice, but if they do stumble on them, they're all marked, 'Made in China,' and could have been put there by anybody, anytime. Given the paranoid disposition of ninety-nine percent of the membership, they will assume the worst about everything and everybody and that one or more of the organizations they obsess over put them there. By the time they get done trying to figure which agency, police department, NSA, CIA, FBI, ISIS, whoever, was watching them, the batteries will have gone dead and the memory chips erased. We'll leave them."

"So, what now?"

"Now we wait 'til the motion sensors are triggered and we record what happens. Then, if our luck holds, we gear up and tomorrow we go in there and bust some chops."

Ruth walked in from cleaning the kitchen. "Chops? What kind of chops?"

"Not what, whose."

"Ike thinks that we will have the goods on Pangborn—"

"You mean assuming you're right about what goes on over there after dark and we can sneak in. That's it, isn't it, Ike? You will go after them."

"Pretty much. Once I have what I need, we will slip in there and knock some heads together."

"Metaphorically."

"If you say so."

"I do say so. Ike, you are out of your jurisdiction. Also, even though you have never practiced it, you're the lawyer. You know damned well if you do anything out of line, they will have their seven-figure-a-year lawyers hand you your guts. If we go in, we go with the local police, or we don't go."

"Ruth—"

"I mean it Ike. We have been shot at, blown up, and abused in an assortment of ways by that bastard and I don't want you screwing up his trip to the slammer by playing your version of *Die Hard.*"

"Yippie-ki-yay."

"Shut up, I mean it."

Ike sighed. Being married to a person with conventional morality had its drawbacks, but Ruth was right. He was an ex-spook and not a lone wolf anymore. Maybe he never was. At any rate, he had to weigh whether he valued his freedom enough to forgo the luxury of splashing Pangborn's brains on the wall. It would not be an easy decision.

"Don't worry. If my hunch is right, I will have the State Police put on notice. Well, that's not quite true. 'An anonymous source' close to the governor will suggest to the director of the State Police that he might make a SWAT team available for a possible raid on the New Star Ranch. It's funny how politics works. As conservative as the governor is, apparently he is not far enough to the right to satisfy Pangborn. Charlie tells me that a large sum of money which he traced to Pangborn ended up in the PAC that tried to oust him in the last election. The governor is still smarting from that. He will have no compunctions about bringing down Pangborn if he's given the opportunity. Frankly, I suspect he won't care much if we turn up anything or not. A well publicized raid by the State Police and the suggestion of a sandal is a publicity bonanza."

"That's mean."

"Do you care?"

"Not even a little bit. And if your hunch is wrong?"

"Plan B."

"Which is?"

"Keep digging. Now help me shove this crate outside for the delivery company to pick up and then I could use a nap."

"A nap? It's nearly six o'clock. Some supper, maybe, but a nap? What's up with that?"

"I think he means a connubial nap," Sam said and reddened.

"Oh, that kind of nap. Let me check my day planner to see if I can fit you in, Sheriff. Are you sure you wouldn't rather have supper?"

"Actually, I meant nap, as in sleeping briefly. Sam, you have been away from Karl too long and your mind is drifting. Get out of here. On the other hand, Ms. Gottlieb, maybe you should check your day planner. I'll grab some sandwiches and that half empty bottle of red and you can help me take care of both."

"Like dinner and a movie, but without the movie. You are such a romantic, Marvin. But how about we take a rain check? It's been a long day."

Chapter Thirty-seven

It was nearly midnight when Billy and Danny took a call from one of the SEAL team. He said he thought someone matching Brattan's description was leaving one of the motels they'd staked out over in Portsmouth after chatting with a "massage therapist" who for a picture of President Grant remembered a loud-mouthed chief. He'd spent some time on her table the day before, she said. Like the rest, it was one of those places where transients crashed between assignments, or while waiting for their RFAD. He said he had him in sight and he seemed headed to the Air Station. Danny told him to stay with him and try to make a positive ID. A few minutes later he called again and said he was ninety-nine percent sure this was the man they wanted and he was holed up at the CPO club. A check with the other watchers came up empty. Danny said he should hold his position. They would be there in a few minutes.

"Okay, Little Brother. If this is your guy, what do we do? You don't have jurisdiction way over here."

"Let's say I am in hot pursuit. I'll arrest him and if he gives us any shit, we can call the Shore Police and they can hold him for impersonating active duty or something until we get us an okay to haul him off to Picketsville and jail. But hot pursuit ought to do it. Why'd you call them other guys?"

"Two reasons. First, he could be slicker that you give him credit for. He could, for example, have friends with him. You and me are good, but why take a chance we lose him? Second, the guys have been scouring the town looking for your dirt bag for, like, fifteen hours. They deserve to be there when we take him down. Also, we need a better plan than barging in and cuffing him. This is a Naval facility and there are things that need to be put in place."

"Like what?"

"We need some official sanction, even if it is a fake. I have a friend assigned to the SPs. I'll call. There is just one other thing worrying me."

"What's that?"

"It's been way too easy."

"What do you mean?"

"Well, you show up late this morning, we spend a couple hours plotting what we need to do, and here is maybe eight hours later and we're done? What are the odds we found that nickel-plated needle? It's been too easy, Billy. Either we are stupid lucky, he is carrying a heap of bad luck, or this ain't him."

"Let's go find out. Maybe, we're that good. Maybe it's both— we're lucky and he ain't."

"Don't count on it."

>>>

The trouble with truly arrogant people, Charlie thought, was they discounted the intelligence of those around them. Brattan was so certain of his ability to disappear it never occurred to him that anyone with an equally devious mind or even a modicum of common sense could figure out what he might do. How difficult is it to guess that and ex-Navy guy would consider hiding out as a sailor. True, there were other equally logical scenarios he might have pursued. He could have gone hunting in the north woods. Gone in for elk as one person, changed his appearance and come out as someone else. He could have headed to Montana with a fake ID. There is enough room out there to hide an army of Martians. He could have faked his own death. As it happened, none of that mattered.

Brattan couldn't have known that the man he knew as the creator of better-than-good fake documents had also done some "off the books" work for the CIA from time to time. When the director of the CIA had heard about the arrangement at the time he'd been understandably upset.

"What the hell are you thinking, Garland? If he figures out what we're up to he can cause us a heap of hurt," he'd said at the time.

"His work, Director, is as good as there is, better even. You should think of it as a symbiotic relationship, like the cellulose-dissolving bacteria in the termite."

"I'm thinking more like the plague-bearing flea on a rat. You better not get caught."

Charlie hadn't and now, grateful for the chance to serve his country, or perhaps not, but rather looking for another chance to call in a favor, he had called Charlie. He might be an artist who made IDs for anyone with sufficient cash, but at the same time, he was no fool. He knew the information would be worth something to the right people. He dealt directly with Charlie in the past and decided he'd call Charlie first. Brattan should have realized that he was not his only customer.

"I heard that this guy Brattan had a BOLO out on him and maybe he is on your Christmas list?" he said.

"He might be. What have you got?"

"I sent him some IDs, fake Navy orders, some other stuff. Is it worth my while to tell you where?"

Charlie agreed on a price which was measured in dollars and the vague promise of future business and the caller gave Charlie the address where the IDs were to be delivered. Once again, Charlie noted, arrogance will almost always displace cleverness. Brattan had had the materials overnighted to him proving that stupid is the sister to arrogance. It was then that Charlie had given the FBI the heads-up which they opted to ignore. Except Special Agent O'Rourke who would have made a call if he hadn't been on the wrong side of the table in an interrogation room in Quantico at the time.

The agent Charlie dispatched to cover Norfolk arrived at the address that afternoon as Brattan returned from a late lunch. Charlie told his agent to sit tight. He wanted to spring the trap only if and when Ike had collected his information. That is, if there was any information that would compromise Pangborn to be collected. Anyway, he said to wait.

About eleven-thirty the agent called in again. Brattan was on the move and he was following him. There was one hitch, he said. He was not the only one on Brattan's tail. Someone else seemed to have him in their sights.

"Can you tell who?"

"Charlie, I have no idea how to do that, short of stopping and asking. I would guess he's military, but then that could be a cover like Brattan."

Charlie frowned and tapped his ballpoint on the scarred surface of his desk. Either the local law had picked up the trail or Pangborn's people had. He didn't believe the first. Most of the people targeted by a BOLO are apprehended at traffic stops or some minor, unrelated event that happens to turn up the wanted man, or someone ratted them out. Therefore, this must be some Fifty-first Star goons who needed to get to Brattan before he was caught and spilled his guts to the police.

"Okay, lay back but be prepared to intervene if you think it's someone from the Fifty-first Star. Wait at least until the Norfolk Shore Police can be called."

Charlie called the Norfolk Naval Station and put them on alert. Nothing to do now but wait.

〉〉〉

"Nothing to do now but wait," Ike said. "Is there anymore wine?"

"Mumph?"

"Sorry, did I wake you? You're losing your touch, there Madam President. I remember when you could—"

"Shut up. It's late and please remember that back in those days, which you remember inaccurately, by the way, I had not spent the better part of a year in a coma, been shot at, and had my house blown up, and had to go on the lam in Idaho. Also, we are not getting any younger, Ike. You want me to be spry? Okay, I want some peace and quiet for a change. No more explosions, blood, and guts for breakfast. You realize that this past year or so I have spent as much time on a leave of absence as I have actually sitting at my desk? It has been jolly, but how long do you think my Board of Trustees is going to put up with it? I could go home and find I have no job."

"Maybe we should both retire, remove ourselves from the line of fire. We could move into your house in Maine. We could live on lobster and clams and my ill-gotten gains from my years as a spy. You could write a book or something. Think of it. No bad guys, no whiney sophomores or their parents. Nobody to arrest, shoot at, or be shot by."

"You do know it's as cold as a witch's whoosis in the winter up there? Like, there's a permanent Nor'easter blowing in off the Atlantic and the temperatures drop to flash freeze."

"We could cuddle."

"Uh huh, like, twenty-four seven. Even you would tire of that eventually. Write a book about what?"

"Oh, I don't know. You are a highly successful university president. You could write *University Administration for Dummies*. You'd make a fortune."

"Been done. What else?"

"Okay, summers in Maine, winters in some nice warm place with white sand beaches and palm trees."

"And write a book?"

"Exactly. *My Life as a Changeling in Picketsville* or *How to Turn a Mediocre College into a Passable University* or *The Vampires of Rockbridge County/My Years as a University President at the Turn of the Century*. Either should sell."

"Very funny. And you will do what?"

"Take many more naps."

"What's that noise?"

Sam had wired the surveillance cameras they'd planted at the range to the large-screen television. One by one eight separate squares lit up. A loud beep told Ike they were online. Someone had entered the bathhouse. The recording tape began to roll.

"Sam," Ike yelled, "I think we're in business."

Chapter Thirty-eight

Danny's friend, Chief Petty Officer Lucy Vandegraaf, was assigned to the Shore Police. The CPO Club at the Air Station was not exactly within her unit's area of responsibility. It didn't matter. The uniform would gain her admittance to the premises and that's all she needed. Danny, with Billy as his guest, strolled in behind her and took a booth across the room from the bar. From that point they had Brattan in view. That is they did if the man seated on a stool midway down its length was in fact him. Billy glanced at the photo spread he had and nodded. The next step would be initiated by Lucy. She draped her jacket over her arm and sidled up to Brattan.

"Say, Chief," she said, "you're new here aren't you?" She waved to the bartender and ordered a beer. A light one.

"You drink that piss?" Brattan asked. "Here, belay that order and bring the lady a real drink. She'll have a sidecar with something that isn't colored water."

"I'm good with this, Chief. Thanks anyway."

Brattan should have known better. This would not be the first mangled pick-up in his career. Unfortunately, like many men of his age and inclinations, he harbored the moronic notion that he was a desirable commodity where women were concerned. He was wrong, of course, but at that moment, the possibility of a sexual conquest short-circuited any cognitive functioning and, as they say, his brains migrated south.

"Little lady, I need to teach you some lessons. Like, when a man offers you a real drink, you say, 'Thank you' and jump at the chance to learn from a master."

"Do they? Gracious! What sort of a thing are you a master at, besides baiting, of course?"

"Huh?"

"Sorry, you remind me of my ex and that sometimes makes me grumpy. So what's your name there, Chief?"

Brattan had to think. After three bourbons, neat, remembering his alias did not come easily to him. Then he had it. "Bart... Bart Hallihan. What's yours, Sweet Cheeks?"

"Lucy Shirpoleze. You on leave?"

"TDY, waiting for reassignment to a destroyer."

"Which one?"

"Umm...not sure yet."

"So, you're a senior chief waiting for a tin can. Wow. I don't meet too many of them in a month. Where were you stationed before?"

"Here and there. Say, you ready for another? A real one this time?"

"Not yet. Where, 'here and there'?"

"You ask a lot of questions for a skirt."

"For a skirt? Yeah, I just love that. Let's just say before I start any kind of a relationship with a guy I need some background. Like where he's from, what he does, where he's been, stuff like that. Don't you agree that's important?"

"Hell, I don't know. I say drink up and see what happens."

"Right. So, your ribbons. Top three, right?"

"Right. There's more where these came from, Honey. You could come by my place and see them if you want."

"Tempting. Maybe later. There's just one thing. If those are the top three, what have you been doing for the last fifteen, twenty years, Chief, lying in a coma somewhere?"

"What?"

"The latest ribbon you're showing looks like Desert Storm era. A lot has gone down since then."

Brattan slid off his stool and stepped back to put some distance between them. "Who the hell are you?"

Lucy slipped on her jacket— blouse, actually—which displayed her badge. "I told you, I'm Lucy, Shore Police. Did I not make that clear? Sometimes I mumble, sorry about that. I need to see some ID, mister, and a copy of your orders."

Brattan pushed away from the bar and started to leave. "Screw you. You ain't getting nothing from me tonight or ever, cop-bitch."

Lucy nodded to Billy and his brother who stood and started toward Brattan. He saw them, guessed why they were heading his way, turned on his heel, and ducked toward the side exit. It was blocked by two beefy SEALS.

"Make a hole," he yelled. Nobody moved. "Get out of my way, sailor, or…"

"Or what, old man? You ain't going nowhere but to jail, I'm thinking."

Brattan pivoted and headed back into the club. He found himself surrounded. "Who are you guys? Let me by."

Billy stepped up and poked Brattan in the chest with his index finger and grinned.

"Jack Brattan. I have a warrant for your arrest pursuant of a BOLO issued by the Sheriff's Office, Picketsville, Virginia. You are the prime suspect in the shooting death of Police Deputy Thomas Frieze, Rockbridge County Sheriff's Department. Under the rules regulating 'hot pursuit,' I am arresting you. If you have problem with that, Chief Petty Officer Navy Policewoman Vandegraaf will book you into the brig for identity theft. If that don't work, we'll think of something else. In any case, you're busted, Brattan and I'm thinking there's a whole lot of folks who want to have a chat with you and your buddies out at the old Five One Star ranch. You up for that? Don't even look cross-eyed at me, dirt bag. You are a cop killer and I'm one second from hoping you make a break for it so I can shoot you right here and now. So, we are going quietly, right? And after you've had a think, you will fall over yourself to help us because otherwise we might just cut you loose and let your friends have a go at you."

"You don't know what you're yammering about. I'm, uh… Senior Chief Bart Hallihan and you better get the f—"

"Shut up, you idiot. You're going to the nearest set of cells I can find and good luck getting a lawyer this time of night. 'Specially since we'll start you in the drunk tank where you won't be offered the opportunity until tomorrow a.m. After that, a couple of hours marinating in cuffs and shackles in the backseat of a police cruiser and then, maybe, we'll let you call your lawyer. Only I ain't so sure you want to do that right now. You remember what happened to the last Fifty-first Star employee who was in custody? Hell, we always did have problems protecting our cell windows. So, you might think twice about letting anybody know where you're at. Okay, police person Lucy, let me Mirandize this mook and then we'll haul his ass off to your brig."

>>>

Nothing good ever comes from a call received after midnight. Consequently Charlie made a habit of putting his phone on silent and disconnecting his land line except during those times when staying connected seemed truly important. Unfortunately, that occurred more often than not. It was after two when he received the call from his man in Norfolk. The police, he heard, had picked up Brattan. It was less clear which police had made the arrest. On the one hand the local Shore Police seemed to be involved with the initial apprehension, but then a civilian cop took over. He's emailed a picture of the event. Did Charlie need him to step in?

Charlie opened the attachment, recognized Billy, and smiled.

"No worries, Harry. Shut it down and come home tomorrow. The right people got our man." Charlie rubbed his eyes and figured the time difference between DC and Idaho and hoped Ike would not mind a midnight call. Ike was still up.

"We have Jack Brattan."

"Who?"

"Oh yeah, we haven't had time to discuss the other half of this operation. He's the guy we think killed the cop who set you up so the bomb could be put in your car."

"Short fat guy? County cop?"

"That's the one."

"I wondered about that. So you got his killer and you're hoping he can finger Pangborn?"

"I do and he can. The question is, will he? Actually, it's your deputy who has him. Somehow your people guessed, as did we, that Brattan would go to ground at a Naval facility. Billy Sutherlin has him in custody. I have to hand it to you, your people are good, Ike."

"They are."

"Are you ready at your end?"

"We'll know in the morning. The tape is rolling and either something will show up there, or we're stuck with Brattan if we want to bring Pangborn to trial. I'm not happy with that prospect, by the way."

"Where's my drone?"

"On its way."

"Will you need any more help?"

"I want to erase you and your people from this op, Charlie. You have enough *tsoris* already for helping us. You can stand by, though. I might need some help persuading the local State Police into running a raid on the ranch if I'm right about what they're up to."

"I can ask the director to call. Governor, or go directly to the police?"

"I don't know. Protocol would suggest the governor first. He could then push on the State Police, but if he doesn't…"

"Maybe both?"

"Governor first. If that doesn't work, tell him the FBI will be notified. I'd guess he would not want the Feds messing in his sand pile and then call the state cops anyway."

"Okay, that's it until tomorrow."

Chapter Thirty-nine

Sleep had been slow in coming. The possibility that Ike was correct in what he believed happened nightly in the ranch's bathhouse forestalled any chance for an easy slide into unconsciousness. So, well before the sun had struggled above the horizon, Sam and Karl, Ike and Ruth, coffee cups in hand, gathered and squinted at the tiny screen as the recording of the previous night's activities in and around the ranch and specifically in the bathhouse unfolded.

A single lamp set in a corner augmented the dawn sunlight as the four figures leaned in to view the screen which flickered sooty images in eight separate sectors. Each square showed activity which took place in front of the surveillance cameras positioned around the ranch the afternoon before. The image quality was not good, but better than they'd expected, given the sacrifices the hook manufacturer had to make in order to squeeze in a video camera. The lenses, no more than a large pinhole somehow managed to capture whatever moved within its cone. One by one, blank sectors brightened as motion triggered them into life. Shadowy figures moved ghost-like from one place and to another. Finally, only two sectors remained lighted as all movement ended elsewhere and whatever happened remained focused in the remaining two. Martin Pangborn and Senator Connors could be easily identified. The others could not—that is, not yet.

And maybe never.

"I can't watch this," Ruth muttered. "I don't want to see it. Jesus, Ike, what are we going to do? We can't just sit here."

"Look, what's done is done. Now…now we need to be sure. No, we don't want to either and wouldn't if I had another option, but God forgive me, I don't. The rest of you are excused. You've seen enough to know what comes next. I have to be certain. Beyond what you see here, the larger question is, how long has this been going on and who else knows?"

Ruth stood and walked to the kitchen table which held the whiskey bottle. She poured a stiff three fingers and drank it in a single swallow.

"Helluva breakfast you got there, lady."

"Hey, I'll join you," Karl said. "How about it, Sam?"

"I'm for pancakes. I need something to counteract the acid reflux this created."

"Okay for you. I don't think I could keep them down."

"What do you mean, who else, Ike? How about the cowboys who you could say delivered the goods?"

"Yes, but not just them. Family? Friends? Somebody had to know, had to have seen the signs. Do parents come with a special set of blinders that prevents them from seeing what their friends or relations are up to? It makes you wonder. Do people really not know this goes on, or is there some subconscious mechanism that allows them to deny what's happening right under their noses? Is the reality so frightening that they elect not to see it?"

"You're asking me or is that a rhetorical question?"

"Both, I guess."

"Then you'd have to ask the people who watched the Nazis create the death camps and did nothing, or the wives who didn't see the incest in their homes, or spouses who were blind to their partner's infidelity. Sometimes the truth is too painful to face and your brain will simply not allow it to surface. I think it's called 'resolving a cognitive dissonance.' It's that or they go crazy. Look, people want to trust those they love and/or admire, so they build filters in their minds that sort out all the things they don't want to know. People protect themselves from the parts of their existence that hurt."

"Cognitive dissonance? Jesus."

"Like that, anyway. All of which allows torture and genocide to continue everywhere from Somalia, Nigeria, Iraq, here, there, you name it. Ethnic cleansing is the *mot du jour*. Sorry, I get carried away, sometimes."

"Got it. You're right, but this is a conversation for another time. Now all of you need to gear up. This afternoon, we will go in there and take the damned place apart and scatter the scum to the winds."

"Jesus. That's it? We go in and…You did say 'we' will? You, me, and what army?"

"By we, I mean the two of us, and Sam and Karl—he's FBI, don't forget. Karl, if this doesn't fall under some interstate criminal behavior statute, nothing does."

"It does. The Mann Act will cover anything and anyone mixed up in this business."

"What about our three fracking friends…? I said fracking, not…what you think I said."

"Our 'health department' officials? Probably not. I think we need to send them back home with the Vulture. Charlie has been a big help. Let's clean up this end so he doesn't get into trouble. We'll still have plenty of other help."

"We will? Who?"

"Charlie will use some 'friends in high places' muscle to prime the director of the State Police. With or without an urging of the governor he'll be only too happy to hustle over here to look at what we have. Unless he has a heart of stone or the IQ of a gnat, by mid-afternoon we will have an army of State Troopers in full riot gear on the ranch grounds and having a round-up of our own."

"Did you say riot gear? Please tell me we aren't going in with guns blazing. I'm not sure I can take another shoot-out, Ike." Ruth did not look happy.

"I hope the blazing bit won't happen. But don't forget, those bozos over at the ranch are seriously armed and primed by months, no years, of antigovernment rhetoric and, therefore, might be tempted to make a stand. So, 'blazing' becomes a possibility."

"I am aware of the possibility. Life is not about possibilities. It is about probabilities. Calculate the odds for me. Will they or won't they?"

"Can't give you the odds. All I can say is, if they do, it won't be nice. Cops, as a general rule, take a dim view of civilians who point guns at them."

"Crap! And you? What does the sheriff of Picketsville think?"

"Believe it or not, I hope they stand down. Most of those people are merely delusional. They don't deserve taking a bullet for that. Having said that, there's a part of me that hopes they will force a confrontation. There are just too many folks with distorted ideas about what constitutes reasonable dissent who need to be brought up short. Then there is the question of acceptable provocation in the public domain. People need to understand that it is one thing to swagger around a supermarket or a Starbucks brandishing an assault rifle, and quite another to have to use it in the sure and certain knowledge they could come up on the hurting end of a fire fight. There is a tendency abroad to trivialize weapons and the carnage they create. There are way too many video warriors lurching around suburban malls with their AK 10s and too few real ones to explain why they're a menace. Once you leave a world defined by comic books and video games and actually face the reality of death at the hands of someone who pulled a trigger a fraction of a second before you did, you might want to rethink the path you took that got you there. But by then, it would be too late. You will become another senseless death. It comes as a shock to folks like those on the ranch to realize that people sometimes shoot back and police always do."

"So says my husband the cop."

"There's more and I could go on, but you already know the rest by heart."

"I think I wrote it. As you are always quick to remind me, it's what we lefty-liberals do. Make speeches about stuff like that. So, what about Pangborn? Will he make a stand with them?"

"Given a choice, I suspect he will slink off and hide behind a phalanx of highly paid legal types. That is, if he is allowed to. That's what people like him do when things get testy. But I hope we get there before he has time to rally his lawyers. If we're lucky we'll nail him *in situ* this time."

"Did you really say, *in situ*?"

"You know what I mean."

"I do. So, what are the odds we'll catch him off guard?"

"If he is totally unaware of what we are doing, as it seems he is, pretty good, but, whether he is or isn't, he's mine."

"Then God help him."

>>>

Jack Brattan was released into Billy's custody a little after eight in the morning. The Shore Police didn't want Brattan. They didn't have jurisdiction to do more than make an arrest. Also, they had no interest in the civilian case and were eager to have him out of their brig. Billy had him cuffed, shackled, on the rear seat of his black and white, and headed west within a quarter of an hour. Billy hummed a tuneless hum for the first fifty miles. Then he spoke.

"So, Brattan, how do you feel about saving what's left of your rear end by talking about your boss?"

"I got nothing to say."

"No surprise there. Well, looky here, the speedometer just informs me that we just drove fifty-one miles. Now don't you think that's a omen or something? Fifty-one miles—Fifty-first Star?"

"Screw you, Barney."

"Now don't go all personal on me there, big shot. I might turn out to be the only friend you got. Murder One is a capital offense, you know. I reckon you need to analyze your position. If you were to, say, give up Mister P, we might could wiggle that charge down a bit and get you life, maybe even with the possibility of parole."

"You don't know shit, Deputy Hick. There is no way in hell that the person you think I work for will ever go down. He's, like, too big, too important. If anybody even tries to make a run at him, he'll have them for breakfast."

"Mercy goodness. All that? That's why you were on the run. Afraid he might take it into his head to squash you like a bug 'fore you could talk to us? So, you're saying you won't talk to us even though you know that if they find you, your old buddies will send you off to La La Land."

"I thought I told you to shut up."

"You did. Okay, what's your feeling about water-boarding?"

"You threatening me with torture?"

"Torture? No, no, we wouldn't do that. I'm just making conversation, here. Since you ain't open to discussing your employer, I thought we might touch on current events, maybe. You know, politics, global warming, stuff like that. So, water-boarding?"

"You're an idiot."

"Some say that. None with all their teeth intact, but they do sometimes say it. Okay, new topic, tell me about that outfit you joined up in, the Fifty-first Star. Is it a good bet? I mean, would a guy like me fit in? I'm just asking 'cause I am naturally curious. What is it they do, besides yahoo around in camouflage with big guns and such, pretending to be the country's saviors?"

"It exists to remove idiots like you from the formula."

"Whoa, from the formula? What formula would that be? Cops? Just cops, or people in general, or just the ones who think differently than you all? That why you dusted Tommy Frieze? How about them other people who're not like you? Maybe it's people who are the wrong color or who go to the wrong churches. Is that the 'formula'? See, I always assumed you all was just a bunch of losers who think carrying a loaded weapon and bullying folks makes you out to be tough and, like, important. Take you, for example. You could start a new group, a sort of 'Bullies Anonymous' thing. You know, people who like to push people around get together and brag how they pushed a cripple down the stairs, fun stuff like that. No? Okay, let me ask you something else. What will you do when people finally get sick and tired of the crap you hand out and push back? Are you going to stand or run?"

Brattan opened his mouth as if to say something and then thought better of it and shut it with an audible slick.

"See, my guess is that the first time somebody says, 'no' to you guys and makes a fist, you will be all running back to momma like little schoolgirls. Am I right?"

Brattan's face turned bright red and he jerked at his chains. Then he sank back in the seat.

"I know what you're trying to do, Huckleberry, and it won't work. Like, there is no way you're going to make me come after you."

"No? Shoot. Well, I reckon it was worth a try, dirt bag. Okay, how about some music? You like country?"

"No."

Billy switched the cars radio on and dialed up a local country music station. "Faith Hill, gotta love her."

Chapter Forty

Later that morning the sun seemed to shine brighter and the air seemed clearer. Not so much cleansing, but at least refreshing. Nevertheless, the images they'd seen on the tape, like acid, had etched their awfulness permanently on their minds. Fortified one way or another, pancakes, strong coffee, or whiskey, all four had managed to compartmentalize them sufficiently to allow them to move on. Ike made the call that would set into motion the steps that should bring the nightmare he and Ruth had endured for the last week and a half to a close. Ruth handed him a final cup of coffee which he drank without tasting.

"Okay, Sheriff, what happens now?"

"We make the calls. We gear up. We…where's Karl and Sam?"

"They are huddling inside. I think Karl is being protective and Sam reminding him she was a cop before she was a NSA nerd and is perfectly capable of taking care of herself. She's cleaning her weapon."

"And you?"

"Gunplay is my least enjoyable pastime, as you know, although we did have some good times back in Maine."

"Which is why we are sitting here wearing wigs and bad haberdashery instead of enjoying a nice luncheon back home at the Crossroads Diner."

"Point taken. Every party has some cleaning up to do afterwards. We forgot to check on that. Let's not make the same mistake today. As for me, I think I will watch from afar, if that is all right with you."

"My preference. You might want to have a chat with Pangborn if the occasion arises. Also, we need to pack up before we go. When this goes down, I want to be able to walk away from here without a trace. The Gottliebs need to vanish."

"We could burn the place down."

"Over the top. I think a good swabbing out and polishing of obvious surfaces for fingerprints will do."

"Finish your calls. I'll start applying the mop."

>>>

Martin Pangborn did not like to be awakened early when he was on vacation. Anyone with the temerity to attempt it had better have a good reason to do so or that person's future as an employee would not last much longer.

"What? This had better be good. What do I need to know at this ungodly hour?" he said and sat up. "Where's my coffee? What do you want?"

"They have Brattan."

"Who has Brattan?"

"The BOLO, remember. Well, some police force in rural Virginia picked him up and has him locked up."

"Rural? Where exactly?"

"You're not going to like this, sir, but it's Picketsville. That's where—"

"I know where the hell that is and before you ask, yes, I know who used to be the sheriff there. So, they think they can squeeze Brattan? He won't talk. He knows better."

"They're saying he might make a deal. They say they have him on murder one, you know, the cop, Frieze. That's a capital offense. If they reduce it to something less, he might, you know, want to talk…not that he knows anything that could hurt you, of course. He doesn't, does he?"

"No. Who the hell is 'they' and who do we have in the area?"

"It's just rumor, maybe, but who can say? Maybe the cops back there are spreading it to smoke out something else. We don't have anyone close anymore because of the Frieze thing."

"Get me Harrison on the phone and wake up the senator. It's time he got the hell out of here. He doesn't need to know what comes next."

Pangborn dressed and hustled a sleepy and disheveled Oswald Connors to the helicopter. It lifted off in a whirl of dust and carried a very relieved senator off to Boise. Next, he picked up the phone intending to set up an intercept in Picketsville. He was busy shouting at the person on the other end of the line when he was told about an unusual gathering of law enforcement vehicles in the area.

"Not my problem. I own the locals and if anything was up, I'd know. Now leave me alone. I have work to do." He was still at it when the police arrived.

> > >

It took longer than Ike expected to get the State Police on board. Their director, as did many of his counterparts across the country, had a reluctance, born of prior experiences, to deal with or accept advice from the federal government. He said he'd listen to what Ike had to say but sounded skeptical. Only after Ike had forwarded a portion of the tape to his cell phone, did the colonel finally pull up to the cabin and meet with Ike. It took another hour and several more phone calls to recount the whole story—how Ike and Ruth came to be in Idaho, what the connection was between them and the ranch and, finally, to map out a plan to take the operation down.

"That's a helluva story, Sheriff. If I didn't know the director of the Central Intelligence Agency personally, I'd say you were nuts and have you in my jail for disturbing the peace, not to mention doing business as a realtor without a license. Health inspectors? Really? So, you have this tape. How'd you get it? Never mind, I don't want to know. Son of a bitch. I heard some talk about the senator, but Pangborn? Jesus. You know some fancy lawyer will have it suppressed as evidence even if we go in there and bust him."

"I do and I don't care. I don't see this getting that far. Civil suits by families, maybe, but I think it is more likely to find its way into the anonymous media stream that seems to rule the news now. TMZ, YouTube, and I don't know where else. I expect once it gets loose it will go viral. There will be no stopping it."

"That is a very mean and nasty thing to do to one of America's more prominent citizens and friend of the former president. I like it."

"I hoped you would."

"I have to tell you, Martin Pangborn has been a pain in my rear for years. He has friends in high places. But you already knew that. Anyway, his friends, that is to say politicians whose election campaigns he helps fund, are after me all the time to turn a blind eye to this or that, especially that bunch of idiots in his so called militia out there at the ranch. They scare the daylights out of the folks hereabouts with their damned guns and crap."

"Glad to find a kindred spirit, Director."

"Yeah, and he tried to get me ousted from my job. Do you believe that? He leaned on the governor pretty hard. I guess he thought he had something on the governor. But the governor has no love for Pangborn so it didn't work. He probably found out that Pangborn funded his opponent in the last election, or something. Besides there'd be too many questions asked if I were pushed out without something big to justify it. Lord knows they tried, though. I've had a private snoop on my case for over a year. Tapped my phone—the works."

"But he failed."

"Yep. Okay, let's put this thing together. I'm going to enjoy this." He pulled his phone off his belt and began making calls. Ike packed his car and briefed the other three.

"We missed a helicopter leaving," the State Police director yelled at Ike. "Who do you think left?"

"I hope it was just the senator. If Pangborn slipped the noose, this is going to be way more difficult. We'll find out soon enough."

Over the course of the next hour and a half, police cars began assembling on the several side roads near the ranch. A correctional facilities bus, equipped with mesh-screened windows joined them, as did several standard school busses and an armored personnel carrier. At three in the afternoon, a front-end loader fitted with a chain hoist lumbered down the road to the ranch followed by a flatbed truck carrying the sort of steel plates used to cover trenches during road repair. The crew monitoring the television surveillance in the ranch house watched astonished as the loader operator lifted them in turn and dropped them over the stop spikes in the "cattle guard" that secured the entrance to the ranch. The moment it finished and backed away, a stream of police cruisers, busses, led by the armored personnel carrier with its complement of SWAT officers, smashed through the gate and rumbled into the ranch.

Chapter Forty-one

Courage is ephemeral. In the imaginings of young boys playing at war, it is a given. Orcs, dragons, aliens, any of the myriad evil-doers who inhabit the fantasies of youth are dispatched without thought of a possible poor outcome. Indeed, in any circumstance except that posed by reality, bravery can be had for the asking. Faced with a real and present danger, however, it is a different story. Why are some men brave and others not? What made Audie Murphy one of the most decorated soldier in World War II, and not the man standing next to him? Why can one woman bear with great serenity the pain and certainty of death from cancer and another collapse in helpless despair? Where does it come from? And once in play, where does it then disappear to? Often courage appears almost as a random event in one's life—unplanned and unexpected. Young men worry if they will be brave if or when they are called upon. Some are certain they will be courageous and fail. Others, equally certain of their cowardice, rise to the occasion. It is a conundrum.

When the convoy of police rolled into the Fifty-first Star compound, every man wearing the star-shaped patch bearing the number fifty-one had to confront his moment of truth. Would he or wouldn't he stand tall? Courage will be fortified by numbers, of course. Colleagues shouting, rallying you onward will add a measure of courage you might not otherwise have. Yet it soon becomes apparent that it is easier to man the barricades than to stand firm in them when the other side approaches, armed and unmoved by your bravado.

The militia, alerted by the crew watching the video of the main gate, formed a double line across the entrance to the compound. Assault weapons locked and loaded, they stood, a menacing front, convinced that the government in this instance, as in Colorado before, would blanch at their determination, their armament, and back away. The Feds, they believed, would not dare start a firefight on their turf. The FBI, they had been told, learned its lesson years ago with the Branch Davidians. A show of force would be sufficient. Thus fortified, they took their positions and waited. The last thing they expected was a full-on assault.

Police have short fuses when it comes to confronting an armed and hostile citizenry. Federal operatives may dither, but police will not. They have a protocol that never varies. They will issue a warning, they will order arms to be put down and, if refused, they will shoot. It is what they are trained to do. Thus, much to the chagrin of the Fifty-first Star, the convoy of police vehicles did not hesitate. It paused only long enough for orders to be given and when ignored, to launch several canisters of tear gas. They waited until the gas had taken effect and then moved forward again. A few of the militia had the foresight to anticipate such a move and had gas masks. The remainder beat a retreat. One shot was fired. It was unclear who pulled the trigger. A hail of rubber bullets from the police scattered the remaining militia and the convoy rolled into the open space between the barracks.

The SWAT team deployed and secured the compound. A confused and teary-eyed militia was rounded up and disarmed. Their obvious leaders were loaded into the correctional system bus, the rest herded into one of the now-empty barracks to be sorted and then loaded into the remaining busses later. The boys, eyes wide as saucers, were similarly rounded up and put on a school bus and sent away for interviewing and identification. As soon as each had been debriefed, their parents would be notified and told to come and take them home. Those identified as victims were sent for evaluation and medical treatment. Martin Pangborn's world teetered at the abyss.

He was having none of it. If his patriots seemed unable to engage, he had no such qualms. Two SWAT team members escorted him into the courtyard, now relatively clear of tear gas. He was met by the director of the Idaho State Police, Ike, Ruth, and Karl.

"What is the meaning of this?" he demanded.

"You are Martin Pangborn?" Karl asked. Without waiting for a replay, added, "We are here to arrest you, sir, and take you into custody."

"And who in the hell are you?"

"Special Agent Karl Hedrick, Federal Bureau of Investigation."

"Special Agent…You are off the reservation, boy. You have no jurisdiction here."

"Actually, he does," the director said, "but that is neither here nor there. You are being placed under arrest by the Idaho State Police and I assure you I do have jurisdiction."

"Arrest? For what, exactly?"

"Ah, well that is where it gets complicated."

"What do you mean, 'complicated' and who exactly are you?"

"Me? I am your worst enemy, Pangborn. As to the charges, well it is a matter of framing them, see? Shall it be for some obvious Health Department infractions or—?"

"This is absurd. You can't just barge in here with a company of State Troopers for that."

"I could if I chose to, but you're right, that would be over the top. We might add conspiracy to commit murder. That would up the ante sufficiently to justify a show of force, wouldn't you think?"

"Murder? Whose murder?"

Ike stepped forward. "Mine, for one."

"And mine." Ruth added.

"Who are you? Wait, you're supposed to be…" Pangborn's eyebrows knit together and he bit his lip. "I have no idea who you are or what you're talking about."

"Oh, I think you recognize the sheriff of Picketsville. Say hello to Ike Schwartz and his wife, both very much alive, no thanks to you. So, then," the director continued, "there is the matter of child sexual abuse. All of these boys are clearly underage. Pederasty, Pangborn. We will arrest you for that."

"What? This is outrageous. You will hear from my lawyers. I will have your badge. I will sue the state for slander if you insist on this. I will—"

"You will please shut up? We have you on tape, Pangborn," Ike said, is voice eerily cool.

"You have…on tape. That is nonsense. You couldn't have. It's impossible."

"But true. You and Senator Connors, last night, in that bathhouse right over there, in fact. Where is the good senator, by the way?"

Pangborn's face turned ashen. He cleared his throat and shuffled his feet in the dust. Around him men clamored their innocence, declared their rights under one section of the Constitution or another and protested against what they referred to as police over-reach. The troopers smiled and herded them along as if they were unruly children caught shoplifting at the Dollar Store. Pangborn's eyes narrowed. He reminded Ike of a fox he'd once had to shoot—crafty, sly, and probably rabid.

"Any such evidence would be either manufactured or obtained illegally. In either case, it will be disallowed in any court of law."

"Court? Sheriff Schwartz, do you think a court will be involved?"

"You mean to view the tape? Oh, no, I don't think so. Mr. Pangborn is correct. It probably wouldn't be allowable. All sorts of legal maneuvering would keep it gagged like forever. After the boys are interviewed, however, it will be a different story. What will they say, do you suppose when the social workers talk to them? Or their parents? It boggles the mind. And what will their parents think? Will they have something to say in a civil court? What would a jury believe? Gosh, what might they do? What do you think would happen, Director?"

"I'm just guessing here, understand, but I'm thinking some-one not happy with Mr. Pangborn, here, might think this is just the tip of the old iceberg and insist on an investigation into all of his affairs. Subpoena his phone records, bank statements, checkbook, who knows what else? Then, God only knows where that might lead. And the parents…well, as you say, it wouldn't surprise me if they sued for damages in a civil court, Sheriff."

"That could involve jail on the one hand and millions of dol-lars on the other. Here's a question for you, Pangborn. I don't expect you will want to answer it, but if any of the boys you misused happened to be a child of one of your own militia, how do you suppose that particular parent will react? Remember, you armed them and assured them that the exercise of justice might not always be exercised through the system you proclaimed cor-rupt. What will the rank and file think of you when they find out what you've been up to out here?"

"What do you mean, find out? Evidence is privileged and my attorneys will seal—"

"Of course. Neither the State Police nor I would dream of violating that principle. No, indeed, we wouldn't. Certainly not. Regrettably, I have to tell you that after I uploaded the tape to my computer back in Picketsville, I was informed that our server has been hacked, by whom I can't say, but it may not be as secure as I would like. You wouldn't know anything about that, would you?"

Pangborn's knees buckled and he collapsed in a heap at their feet.

The State Police director stepped back and watched him fold. "It seems like you might have touched a nerve there, Ike. Are you alright, Mr. Pangborn?"

"More than one nerve, I think," Ike added. "Pangborn, do you do know the only reason you are alive and not rotting in the pasture with one of your cows, is my wife has a soft streak and persuaded me to not shoot you on sight? Just saying. But now that I think about the probable consequences you now face, I'm guessing you might be wishing I had pulled the trigger."

Chapter Forty-two

Jack Brattan had a problem to solve. Actually, he had several problems to solve. If he had been an animated character in a cartoon, the space above his head would have been filled with a series of light bulbs which glowed and then blinked out as one bad idea after another popped into his head. He sat with his back pressed against the cell wall. The window on the wall had been situated high, and because it was a cell window, it had been fitted with both thick Plexiglas panes and bars. Still, it made him nervous. He didn't trust either the bars or plastic and knew that if Pangborn believed he might talk, neither the bars nor the Plexiglas would be sufficient to prevent something lethal from sailing through. If he insisted on being placed in a different cell, he would have to tell his jailers why. They probably knew anyway, but he didn't want to give them the satisfaction of seeing him squirm. So, were these hick cops smart enough to put two and two together about the other stuff? He didn't know. He needed a lawyer, but to call on the ones he knew would be to put him squarely in Pangborn's court. He'd know where he was and that could lead to the problem with the window even sooner. Maybe he already knew. Or maybe not. Where was Pangborn? What did he know?

He felt like kicking himself for not having a back-up plan. He should have figured this out years ago when he'd seen what the Fifty-first Star was capable of. Seen? Been party to what happens to people who threatened the organization. He paced. Shoulda, coulda, woulda, too late now. Was that a shadow outside the window? So absorbed in his problems that he didn't notice when Billy Sutherlin strolled up to his cell with a tray of food.

"Here you go, Brattan, dinner from the Crossroads Diner. It's the best food in town. Say, you looked a little peaked. You're not worrying about something, are you? Hate to see you spoil your appetite."

Brattan had developed a facial expression which in the past had been deemed by those exposed to it as terrifyingly intimidating. He called it "The Stare." Eyes unblinking, face frozen, he swiveled his head around and focused it on Billy.

The cop did not respond. Well, he wouldn't. There were bars between them. Still, it ought to shut him up. It didn't.

"So, here's some news for you, Big Guy. Your boss…maybe your ex-boss by now, that is, just got busted. You'll never guess what for."

Brattan sat still, the stare intact.

"Okay, so here is how it goes down, Jackie boy. Pangborn is toast. The Fifty-first Star is toast. If you're thinking his big-shot friends are going to pull his chestnuts out of the fire, you're wrong. Whoever they are, they will be putting some serious distance between him and them as fast and as far as possible. You want to know why?"

No response.

"Right. Your boss has a problem, see? He likes little boys. Did you know that?"

Blink.

"Whoa. Maybe you and him shared that twisted lifestyle. Did you?"

Rapid blinking.

"Oh, oh. My friend, you could have a serious problem. See, he might be able to bring enough money and influence to bear to keep hisself out of a prison's general population, but you surer'n hell don't. You do know what happens to baby rapers in prison?"

"I want my phone call and lawyer."

"'Course you do. Who you want to call? Some of Mister P's? You can do that, but do you think they will want to talk to you? On the other hand, are you sure you want to talk to them? I mean you need to think about your options first. Am I right? Pangborn in cuffs is a different fish than one out and about. Might smell the same and all, but different in important ways. You could be thinking about a deal, right? I would if I was you. 'Course, I ain't, which is a blessing. You sure as hell don't want to go into prison with people knowing who it is you have an attachment to. No sirree. It's a problem, for sure. By the way, we can always set you up with the public defender. You could talk to him. He's pretty good, at least when he's sober, he is. Well, shoot, you got a lot to mull over. You'll want to think about all this, I reckon. I'll give you some alone time and check back later. Enjoy the meat loaf."

◇ ◇ ◇

Pangborn staggered to his feet, some of his bravado restored. He dusted off his sleeves and scowled.

"You know something, Pangborn?" Ike said. "I promised myself that when I found out who tried to blow up both of us, I would put a bullet in his brain. I would not argue, I would not bargain, and I would not concern myself with the niceties of due process. I would just blow his brains out and walk away. Irrespective of the idea that you'd probably be better off if I did, as I said just now, you should note that I am armed and still thinking about doing it anyway, you son of a bitch. On the other hand, my wife worries that if I were to do that and without some reasonable, that is to say within the bounds of legal, provocation, I, not you, would end up in front of a judge. So, I will not shoot you, unless you try to make a break for it. You won't will you? No? Well then, he's all yours, Director."

"Ike," Ruth said, "I've changed my mind. Shoot the fucker."

"Ruth, we talked about this."

"I know. Sorry. Shoot the bastard. Better?"

"Much."

Ike cocked his automatic and aimed it at a point between Pangborn's eyes.

"Do something," Pangborn yelled, "you're the police here. Make them stop."

"What? You want me to stop this man here from shooting you or the woman from using bad language? Hell, she already apologized. I'm okay with that. As for the shooting, I don't know. It would save the state a ton of money if we didn't have to try you. Then there is the pain and suffering a trial would cause. Kids would have to testify. You know how the tabloids blow everything out of proportion. Terrible. No, I think shooting you right now would be better for everyone. Go ahead, Sheriff, dust the son of a bitch."

A dark stain bloomed in Pangborn's pants as he lost control of his bladder.

"Oops. Looks like you got a little problem there, Martin. Say, is it too late to hit you up for a contribution for the policeman's fund? No? Oh well, I ain't too sure I want one from you, all things being considered. We generally don't accept donations from convicted felons, which is what you are about to be."

Pangborn began to babble.

"You going to shoot him or not, Sheriff? No? Okay. Sergeant, haul this bag of crap away."

Two state troopers dragged a limp Pangborn to a cruiser, shoved him in and read him his rights. The convoy reassembled and pulled out. A half hour later more busses arrived to remove the remainder of the cadre of militia, the women, and even the ranch hands.

◇◇◇

A call by the State Police commander to the governor, who in turn called the federal judiciary for advice, resulted with a make-do court set up in a nearby high school gym. Pro bono lawyers, private attorneys, and prosecutors sorted through the number of detainees. By mid-afternoon the following day, the majority of the men and women arrested at the ranch were released on their own recognizance, in jail, or awaiting bond hearings. The core leaders, those with outstanding warrants and Pangborn, were held over with bail set at sums ranging from the mid-five figures to eight figures for Pangborn.

By nightfall most of the relatively innocent were out and on their way home. Seven boys remained in the custody of Child Protective Services, and Pangborn, in an orange jumpsuit, angrily paced in a jail cell, having failed on four separate occasions to contact either his attorneys or arrange bail.

The news of the raid and the rumors surrounding its cause circulated rapidly, the electronic and social media being what they are. The next morning scandal sheets, YouTube, and their clones, alternates, and wannabes were gleefully reporting a *gemischt* of innuendo, half truth, and outright lies about Pangborn, the Fifty-first Star, and its leaders. The one person not already under indictment and who knew the whole, unadorned truth, took his own life.

The afternoon news carried the story of the sudden and wholly unexpected suicide of the junior senator from Idaho. No details were immediately available.

❯❯❯

Jackson Shreve sat in stunned silence as the news came in over the TV. Pangborn did what? He'd been loyal. As much, maybe more than any of the others, and how was he treated? Like dirt. Okay, the accidental opening of the gate was on him, but did that warrant a trip to Wyoming and exile? And alone? His wife and boy were back in Idaho. "When the whole family is involved," Pangborn had declared in one of his speeches, "it showed true patriotism" or something like that. Jackson couldn't remember it exactly, only that he had been impressed by the man. So, his family committed. For what? Not for this. How could he? How could he do something like that to anyone? His wife and his son and only child were still there. You do your damndest to raise them up right, to respect the flag and the Constitution, to be patriotic Americans. That's what the Star is all about, right? So, where is it part of what we are defending to include that stuff? An intense buzzing grew in his ears, no in his brain, louder crowding his thoughts. Buzz and drown them out. Some things need never to be thought about.

Buddy!

Jackson Shreve stared at the television in disbelief. It couldn't be. It was. Who...Buddy? His wife called and said they were holding Buddy for tests. What tests? Buddy hadn't done anything. This was police harassment and he wasn't going to stand by and...What tests? His mind blanked out, the buzzing ratcheted up to a dull roar. Nothing stirred behind those watery blue eyes for ten minutes. Then he knew. Tests. Buddy was one of the boys they hinted at on the news. His son. He'd dedicated his son to the cause, enrolled him in Pangborn's Young Pioneers. Pangborn promised they would be the vanguard of the future leaders of the country. But that isn't what he meant at all. The lying bastard.

Jackson felt dirty. Dirty and used, as dirty and used as his son. Abused and discarded. At that thought he began to weep. He wept for Buddy, for himself, but mostly at the enormity of betrayal he'd experienced. He sat in the dark, the television on but unheard for hours. Sometime before dawn, he stood and went to the cabinet where he kept his weapons. He needed to get them ready for what came next.

Chapter Forty-three

Ike and Ruth flew to Raleigh, North Carolina and returned the plane the Agency had leased for them. They rented a car and motored north and west to Picketsville. Before they left Idaho, Ruth managed to open her e-mail account.

"Okay, it happened, Ike. I told you it might and it did."

"Told me what?"

"I said there would be a limit to how much my Board of Trustees would accept from a basically absentee president. I am commanded to appear before them. There is, this message says, not subtly, by the way, that my continued tenure as president is being questioned. They want to fire me."

"Well, it would appear that attending my own funeral is not the only item on our agenda."

"So it would seem. This is no good, Ike. So, while I figure out my speech for the Board, what do you plan to say to all the mourning folks when they show up all teary eyed at your memorial service and see you alive and kicking?"

"Good question. I could quote Mark Twain. You know the line, 'The news of my death has been greatly exaggerated.' Or I could just yell, 'So sorry, big mistake, the drinks are on me.' I don't know. Should we send in an advance party?"

"Maybe. It depends on whether you can afford to buy that many drinks."

"You think many people will plan to attend?"

"Oh, no more than a couple of hundred."

"How about we skip it and take off for parts unknown? Being dead has its perks. Like no one will come after me anymore. I could get used to being dead and you wouldn't have to be fired, you'd quit."

"Life as a zombie? I don't know. What's in it for me?"

"No more budgets to finagle, no board meetings to drive you insane, forget the humiliation of begging for money at fund-raisers with pushy alumnae, no federal guidelines to worry about, not to mention tenure decisions, weepy sophomores—"

"I think we had this conversation before, but I take your point. Tempting as that may be, and it is, no, not just yet."

"You may never get a chance like this again."

"Still taking a pass. I don't run from problems any more than you do. Hey, this is a convertible. Let's put the top down."

"I'd rather not."

"Because?"

"It's dangerous. We're exposed in an open car. Anyone who's a decent shot and has the right equipment could blow us away in a heartbeat."

"That's it? You think there are still people who are gunning for us even now?"

"Maybe. Okay, probably not. Hey, it's force of habit. I never put convertible tops down."

"You are such a wuss. Listen, Ike, be serious a minute. We need to talk. All this daring-do and action hero stuff has got to stop. I can't be looking over my shoulder the rest of my life. You said you knew a way for it to go away. I'm not talking about joining the zombie nation. So, can you make it all go away?"

"I don't think I said 'all.' What I believe I said was, with some help from my friends, I might be able to reduce to near insignificance the instances when my past would rear its ugly head and bring down bad juju. That is, I could be erased from the Agency's files and all connection with it to me would disappear. That would not keep a lunatic with bad memories from finding me, or some super hacker with issues. Perhaps we should ask to be put in the witness protection plan."

"I just said, I'm not ready to give up fighting to keep my job, although, if I don't put an end to this Murder Incorporated, I really will be fired, assuming I can quiet their jets when we get back. There has got to be a limit for what the Board of Trustees will put up with."

"You do know that as long as I am sheriff, I am stuck with being a potential target for anyone ranging from the criminally insane felon who thinks I am the cause for all of his bad karma to the merely disgruntled who has had his driver's license revoked because I served him with a DUI. Since I and you are now us, that means we will never be wholly safe."

"You could retire from sheriffing."

"I could. I do not need to run for reelection next time around. Frank is perfectly capable of running the department."

"Yes he is. The difficulty with that is, can he get elected? Recall that our mayor harbors plans to return the town to the bad old days of cronyism and corruption."

"True. Maybe I should run for mayor."

"You don't mean that."

"You're right, I don't. We will have to revisit this problem later. There must be better options. We're the good guys, right? But right now I need to figure out how to manage a church service set up to mourn my demise and you need to figure out how to explain your non-widowhood, not to mention your cavalier approach to presidenting."

"For the second part, I do. As for the first, maybe I don't. Knocking you off would solve both our problems."

"Frank would arrest you."

"For what? You're already officially dead. How can I be arrested for your murder if you are already dead?"

"Interesting legal point. I'll have to think about that."

◇◇◇

Jack Brattan had his "mull," as Billy had put it. The public defender advised him to be quiet, plead not guilty, and take his

chances. He said the case against him that the local police had
him for murder hinged on connecting him as the person who
leased the car seen in the video of the shooting to establishing
him as the shooter. There was no image of the person in the car,
much less one of him. Worst case, the lawyer said, would be as
an unwitting accomplice. It was, he maintained, a weak thread
at best. With allowances for reasonable doubt, Brattan would
surely beat any murder one charge and probably any lesser ones.
He thanked the lawyer and said he'd think it over. His problem
was not what the local police and judiciary could or could not
prove. The state would not have to establish the connection.
Pangborn would do it for them. If he was in custody, as the
hick deputy said, nothing could save Jack's hide. Pangborn had
a larger pile of chips in this game. That included stuff on Brattan that could send him to death row in at least three states.
Then there was compromising information he could supply on
dozens more in high places—really high places. He would be
in position to cut an attractive deal. That deal would include
chopping Jack off at the knees with a bushel of politicians and
other influential people. Pangborn would see to it that he went
down for the Frieze shooting and all those other things as well.

Jack's best play, he thought, would be to make a preemp-
tive strike. He would spill his guts to these local yokel cops
and make his own deal before Pangborn got a chance to bury
him. Hell, he knew enough to have the bastard put away for,
like, a million years. He called his lawyer and sent him off to
the county prosecutor. In return for giving them an airtight
indictment incriminating Martin Pangborn, he only asked for
a reduced charge and a minimum security prison. He hoped the
cops wouldn't figure out he had no real leverage. That what he
knew about Pangborn could be shot down by any one of the
attorneys Pangborn kept on retainer. With any luck, the rubes
never would figure it out.

His luck held. He caught a busy prosecutor and a judge in
a good mood. Pangborn's attorneys, along with the majority of
his powerful friends refused to acknowledge him publicly or

privately. Jack would plea bargain and receive fifteen to twenty with a chance at parole and be shipped off to the nearest minimum security prison. A fistfight and a suspicious shakedown of his cell which produced a handmade blade would result in a transfer to the state prison and thence into its general population. He would be found dead, his head stuffed in a toilet bowl, a month after that.

>>>

His first shot nicked Pangborn's ear. Jackson had choked and jerked the trigger. He knew better than to do that. Hell, he'd been trained by the best the Fifty-first Star had to offer. *Too anxious, need to slow down, take the time.* People screamed and scattered as the report echoed across the street. Pangborn seemed frozen in place. *Stay that way, you bastard.* He would not jerk the trigger this time, he told himself. He worked the rifle's bolt and ejected one shell, locked in another, and settled the crosshairs on the man's core. *Breathe in, pause…* he let his breath out. *Slowly, slowly and…squeeze.* An officer of some sort yanked Pangborn to one side at the precise moment the rifle discharged and his second shot caught Pangborn in the arm. Jackson cursed and yanked the bolt back again to put a third round in the chamber. He scanned the area through his telescopic sight, searching for Pangborn, but couldn't find him. Where did he go? A volley of returning fire came from somewhere opposite. Bullets chipped the concrete around him. He didn't notice or care. Where was Pangborn? Where was the pervert? He found him. Two cops were trying to stuff him into the backseat of a patrol car. He drew a bead on him and fired.

A state policeman, who took it on himself to stop the crazed gunman in the parking garage across the street from the courthouse raced up the staircase. He didn't know how he'd managed to reach the third level so quickly. But he did and was able to drop Jackson Shreve with a single shot to the head at that precise moment his rifle recoiled from his third and final attempt to kill the one man whom he'd come to see as the devil incarnate.

Jackson Shreve, a member of the Fifty-first Star and patriot, would not see the green-tipped and probably illegal round smash into Pangborn's fifth cervical vertebrae. In a way, he'd done him a favor. Pangborn would never experience the terror of being in a prison's general population where his life would be at risk daily, hourly. He would, instead, be incarcerated in a moderately pleasant facility where he would share a room with only one other prisoner. The bad news: he would spend the remainder of his days as a quadriplegic, his continued existence dependent on the goodwill offered by people, most of whom despised him.

> > >

In another part of the country where things were comparatively less complicated, Ruth twisted in the car's seat and studied Ike. "Tell me something, Sheriff. Before we face the music in Picketsville, why did you call in the State Police back there? The way you were talking, I expected that the minute you had the evidence you needed, you'd storm onto the ranch and splatter Pangborn across the Idaho countryside. What happened?"

"Maybe I heeded your very good advice."

"Possible, but barely so."

"Okay, you were right. And recall what I said to Pangborn at the time. You know, it is a funny thing about society in this quarter of the twenty-first century. You can abuse the system to the point where your greed is responsible for the economic collapse of the nation thereby bringing ruination to millions of people or, like Pangborn in his heyday, destroy people's livelihoods and futures. You can be arrogant and bellicose enough to require the deployment of troops into combat or drone attacks on innocent villagers in parts of the world about which you know little or nothing. You can start a war, torture, maim, and destroy people willy-nilly and then retire with a golden parachute, a Nobel Peace Prize, or maybe even a Presidential Library. You may be vilified, but you will endure, equally praised and despised."

"Ike…"

"However, if you are caught sexually abusing children, you are branded a monster to the end of your days. Your friends will not acknowledge your existence ever again. Your career, if you have one, will be trashed. You will be tracked, monitored, distrusted, and abused in turn for the rest of your hellish life. If Pangborn goes to jail, as I am now sure he will, he may not last a year. If he manages to avoid it, he will have a target on his back the size of Texas. One year or twenty, free or incarcerated, his end, when it comes, will be painful and mortifying."

"Wow. So you didn't shoot him because...?"

"Shooting him would be a mercy killing and mercy killing is only legal in four or five states and Idaho is definitely not one of them."

"Right, and you are the sheriff, charged with upholding the law."

"I am."

"Okay, I get it. Pangborn gets a living hell before he lands there permanently. Wow, I like it. Now Ike, can we put the top down and live dangerously one last time?"

Ike pulled over. When the top had locked down, Ruth sat back and gazed up at the sky.

"Open sky. No more hiding. What a relief. You don't realize what freedom to move about can be until you lose it."

Ike's phone buzzed. "It's Charlie. What?...Crap...Okay."

"What did he say?"

"Someone got to Pangborn. One of his own shot him."

"He's dead?"

"No, Charlie says he's tetraplegic. What the hell is tetraplegic?"

"It means he's paralyzed from the neck down, a quadriplegic. The wordsmiths in charge of important topics like how we classify things and then name them, in this case medical terminology, were uncomfortable with the American habit of mixing Greek and Latin prefixes and suffixes. *Quadra* is Latin for four and *tetra* is the Greek. Since *plegia* is Greek, it needed a Greek stem. So, substituting *tetra* for *quadra* harmonizes the languages, gives you tetraplegic. See? Simple."

"Wow, I'm glad we cleared that up. Imagine the potential damage to our youth mixing our classic languages could have."

"Now, now, no need to be snarky. We have survived near death. Some very bad people have been removed from general circulation, and a potential domestic terrorist organization has been dismantled. Be happy."

"I am happy. On the one hand our villain has been spared a horrific death in jail, but on the other, he will receive far worse than that—a life in which he will be reminded daily that he is wholly dependent on the willingness of people he loathes to keep him alive."

"Let's call it a toss-up Look, there's a big bird circling up there. Is that a big hawk?"

"It's a buzzard."

"Or a vulture. You don't suppose...?"

"Suppose what?"

"I'm going with vulture." Ruth twisted in her seat and waved at the bird.

A Brief Author's Note

This is the second book which has child abuse as a secondary theme. It will be the last. I have persisted this far because one thing bothers me about it. It happens often, and that is bad, but one might argue that it seems integral to the human condition and cite incidents stretching back into ancient history to confirm that sad fact. That doesn't excuse it, only puts it in perspective. What is most disturbing to me is not the fact it exists, as awful as that is, but that it goes on with the full knowledge of otherwise responsible people and thus, too often, goes unreported and unpunished. Why this should be is a problem to be unraveled by keener minds than mine. Perhaps more dollars spent on childhood protective services would help, or reducing the divide between those who have and those who have not. I don't know, but in any event, it is clear to me that as long as the political system places economic growth ahead of human welfare, it will endure.

This book is dedicated to all those victims who have thus been robbed of their innocence and discarded by an uncaring society.

To receive a free catalog of Poisoned Pen Press titles, please provide your name and address in one of the following ways:

Phone: 1-800-421-3976
Facsimile: 1-480-949-1707
Email: info@poisonedpenpress.com
Website: www.poisonedpenpress.com

Poisoned Pen Press
6962 E. First Ave. Ste 103
Scottsdale, AZ 85251

CPSIA information can be obtained at www.ICGtesting.com
Printed in the USA
BVOW05s1028171215

430537BV00004B/106/P

9 781464 204784